Alexander McCall Smith

THE CAREFUL USE OF COMPLIMENTS

Alexander McCall Smith is the author of the international phenomenon The No. 1 Ladies' Detective Agency series, the Isabel Dalhousie series, the Portuguese Irregular Verbs series, and the 44 Scotland Street series. He is professor emeritus of medical law at the University of Edinburgh in Scotland and has served on many national and international bodies concerned with bioethics.

www.alexandermccallsmith.com

BOOKS BY ALEXANDER MCCALL SMITH

THE CAREFUL USE OF COMPLIMENTS

Alexander McCall Smith

ANCHOR BOOKS

A Division of Random House, Inc.

New York

FIRST ANCHOR BOOKS EDITION, SEPTEMBER 2008

The Library of Congress has cataloged the Pantheon edition as follows:
McCall Smith, Alexander.
The careful use of compliments / Alexander McCall Smith.
p. cm.
1. Women editors—Fiction. 2. Art dealers—Fiction. 3. Art—Forgeries—Fiction.
I. Title.
PR6063.C326C37 2007
823'.914—dc22
2007015073

Anchor ISBN: 978-1-4000-7712-0

www.anchorbooks.com

This book is for Daniel Shuman

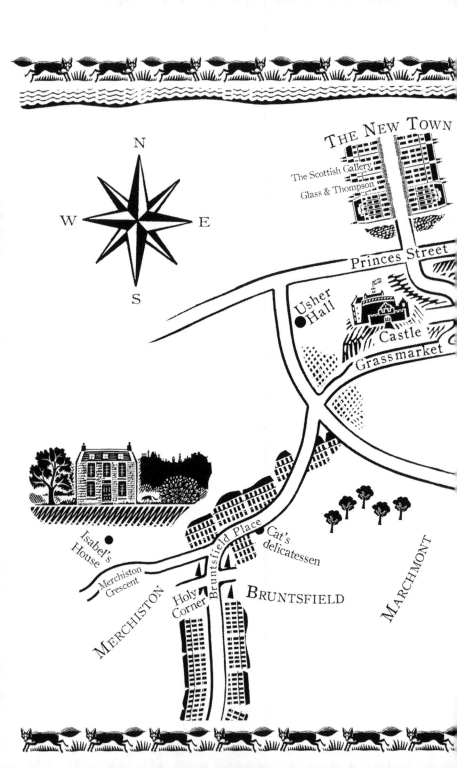

FIRTH OF FORTH

Scottish National
Portrait Gallery

The Scott
Monument

London Road

Holyrood
Palace

Arthur's Seat

Salisbury
Crags

Royal Mile

HOLYROOD

University

THE
MEADOWS

AN
Isabel Dalhousie
EDINBURGH
MAP

CHAPTER ONE

"Take one hundred people," said Isabel.

Jamie nodded. "One hundred."

"Now, out of those one hundred," Isabel continued, "how many will mean well?"

It was typical of the sort of trying question Isabel asked herself, in the way in which we sometimes ask ourselves questions that admit of no definitive answer. She was an optimist when it came to humankind, unfashionably so, and so she thought the answer was ninety-eight, possibly even ninety-nine. Jamie, the realist, after a few moments' thought, said eighty.

But this was not a question which could be disposed of so easily; it raised in its wake other, more troubling questions. Were those one or two people the way they were because of the throw of the genetic dice—a matter of patterns and repeats deep in the chemistry of their DNA—or was it something that went wrong for them a long time ago, in some dark room of childhood, and stayed wrong? Of course there was quite another possibility: they *chose*.

She was sitting in a delicatessen when she remembered this conversation with Jamie. Now, from that convenient vantage

point, she looked out of the window—that man who was crossing the road right then, for example; the one with the thin
mouth, the impatient manner, and the buttoned collar was perhaps one of that tiny minority of the malevolent. There was
something about him, she felt, that made one uneasy; something in his eyes which suggested ruthlessness, a man who
would not wait for others, who did not care, who would suffer
from road rage even while walking . . . She smiled at the
thought. But there was certainly something unsettling in his
demeanour, a hint of poisoned sexuality about him, she felt; a
whiff of cruelty, something not quite right.

She looked away; one did not want such a person to see one
staring; nor, she reminded herself, did she want to catch herself
engaging in such idle speculation. Imagining things about perfect strangers might seem a harmless enough pursuit, but it
could lead to all sorts of ridiculous fantasies and fears. And
Isabel was aware that of all her manifold failings, thinking too
much about things was one of the most egregious.

Of course a delicatessen in Edinburgh was not the most
obvious place to entertain such thoughts on the nature of good
and evil, but Isabel was a philosopher and knew full well
that philosophical speculation came upon one in the strangest
places and at the strangest times. The delicatessen was owned
by her niece, Cat, and in addition to selling the usual things
that such shops sold—the sun-dried tomatoes and mozzarella
cheese, the fresh anchovy fillets and the small bars of Austrian
marzipan—this delicatessen served coffee at the three or four
small marble-topped tables that Cat had found on a trip to the
Upper Loire valley and that she had carted back to Scotland in
a hired self-drive van.

Isabel was sitting at one of these tables, a freshly made cap-
puccino before her, a copy of that morning's *Scotsman* news-

paper open at the crossword page. Her coffee had been made by Cat's assistant, Eddie, a shy young man to whom something terrible and unexplained had happened some time ago and who was still awkward in his dealings with Isabel and with others. Eddie had gained in confidence recently, especially since he had taken up with a young Australian woman who had taken a job for a few months in the delicatessen, but he still blushed unexpectedly and would end a conversation with a murmur and a turning away of the head.

"You're by yourself," said Eddie, as he brought Isabel's coffee to her table. "Where's the . . ." He trailed off.

Isabel smiled at him encouragingly. "The baby? He's called Charlie, by the way."

Eddie nodded, glancing in the direction of Cat's office at the back of the delicatessen. "Yes, of course, Charlie. How old is he now?"

"Three months. More or less exactly."

Eddie absorbed this information. "So he can't say anything yet?"

Isabel began to smile, but stopped herself; Eddie could be easily discouraged. "They don't say anything until they're quite a bit older, Eddie. A year or so. Then they never stop. He gurgles, though. A strange sound that means *I'm perfectly happy with the world.* Or that's the way I understand it."

"I'd like to see him sometime," said Eddie vaguely. "But I think that . . ." He left the sentence unfinished, yet Isabel knew what he meant.

"Yes," she said, glancing in the direction of Cat's door. "Well, that is a bit complicated, as you probably know."

Eddie moved away. A customer had entered the shop and was peering at the counter display of antipasti; he needed to return to his duties.

Isabel sighed. She could have brought Charlie with her, but she had decided against it, leaving him instead at the house with her housekeeper, Grace. She often brought him to Bruntsfield, wheeling him, a wrapped-up cocoon, in his baby buggy, negotiating the edge of the pavement with care, proud in the way of a new mother, almost surprised that here she was, Isabel Dalhousie, with her own child, her son. But on these occasions she did not go into Cat's delicatessen, because she knew that Cat was still uncomfortable about Charlie.

Cat had forgiven Isabel for Jamie. When it had first become apparent that Isabel was having an affair with him, Cat had been incredulous: "Him? My ex-boyfriend? You?" Surprise had been followed by anger, expressed in breathless staccato: "I'm sorry. I can't. I just can't get used to it. The idea."

There had been acceptance, later, and reconciliation, but by that stage Isabel had announced her pregnancy and Cat had retreated in a mixture of resentment and embarrassment.

"You disapprove," said Isabel. "Obviously."

Cat had looked at her with an expression that Isabel found impossible to interpret.

"I know he was your boyfriend," Isabel continued. "But you did get rid of him. And I didn't set out to become pregnant. Believe me, I didn't. But now that I am, well, why shouldn't I have a child?"

Cat said nothing, and Isabel realised that what she was witnessing was pure envy; unspoken, inexpressible. Envy makes us hate what we ourselves want, she reminded herself. We hate it because we can't have it.

By the time that Charlie arrived, tumbling—or so it felt to Isabel—into the world under the bright lights of the Royal Infirmary, Cat was talking to Isabel again. But she did not show much warmth towards Charlie; she did not offer to hold him or to kiss him, although he was her cousin. Isabel was hurt by this, but decided that the best thing to do was not to flaunt Charlie before her niece, but allow her to come round in her own time.

"You can't carry on disliking a baby for long," said Grace, who, imbued with folk wisdom, was often right about these things. "Babies have a way of dealing with indifference. Give Cat time."

Time. She looked at her watch. She had put Charlie down for his nap almost two hours ago and he would be waking up shortly. He would want feeding then, and although Grace could cope with that, Isabel liked to do it herself. She had stopped breast-feeding him only a few days after his birth, which had made her feel bad, but the discomfort had been too great and she had found herself dreading the experience. That was not a way to bond with one's child, she thought; babies can pick up the physical tension in the mother, the drawing back from contact. So she had switched to a baby formula.

Isabel would not leave the delicatessen without exchanging a few words with Cat, no matter how strained relations might be. Now she rose from her table and made her way to the half-open door to the office. Eddie, standing at the counter, glanced briefly in her direction and then looked away again.

"Are you busy?"

Cat had a brochure in front of her, her pen poised above what looked like a picture of a jar of honey.

"Do people buy lots of honey?" Isabel asked. It was a banal question—of course people bought honey—but she needed something to break the ice.

Cat nodded. "They do," she said, distantly. "Do you want some? I've got a sample somewhere here. They sent me a jar of heather honey from the Borders."

"Grace would," said Isabel. "She eats a lot of honey."

There was a silence. Cat stared at the photograph of the jar of honey. Isabel drew in her breath; this could not be allowed to go on. Cat might come round in the end—and Isabel knew that she would—but it could take months; months of tension and silences.

"Look, Cat," she said, "I don't think that we should let this go on much longer. You're freezing me out, you know."

Cat continued to stare fixedly at the honey. "I don't know what you mean," she said.

"But you do," said Isabel. "Of course you know what I mean. And all that I'm saying is that it's ridiculous. You have to forgive me. You have to forgive me for having Charlie. For Jamie. For everything."

She was not sure why she should be asking her niece's forgiveness, but she was. When it came to forgiveness, of course, it did not matter whether somebody was wronged or not—what counted was whether they felt wronged. That was quite different.

"I don't have to forgive you," said Cat. "You haven't done anything wrong, have you? All you've done is have a baby. By my . . ." She trailed off.

Isabel was astonished. "By your what?" she asked. "Your boyfriend? Is that what you're saying?"

Cat rose to her feet. "Let's not fight," she said flatly. "Let's just forget it."

If this had been said with warmth, then Isabel would have been comforted by these words, and relieved. But they were said without passion, and she realised that this was far from a rapprochement; this was a mere changing of the subject. She wanted to protest, to take Cat in her arms and beg her to stop this, but a barrier of animosity, one of those invisible clouds of feeling, stood between them. She turned away. "Will you come round to the house sometime?" she asked. "Come and see us."

Us. She was getting used to the first person plural, but here, of course, in this atmosphere, it was heavy with significance, a land mine of a word.

She left Cat's office. Outside, from behind the counter, Eddie looked up and exchanged glances with Isabel. For a young man who everybody imagined understood nothing, he understood everything, thought Isabel.

"HE WAS YELLING his head off," Grace said. "So I gave him his feed. And since then he's been perfectly happy. Look."

Grace had been cradling Charlie in her arms and now handed him over to Isabel in the hall.

"Looking at him now," said Isabel, "you wouldn't think it, would you? So much volume in those tiny lungs."

She carried him through to her study and sat down in the chair near the window. It still felt strange to her to have Charlie in her study, her place of work. Babies belonged to a world of blankets, colour, softness, not to this place of paper, files, telephones. And philosophy, which is what Isabel did as editor of the *Review of Applied Ethics,* seemed so far removed from the world of infancy. Would Immanuel Kant have known how to hold a baby? she asked herself. It was highly unlikely; babies were too irrational, too messy for him, although he would have acknowledged, of course, that each baby should be treated as an end in its own right, and not as a means to an end. So one should have a baby because one wanted that baby to be born and to have a life, not because one wanted the pleasure oneself of having a baby; that was implicit in any Kantian view of the matter. But even if he had acknowledged the essential value of every baby, would Kant have had the faintest idea how to *deal* with a baby? Would he even have known which side was up? That was the cold and formal face of philosophy, Isabel thought; something far removed from the world that ordinary people knew; their world of struggle, and messy passions, and unresolved pointless differences, such as her difference with Cat. That was Kant's child-unfriendliness established; Hume would have known about children, she decided. He would have found babies good company because they were full of emotions, unexpressed perhaps, or made known only in the crudest of manners, but emotions nonetheless. And Hume, the Good Davey as he was called, was easy company, of course, and would have been liked by babies.

Content in his mother's arms, Charlie now seemed to be dropping back to sleep. Isabel watched as his eyelids fluttered and then closed. She could watch him for hours, she thought, whether he was awake or asleep; it was difficult to believe that she—and Jamie, of course—had created this little boy, this person, had started a whole future on its track. That struck her as little short of a miracle; that a few small cells could multiply and differentiate and create an instrument of thought and language, a whole centre of consciousness.

Grace watched her from the doorway. "Would you like me to take him up to his cot?" she asked. "So that you can work?"

Isabel handed the sleeping child over to Grace and went to her desk. Charlie's birth had had little impact on the *Review of Applied Ethics;* in her determination to be prepared well in advance, Isabel had put together two special issues during her pregnancy—an issue on moral particularism in the work of Iris

Murdoch ("the moral dilemmas of Oxford types," Jamie had called it) and one on the morality of boundary controls. The Murdoch issue had gone to press shortly after Charlie's birth, and the second would be published within a month or two. It had caused her some anxiety, this second one, because the topic was such an uncomfortable one. States are entitled to have some control over their borders—there is general agreement on that—but when they try to keep people out, then passions are raised and accusations of heartlessness made. Auden had a poem about this, which she quoted in her editorial. He had written from the perspective of a displaced person who hears the rhetoric of hate of his persecutors; and there is that arresting line that brings it home so strongly: "He was talking of you and me, my dear," says the man to his wife. You and me: at the end of every bit of exclusion, every act of ethnic cleansing, every flourish of heartlessness, there is a you and me.

And yet, she reflected, that was written in an era of Fascism. Modern states and their officials act very differently; they have to make difficult decisions against a backdrop of human rights laws and openness. We could not *all* go and live in the United States or Canada or Australia, or some other popular country, even if we wanted to. At some point the people already there were entitled, were they not, to say that there were limited resources for newcomers, that their societies could take no more. Or they could argue that even if they had the space, they were entitled to preserve the existing culture of their country by controlling the extent to which others came to it; we live here, they might say—it's ours and we can decide whom to invite in. But then somebody might point out that the current possessors themselves, or their ascendants, had probably taken the land from somebody else, and it was not clear why that should give

to be printed out for her perusal. This meant that a river of paper entered the house each month, swirled in eddies about her study for a week or so, and then was guided out in a stream of recycling bags. The rejected manuscripts, those that she judged unworthy of the editorial board's scrutiny, were often the work of doctoral students, anxious for their first publication. Isabel was gentle in her rejection of these, expressing the hope that the authors would find somebody else willing to publish their work. She knew that this was unlikely, that the *Review* may have been their fifth or sixth port of call. But she could not be brutal; she had been a doctoral student herself once and re-membered what it was like.

She took an envelope off the top of the pile and slit it open. "Dear Ms. Dalhousie, The enclosed paper may be suitable for publication in the *Review of Applied Ethics* and I should be grateful if you would consider it. The title is 'The Concept of Sexual Perversion as an Oppressive Weapon' and in it I examine some ideas which Scruton advanced in his book *Sexual Desire*. As you know, the concept of perversion has been subjected to critical reassessment . . ."

She sighed and laid the paper aside. She received numerous submissions on the subject of sex; indeed, some philosophers seemed to imagine that applied ethics was more or less exclu-sively concerned with sex. Often these papers were interesting, but on other occasions they were distinctly scatological and she wondered whether she should be reading them with gloves on. The absurdity of this struck her as quickly as the thought itself came to her, but it was amusing to think of editors handling such material with the protection of gloves, as if the grubbiness of the subject matter might rub off or infection might leap from the page.

A few days previously she had received a paper entitled "On the Ethics of Pretending to Be Gay When You Are Not." If she had been taken by surprise by this title, then that was clearly the author's intention. We expect the issue to be the ethics of pretending to be straight when you are not, he wrote, but that assumes that there is something shameful about not being straight. The conventional question, then, connives in the marginalisation of the gay, and therefore any consideration of this form of *passing* should be from a viewpoint which recognises that some may wish to pass for gay rather than the other way round.

She smiled at the recollection of that paper, which she had circulated to the members of the editorial board for their verdict. The board would recommend publication, Isabel thought, even if they were not impressed by the content. "That's exactly the sort of paper we should encourage," one member of the board had already written. "We need to show people that we are not, as some suggest, old-fashioned in our approach." This comment had come from Professor Christopher Dove, a professor of philosophy at a minor English university, and a man with a reputation for radicalism. It had been a dig at Isabel, who was herself thought by Dove to be old-fashioned. And she had risen to the occasion in her reply. "Thank you for your support," she had written. "I wondered whether members of the board were ready for this sort of thing. I'm glad to see they now are."

She picked up the next item, a bulky brown envelope which would contain, she thought, a catalogue of some sort. It did: *Lyon & Turnbull, Forthcoming Sales.* Lyon & Turnbull were a prominent Edinburgh auction house at whose sales Isabel had bought the occasional item, thus entitling her to their catalogues. This one was for a sale of furniture described as "good

antique furniture" and paintings, neither of which Isabel actually needed—in fact the house had too much furniture and too
many paintings. But she found auction catalogues irresistible,
even if she had no intention of buying anything.

She skipped through the pages of furniture, pausing only to
study more closely a set of library steps in mahogany, with brass
fittings. The estimate seemed discouragingly high, and she
moved on to the paintings. That was where she stopped. Lot
number 87 was a painting of a man standing on a shore, a stack
of lobster creels just behind him, and behind the creels a mountain rising sharply. It was unmistakably the landscape of the
Western Highlands of Scotland, with its grey rocks protruding
from thin soil, the verdant green of the grass, the gentle, shifting
light; and the man's face, with its weather-beaten look, further
proclaimed the place. She looked at the description underneath:
Andrew McInnes, Scottish, b. 1958, *Sea Livelihood*. Below this,
in smaller type, the auctioneers went on to explain: "McInnes
was perhaps the most talented of the students to have passed
through the Edinburgh College of Art in the last years of
Robin Philipson's tenure as principal. He rapidly acquired a
substantial reputation, and this was reflected in the prices
achieved by his paintings during the years immediately before
his death."

Isabel studied the painting intently. It was the expression on
the man's face that interested her. This was a man who knew
hardship, but was not bowed by it. And there was a kindness
too, a gentleness that was sometimes squeezed out of those who
wrested their living from a hard place—the sea or a windswept
island.

She reached for the telephone and dialled Jamie's number.
At the other end of the line, the phone rang for a long time and

she was about to put the handset down when Jamie suddenly answered. He sounded breathless.

"You've just run up the stairs," she said. "Do you want me to call back later?"

"No, I'll be all right. I heard it when I was on the way up and then I couldn't get my key into the lock for some reason. But it's all right now."

Isabel looked at her watch. It was eleven thirty. She could put Charlie into his baby sling and take him with her; he slept very contentedly in the sling because, she thought, he could hear her heartbeat and he imagined he was back in the womb, back to the simpler life that perhaps he remembered—just— and missed.

"Would you like to see your son for lunch?" she asked.

"Of course," Jamie answered quickly. She knew he would say that, and it gave her satisfaction. He loved Charlie, which was what she wanted. It did not matter whether or not he loved her—and she did not know whether he did—the important thing was that he loved Charlie.

"And we could drop into Lyon & Turnbull beforehand," Isabel suggested. "There's something I want to look at."

"I'll meet you there," said Jamie.

She put the telephone down and smiled. I am very fortunate, she thought. I have a child, and I also have a lover who is the father of the child. I have a large house and a job that allows me to do philosophy. I am happy.

She moved to the window and looked out into the garden. The summer profusion of shrubs made shadows on the ground below. There was a fuchsia, laden with red and purple flowers, and beside it a large rhododendron bush, popular with small birds. When they alighted on the foliage of the rhododendron,

these birds made the topmost branches bend almost imperceptibly under their tiny weight. But now the lower branches, those
right down by the ground, moved suddenly, and for another reason. *And I have a fox,* she whispered. *I have a fox who watches
over my life.*

❖

CHAPTER TWO

SO," SAID JAMIE. "Which one is it?"

He asked the question in a way which suggested that he was not really interested in the answer. And the reason for that was in his arms: Charlie, his son, looking up at his father's face, struggling to focus.

"Over there," said Isabel, pointing to the other side of the saleroom. "I've already had a quick look at it."

Jamie hardly heard the answer. He had strapped Charlie's sling onto his front now, and was gently tickling the child under the chin. "He likes that," he said. "Look, he's going all cross-eyed."

Isabel smiled indulgently. "Yes. He's pleased to see you. That is, if he can see you properly, which I'm never really sure of. I suppose he can, even if colours are still a bit confusing at that age."

"He knows me," said Jamie mock-defensively. "He knows exactly who I am. If he could say *Daddy* he would."

Isabel took Jamie by the arm and steered him gently across the room to stand in front of a large painting in a gilded frame. "What do you think of this?"

Jamie looked at the painting, watched by Isabel. "I

rather like it," he said. "Look at that man's face. Look at the expression."

"Yes," said Isabel. "It says rather a lot, doesn't it?"

Jamie glanced away for a moment; Charlie had seized the finger of his right hand and was attempting to put it in his mouth. "You mustn't," he said. "Unsanitary."

"Everything about children is unsanitary," said Isabel. She turned back to the painting and pointed to its top right-hand corner. "Look over there. He's really caught that west coast light."

Jamie leaned forward to peer at the canvas. "The Inner Hebrides?" he said. "Skye?"

"Probably Jura," said Isabel. "He lived there for a while. Jura scenes became his trademark, rather like Iona and Mull were for Samuel Peploe."

"Who?" asked Jamie. "Who was he?"

Isabel handed him the catalogue. "Andrew McInnes. There's something about him here. Look."

Jamie took the catalogue and read the few lines of description. Then he handed it back to Isabel and looked at her enquiringly. She noticed his eyes, which were filled with light; that brightness which attracted her so strongly, which spoke of a lambent intelligence.

"I'm sorry," she said. "You must be wondering what I'm going on about." As she spoke to Jamie, she reached out and touched Charlie, who was gazing intently at her. "Do you know that painting I have on the stairs, halfway up? On the landing? It's by the same Andrew McInnes. It was one of his earliest works. My father bought it."

Jamie looked thoughtful. "Kind of," he said hesitantly. "I think so. On the left as you go up?"

"Yes," said Isabel. "That's it."

"I haven't really studied it," said Jamie. "I suppose it's just one of those things one walks past."

Isabel gestured towards the painting. "It's much smaller than this, of course. About one quarter the size. But it's exactly the same subject. Almost identical. That man and those hills. The lobster creels. Everything."

Jamie shrugged. "Artists paint the same thing over and over again, don't they? The same models. The same scenes. They can be creatures of habit, can't they?"

Isabel agreed. There was nothing surprising in finding paintings that were very much the same as one another, particularly if one was smaller. Her small painting was evidently a recurrent image in the artist's mind, and that was nothing unusual. What she wanted from Jamie, though, was encouragement to bid for the larger version. Should she?

"It's up to you," said Jamie. "But . . . look at the estimate. Twenty-five thousand. Isn't that rather a lot?"

"They know what they're talking about," said Isabel. "He's sought after. He's not cheap."

Jamie frowned. "But twenty-five thousand . . ." He was trying to recall what he made each year as a part-time teacher of bassoon and an occasional performer. It was not much more than that, if it was any more at all; of course there was the small legacy he had received from his aunt, and the flat, which had come from her too, but even then he had to watch his money carefully, as most people did. He knew that Isabel was not hard up, but to be able to spend twenty-five thousand pounds on a painting astonished him. People paid that, of course; some considerably more. But these were not people *he knew*; that was the difference. He glanced at her, as if with new eyes; she did not look wealthy, and there was none of that irritating self-assuredness that sometimes hung about the rich, an air of power, of being able to take things for granted. Jamie had noticed that in the parents of some of his pupils. They were often well-heeled for the simple reason that the bassoon was an expensive instrument and there were many parents who could not afford to buy one. Most of these people were modest in their manner, but some condescended to him or showed a general arrogance in the way they expected everyone to fit in with their whims. The mothers in the expensive four-wheel-drive vehicles were the worst, he had decided. Why did they need these fuel-hungry contraptions in their urban lives? To barge their way past other, smaller cars, or to make a statement about who they were and what they had?

One of these mothers was interested in him. He had noticed it because she had made it so obvious, arriving early to collect her son from his lesson in the flat—the boy could easily have gone downstairs to meet his mother on the street, as the others did, but she came up, rang the bell, and waited in the kitchen until her son's lesson was finished. Then she engaged Jamie in conversation, quizzing him about her child's progress, while the boy himself lurked in the background, clearly embarrassed, eager to leave.

She stood close to Jamie while she spoke to him; the sort of invasion of the unspoken limits of bodily space that can be so disconcerting. He moved away slightly, but she followed him, inching nearer. He glanced at his pupil, as if for rescue from that quarter, but the boy looked away, his embarrassment compounded by the complicity that had now arisen between them.

Jamie's deliberate distance seemed only to spur this woman on, and she had invited him to join her for coffee after the lesson. He had replied that he could not, as there was another pupil, and then he added, "And I don't think it would be a good idea anyway." She had looked at him mischievously, and then, as if oblivious to the presence of her son on the other side of the room, had said, "It may not be a good idea, but it's always fun." After that, he had asked her not to come up to fetch her son, but to wait for him downstairs.

She had been outraged. "Who exactly do you think you are?" she had hissed.

"Your son's bassoon teacher," he said.

"Ex–bassoon teacher," she said, and she had withdrawn her son from further lessons.

Isabel had laughed when she heard of this. "I can see her," she said. "I can just see her saying that."

"But I haven't told you who she was," Jamie protested.

"But of course I know," said Isabel. "Remember that this is Edinburgh. I can work it out. It's . . ." And she had named the name, and got it right, to Jamie's astonishment.

"Too much money," Isabel went on. "She's incapable of handling it. She thinks that it buys bassoon lessons—and the bassoon teacher."

Isabel was not like that at all. But now this talk of spending twenty-five thousand pounds on a painting made Jamie feel vaguely uneasy.

"Should you spend that much?" he asked, but he went on to answer his own question immediately. "Of course, if you can afford it, then that's your business."

Isabel detected a note of disapproval in his tone; she had not expected this reaction. They had never discussed money; the subject simply had not arisen between them. And if there was a yawning disparity between their respective financial positions—which there was—it seemed to her that it was quite irrelevant. Isabel had never judged people by their means; it simply was not an issue with her. But at the same time, she realised that it could be difficult for Jamie. Money gave power over people, no matter how tactful one was about it. With money you could get the attention of others; you could ask them to do things.

"I can afford it," she said quietly. "If I want it. But the problem is . . . well, I feel guilty." She paused. "And you're not helping much."

He frowned. "Not helping? I don't know what you mean."

"You disapprove of the fact that I can buy that," said Isabel. "You're making it rather obvious."

Jamie's surprise was unfeigned. "Why should I disapprove? It's your money. What you do with it—"

"Is my business," Isabel interjected. "If only that were the case. But it isn't, you know. People watch what other people do with their money. They watch very closely."

Jamie shrugged his shoulders. "Not me," he said. "I don't. If you think that I do, then you're wrong. You really are."

Isabel watched his expression as she spoke. She had misjudged him; what he said was true—he had no interest in what she did with her money; there was no envy there.

"Let's not argue," she said. "Especially in front of Charlie."

Jamie smiled. "No. Of course." The discussion had made him feel uncomfortable, as it had raised something which had not been present in their relationship before: a financial dimension. As they left the auction house, with Charlie returned to his sling on Isabel's front, Jamie thought about what had been said. And there was something else worrying him, something else that had not been spoken about but that had to be discussed at some point. Who was financially responsible for Charlie? He had not thought about this, in the drama of Isabel's pregnancy, but a few days previously it had occurred to him that now there would be bills. He had seen an article in the paper about the cost of a child until it reached the age of independence, and the figure had been daunting. Tens—scores—of thousands of pounds were needed to feed, clothe, and educate a child, and the age of independence itself seemed to be getting higher and higher. Twenty-five-year-olds still lived with, and on, their parents, and the paper cited one case of a daughter of thirty-two, still in full-time education, still being supported by her father. Was Charlie going to be that expensive? And if he was, would he be able to pay his share?

They were going for lunch in the restaurant at the Scottish National Portrait Gallery, which was on Queen Street, a short walk from the auction house. Outside, in spite of the fact that it was June, the wind had a note of chill in it, a wind from the east, off the North Sea. Isabel looked up at the sky, which was clear but for a few scudding clouds, wispy, high-level streaks of white. "It's so bright," she said, shivering as a gust of wind swept up Broughton Street and penetrated the thin layer of her jersey. "Look at that sky. Look up there."

Jamie stared up into the blue. He saw a vapour trail, higher than the clouds, on the very edge of space, it seemed, heading westwards towards America or Canada. He thought of the shiny thin tube suspended, against gravity, in that cold near-void; he thought of the people inside. "What do you think of when you see those jets?" he asked Isabel, pointing up at the tiny glint of metal with its white wisp of cotton wool trailing behind it.

Isabel glanced up. "Trust," she said. "I think of trust."

Jamie looked puzzled. "Why would you think of that?" Then he started to smile; he knew the answer, and Isabel was right. "Yes, I see."

They turned the corner onto Queen Street. On the other side of the street, a block away, rose the red sandstone edifice of the Portrait Gallery, an ambitious neo-Gothic building which Isabel had always liked in spite of what she called its "Caledonian spikiness." The gallery restaurant, tucked away and old-fashioned, was popular with people who wanted to sit, four to a table, in high-backed chairs reminiscent of suburban dining rooms. Isabel liked it because of its welcoming atmosphere and the overflow paintings from the main gallery hanging on its walls.

"I like coming here," said Jamie, as they sat down at their table. "When I was a boy, I used to be brought here to see the pictures of the kings and queens of Scotland. I was interested in seeing Macbeth, but of course we haven't a clue what he looked like."

"A much maligned king," said Isabel as she loosened Charlie's sling. "Shakespeare cast him as a weak man, a murderer, but in fact he had quite a successful reign. Scotland prospered under Macbeth."

"*She* was the problem," said Jamie.

Isabel doubted this. It was only too easy to blame women, she thought, although she had to admit, if pressed, that there were some women who deserved any blame that came their way. Mrs. Ceauşescu was such a case, as she pointed out.

"She was shot, wasn't she?" said Jamie.

"I'm afraid so," said Isabel. "And nobody deserves that. Not even the most appalling tyrant, or tyrant's wife. She pleaded for her life, we are told, as did her husband, in his long winter coat, standing there in front of those young soldiers. He said that they should not shoot his wife, as she was a great scientist. At least he tried to do something gentlemanly at the very end."

They were silent for a moment; Romania and firing squads

seemed a world away from the atmosphere of the Portrait Gallery. Jamie looked at Charlie. The cruelties of the world, its viciousness, seemed so dissonant with the innocence of the child. He returned to kings.

"George IV," he said. "That was another favourite picture of mine. Ever since I heard that the artist who painted the picture of his arrival in Edinburgh showed him in his kilt but without the pink tights that apparently he wore when he arrived in Scotland."

Isabel laughed. "That sounds almost as bad as those Soviet portraits. I saw one in the State Gallery in Moscow years ago. It was a collective portrait of the politburo or some such group. The ones who had been discredited or executed were simply painted out and replaced with large flower arrangements. But the contours of the paint showed that something had been done. Such a bad sign—the appearance of flowers in official portraits."

Jamie looked at her quizzically. He was not quite sure how to take remarks like that from Isabel. It was, he said, her Dorothy Parker streak. "But I'd never take a streak from another woman," Isabel had protested.

"There you go," said Jamie.

But now there was this odd remark about flowers. "Why flowers?" he asked.

"Well," said Isabel, "look at political broadcasts by presidents and prime ministers. The shaky ones, those one thinks are lying, or at least being economical with the truth—they bedeck the tables behind them with large floral arrangements. I take that as a sure sign that there's something fishy going on. Flags and flowers. They're stage props. And soldiers. Being seen talking to the troops is very good for votes."

The waitress arrived and they gave their order. Jamie reached across the table and touched Charlie's arm.

"So small," he said. "Like a little doll."

Isabel smiled and let her hand touch Jamie's. He curled his fingers round hers, briefly.

"Thank you," she said quietly.

"Thank you for what?"

"For not going away."

He gave a start. "Why should I go away?"

She nodded in the direction of Charlie. "Not every man stays," she said. "You might easily have preferred . . . preferred your freedom."

He stared at her. Had she misjudged him that badly? He felt an irritation, a crossness, that she should think that of him. And Isabel, watching him, immediately sensed that.

"I'm sorry," she said. "I've offended you. I didn't mean to. It's just that . . . well, you're younger than I am. You need your freedom. You don't need to be tied down."

Jamie swallowed. He looked about him briefly; the restaurant was busy, as it always was at lunchtime, but in the general hubbub it did not look as if anybody might overhear their conversation. "Of course I wouldn't make myself scarce," he said. "I told you that—right at the beginning. I told you when Charlie arrived. I was there, wasn't I?"

"Of course you were," said Isabel soothingly. "Please don't be angry with me. Please." And she thought, I'm making a mess of this. It's exactly the same as my relationship with Cat. I make a mess of things by saying things that I don't need to say.

Jamie was staring at the table, tracing on its surface an imaginary pattern with a forefinger. He looked up, and Isabel saw that he was flushed. "Jamie," she said. "Please . . ."

He shook his head. "No. I want to say something. I should have said it before. Now I'm going to say it."

She held her breath. I shouldn't have imagined that this would last, she thought; now I'll find out what I always feared. To have had him, now to lose him; it was inevitable.

"Isabel," he said. "I'd like you to marry me." He paused. "I think we should get married."

For a moment she thought that she had misheard him. But then he repeated it. She was surprised, but not surprised. She had wondered whether he might say this, ever since she announced to him that she was pregnant. She had been unable to stop herself from entertaining the possibility, and had considered, at length, what her response would be. And now that the moment had come, she found herself hesitating. What if she said yes right there and then?

Instead she said, "It's a rather public proposal, isn't it, Jamie?" She gestured about her.

Jamie blushed. "I'm sorry. But it's just that you brought up the whole issue of my being around. I felt that I had to say something."

She reassured him. "Yes, I understand."

"And?"

"I know you feel you have to ask me," she said. "But I think we should wait. I really do. Let's wait some time and see how things go. That makes more sense, you know."

He did not say anything for a minute or two, and she imagined that he was wrestling with himself. If he really wanted to marry her, she thought, he would press her again. But if he had merely proposed out of a sense of duty, then he would probably accept her suggestion with some relief.

"All right," he said at last. "Let's see."

She realised how tense she had been; now she relaxed. But she felt a certain sadness that he had gone along with her suggestion, even though she knew that this was the right thing to do, and that quite the wrong thing for her to do would be to allow him to marry her. And that, in a way, was the burden of being a philosopher: one knew what one had to do, but it was so often the opposite of what one really wanted to do.

CHAPTER THREE

BY THE TIME Grace arrived at the house the next morning, Isabel had bathed Charlie, given him his breakfast bottle, and was standing in front of the drawing-room window, encouraging him to look out over the garden. She was not sure how much he saw, but she was convinced that he was interested and was gazing fixedly at one of the rhododendrons. As she held Charlie before the window and rocked him gently, Isabel saw Grace walking up the front path, although Grace did not spot her. Grace had a newspaper tucked under her arm and was carrying the white canvas tote bag that accompanied her to work each day. This bag was often empty, and hung flaccid from Grace's arm, but on occasion it bulged with tantalizing shapes that intrigued Isabel and that she wished she could ask Grace about. She knew, though, that there was usually at least a book in the bag, as Grace was a keen reader and had a sacrosanct lunch hour during which she would sit in the kitchen, immersed in a novel from the Central Library, a cup of tea getting steadily colder in front of her.

Since Charlie's arrival, the nature of Grace's job had changed. This change had required no negotiation, with Grace assuming that Isabel would need help with the baby and that naturally this would take priority over her normal, more mundane duties of cleaning and ironing.

"I'll look after him while you're working," Grace had announced. "And also when you want to go out. I like babies. So that's fine." The tone of her voice indicated that there needed to be no further discussion.

Isabel was happy with the new understanding, but even had she not been, she would have hesitated to contradict Grace. Although Isabel was nominally Grace's employer, Grace regarded herself as still working for Isabel's father, who had died years before and in whose service as housekeeper she had spent all her working life. Either that, or she thought of herself as being employed in some strange way by the house itself; which meant that her loyalty, and source of instructions, was really some authority separate from and higher than Isabel.

The practical consequences of this were that Grace occasionally announced that something would be done because "that's what the house needs." Isabel thought this a curious expression, which made her home sound rather like a casino or an old-fashioned merchant bank—in both of which one might hear the staff talking about *the house*. But for all its peculiarity, the arrangement worked very well and indeed was welcomed by Isabel as a means of putting the relationship between herself and Grace on a more equal, and therefore easier, footing. Isabel did not like the idea of being an employer, with all that this entailed in terms of authority and power. If Grace regarded herself as being employed by some vague metaphysical body known as the house, then that at least enabled Isabel to treat her as a mixture of friend and colleague, which is precisely how she viewed her anyway.

Of course the circumstances in which the two women found themselves were different, and no amount of linguistic sleight of hand could conceal that. Isabel had enjoyed every advantage in education and upbringing; there had been money, travel, and, ultimately, freedom from the constraints of an office job or its equivalents. Grace, by contrast, had come from a home in which there had been no spare money, little free time, and, in the background, the knowledge that unemployment might at any time remove whatever small measure of prosperity people might have attained.

Grace went into the kitchen, put the tote bag down on a chair, and made her way into the morning room.

"I'm here," Isabel called out. "In the study."

Grace entered the room and beamed at Charlie. "He's looking very bright and breezy," she said, coming up to tickle Charlie under the chin. Charlie grinned and waved his arms in the air.

"I think he wants to go to you," said Isabel.

Grace took Charlie in her arms. "Of course he does," she said.

It was not the words themselves, Isabel realised—it was more the inflection. Did Grace mean that it was no surprise that Charlie should want to go to her rather than stay with his mother? That was how it sounded, even if Grace had not meant it that way.

"He actually quite likes me too," said Isabel softly.

Grace looked at her in astonishment. "But of course he does," she said. "You're his mother. All boys like their mothers."

"No," said Isabel. "I don't think they do. Some mothers suffocate their sons, emotionally. They don't mean to, but it happens." She looked out of the window. She had seen it in her family, in a cousin whose ambitious mother had nagged him until he had cut himself free and had as little as possible to do with her. He had been civil, of course, but everybody had seen it—the stiff posture, the formal politeness, the looking away when she spoke to him. But had he loved her, in spite of this? She remembered him at his mother's funeral when he had wept, quietly but voluminously, and Isabel, sitting in the row behind him, had put her hand on his shoulder and whispered to him in comfort. We leave it too late, she had thought; we always do, and then these salutary lessons are learned at the graveside.

"Mothers always mean well," said Grace. "As long as they don't try to choose their son's wife. That's a mistake."

Charlie looked up at Grace and smiled. I have enough, thought Isabel; I have so much that surely I can share him.

Grace turned towards Isabel. Her face, Isabel noticed, seemed transformed by the close presence of the baby, her look at that moment one of near pride. "Do you want to work this morning?" she said, looking in the direction of Isabel's overcrowded desk. "There's not much to do in the house. I could look after Charlie."

Isabel felt a wrench. Part of her wanted to answer that she would decide for herself, in good time, whether she wanted to work or whether she wished simply to be with Charlie; but another part of her, the responsible part, felt she should deal with the pile of correspondence that she had started to tackle the previous day but that she had abandoned in favour of the auctioneer's catalogue. There *were* two horses in the soul, she thought, as Socrates had said in *Phaedrus*—the one, unruly, governed by passions, pulling in the direction of self-indulgence; the other, restrained, dutiful, governed by a sense of shame. And Auden had felt the same, she thought; he was a dualist who knew the struggle between the dark and the light sides of the self, the struggle that all of us know to a greater or lesser extent.

She sighed. "Work," she said. She had never sighed over the prospect of work before; but now there was Charlie.

As Grace took Charlie from the room, Isabel sat down at her pile of mail. It had grown that morning by five letters, pushed through the letter box by the postman on his morning round, all of them concerned with *Review* affairs. She disposed of the top two quickly. One was a request for a further supply of offprints of her article by an author who had lost her carefully husbanded supply which the *Review* gave on publication. The offprints had been mislaid in the course of a move following the breakup of a relationship. Isabel had stumbled over this. Why was it necessary for her to be told that the move had been prompted by this? Was it an attempt to engage her sympathy so that the offprints would be given free, or was it an excuse for the loss itself—a life thrown into disarray by the bad behaviour of another? Isabel looked up at the ceiling and pondered this; if one was to err, then it was better to err on the side of generosity. The offprints would be free, and she wrote a note to that effect. The second letter asked why a book review of *Virtues in a Time of Trial* had not yet appeared; that, too, was easily dealt with. The reviewer had died, of old age as it happened, before writing the review. A new reviewer had been approached and the review would appear in due course.

Ten minutes: that was all it took to read and reply to these letters. At this rate, Isabel thought, she would be finished in an hour, possibly even earlier. But then came an innocent-looking envelope, addressed in handwriting, and postmarked London.

She slit open the envelope and began to read the letter. The letterhead, once exposed, told her who the sender was—the oddly named Professor Lettuce, professor of moral philosophy at one of the smaller universities in London, and chairman of the *Review*'s editorial board. In general, Robert Lettuce played a small role in the affairs of the *Review*, being content to allow Isabel to run everything. She reported to him and the board from time to time and he, in due course, reported to the *Review*'s owners, a small academic publishing firm. This firm published textbooks in veterinary science and biology; the *Review of Applied Ethics* came into its possession almost by accident when it bought the building occupied by the private trust that owned the *Review*. In the trustees' relief at selling a building that had been a drain on finances, the *Review* had been thrown into the sale as a gesture of goodwill. The new owners were lukewarm about their ownership and had occasionally mentioned their willingness to sell the *Review*, should a suitable purchaser be found. But no purchaser had ever expressed more than a passing interest in a concern that made very little profit, if any at all. So there had been no change in ownership.

She read halfway through the letter, put it down for a few moments, and then picked it up to read the remainder.

Dear Isabel,

As you know, I've enjoyed working with you over the last five years. [He's going to resign, she thought as she read this.] We have had very few disagreements, and I must say that I have always been very impressed with your editing of the *Review*. Under your editorship, the circulation has increased considerably—some would say dramatically—and the journal has been redesigned. Remember how awfully dull it looked when we first started, with that curious mauve cover? [Actually, thought Isabel, you were against the change. I had to persuade you; you liked mauve, as I recall.] And I have always appreciated the single theme idea, which was your brainchild and which has been, in my view, a great success.

But, Isabel, as I am sure that you appreciate, there is always a case for change, as well as for variety, and at the prompting of a couple of members of the board I carried out a sounding of the others to see whether people felt that it was time for a fresh incumbent of the editorial chair. I did not imagine that there would be much support for this, but unfortunately I was proved to be quite wrong on this. The view, I'm afraid, was pretty much unanimous: it's time for a change.

I know that you will be both surprised and upset by this: both of these reactions were mine too. But I know, too, that you will understand that in voting for a change the members of the board are in no sense passing adverse judgement on your considerable achievements at the helm of the *Review*.

There was some enthusiasm for an immediate change of editor, but I took the view that the best thing to do would be for you to remain in the post for the rest of the year (if you are willing) and then we can start the next calendar year with the new person. That will give you time to look for something else, and also will provide continuity, which is so important.

As to your successor, Christopher Dove has offered his services and this choice is broadly acceptable to the rest of the board. No doubt you and he will be able to get together at some point to discuss the technicalities of the changeover.

And there the letter had ended, with Lettuce's signature underneath and a pencilled postscript asking Isabel whether she had read the "wonderfully perceptive" obituary of the reviewer who had died before getting round to reviewing *Virtues in a Time of Trial.* "An excellent piece," wrote Lettuce. "Did you know he was an accomplished violinist *and* a glider pilot in his earlier years?"

Isabel's emotions were complex. She was shocked by the unexpectedness of the news, by the sheer surprise of being told that what she had taken for granted, her job, was being taken from her. Then there was a sense of disgust at the obvious plotting that must have been going on. Dove—he was the one, she decided. It had occurred to her before this that Dove probably coveted her post as editor; he was ambitious and the editorship of an established journal would help him on his climb up the pole of academic success. He was currently at an obscure university, one so low in the pecking order that it appeared in no tables at all. She had been told by a friend who knew him that he really would like to be elsewhere altogether, at Magdalen College, Oxford, of which he was a graduate. That involved an ascent on an Alpine scale, and the editorship of the *Review* would help. He would have been in touch with other members and poured poison in their ears, dangling some sort of carrot perhaps, cajoling, and enough of them had been craven enough to go along with this. Not one, she thought, not one had contacted her to discuss the issue; that was almost the most difficult thing to bear.

And as for Lettuce himself, he might have telephoned to break the news personally, he might even have bothered to travel to Edinburgh to discuss it with her. Instead, he had written this relatively impersonal letter—a document which amounted to a letter of dismissal. It had been made worse by the fact that he had appended a chatty postscript. That is a hallmark of guilt, she thought; he who feels acutely guilty attempts to establish that all is actually well by resorting to the quotidian remark that has nothing to do with the real business. That is exactly what Lettuce had done.

Isabel let the letter drop to the floor. It fell facedown, but the ink from the signature had seeped through the cheap paper to provide faint mirror-writing on the back. Ecuttel. That was a far better name for him, far more sinister than Lettuce. Ecuttel and his lackey, Evod. The thought made her feel slightly better, but only slightly; engaging in such childish fantasies is merely a way of protecting ourselves from the sense of hurt that comes from betrayal or injustice. But it works only for a moment or two.

GRACE WAS IN THE KITCHEN, sitting in front of Charlie, who was strapped into a reclining baby chair placed on top of the table. She was holding a knitted figure of what looked like a policeman and moving it up and down to get Charlie's attention. She looked up when Isabel came into the room but then transferred her gaze back to the baby.

"Fed up already?" Grace said. "Look at this. He loves this little policeman. I think it must be the dark blue. He thinks it very funny."

Isabel nodded. She looked at Charlie, and then looked back at Grace. She wanted to say to her, "I've been sacked. I'm the victim of . . ." But what was she the victim of? A palace coup was perhaps the best way of describing it. Or maybe she should call it a putsch, which had a more strongly pejorative air to it, a hint of violent overthrow. That was perhaps overstating matters a bit . . .

"I've been—"

Grace interrupted her. "I think he's tired," she said. "Look, his eyes are shutting. There he goes."

No, thought Isabel. I'm not going to tell her. I shall keep this humiliation private. Then, later this year, I shall simply announce that I have given up the editorship of the *Review,* which will be true, and if anybody should ask the reason I shall tell them. But until then I shall continue as before.

Grace now turned to Isabel. "Sorry, you've been what?"

"I've been thinking of going into town," said Isabel. "If you're happy enough looking after Charlie."

Grace reassured her that this would be fine.

"Thank you," said Isabel, and left the kitchen, lest Grace should see the tears that had come into her eyes. She had never been dismissed before and was unused to the particular form of pain it entailed. It was as bad as being left by a lover, or almost as bad, she thought, and in her case she did not even depend on the tiny salary she drew as editor, an honorarium really. What, she wondered, would it be like to lose the job that brought food to the family table, as happened to people all the time? That was a sobering thought, sufficient to forestall the self-pity of one in her position—and it did.

CHAPTER FOUR

SHE WALKED INTO TOWN. Isabel very rarely took her green Swedish car into the city because of parking problems. She suspected, though, that she would use it more now that Charlie had arrived; babies required such a quantity of paraphernalia that the car, she thought, would become more and more tempting. She believed in public transport, and acted accordingly, but she was not one to become obsessed with the issue of her carbon footprints, or to lecture others on theirs. And the green Swedish car, she reminded herself, was green in another sense—unlike those intimidating machines which some people drove; those monsters with their tanklike bulk from which small, urban people stared down. Isabel had read of a man who had entered on a private crusade against these vehicles, attaching notes to their windscreens telling their owners just how irresponsible their choice of car was. She could understand that, even if she could never do it herself: it was one thing to think such things, another to tell other people what one thought.

But concern for the environment was not the only reason she chose to go by foot that morning; she wanted to put her thoughts in order, and it would be easier to do that while walking, making her way across the Meadows, the large park that divided the Old Town of Edinburgh from its southern suburbs. She had taken that path so many times before, and in so many moods. She remembered once, after a concert in the Queen's Hall, she had walked home fighting back tears and had been stopped by a young woman and asked if she was all right. Those tears had been for the impossibility of her relationship with Jamie, whom she had seen during the concert intermission with a young woman she had assumed to be his girlfriend. It had never occurred to her then that not all that long afterwards they would become lovers and she would have his son. She would not have believed it; would have considered it utterly impossible. And now . . .

Nor would she have dreamed, she thought, that she would be walking across the Meadows, brooding with bitterness over her dismissal from the job to which she had devoted so much. This would not have occurred to her because she would never have imagined that anybody else would actually *want* to be the editor of the *Review.* Nor would she have imagined that anybody would have thought that she had done the job badly. She had not. She had made a success of it, and had taken very little for her efforts.

Well, now it had happened and she wondered whether she should simply accept her dismissal as a fait accompli, or whether she should fight back. One thing she could do was write to Professor Lettuce, asking him to explain exactly why he thought a change of editor would be a good thing. Would Christopher Dove adopt a different editorial policy, and if so, how would that policy differ from her own? Of course he would find the words to deal with that by talking about something else and not answering her questions—he was very skilled at that— so perhaps it would simply be a waste of time.

She reached the start of Jawbone Walk, at the entrance to

which giant inverted whale jaws served as an arch. Many Scots had been whalers, and these bones had been presented to the city by Shetland and Fair Isle knitters who had used them in an exhibition in the nineteenth century. Isabel thought that knitting and whaling did not sit together well; she did not like this reminder of something that she would have preferred to forget—our relentless pursuit of those gentle creatures, almost to the point of extinction. But the city was full of uncomfortable reminders of how things in the past were otherwise than one might wish they had been: memorials to wars which should never have been fought, statues of men who presided over so many remote cruelties—that was what came of having an imperial past. And Scotland had been an active participant in all that, supplying many of the soldiers, the engineers, and the officials who kept that vast imperial conceit going; nor did one have to look far to see the reminders. Old battles . . .

I'll fight back, she thought. I'll write to the publishing company and tell them that I'm being unfairly dismissed. There are industrial tribunals, are there not, and these could order my reinstatement; but are they intended to protect people like me? Somehow I think not.

By the time she reached the High Street and had begun her descent of the Mound, Isabel's mood had changed and she had resolved that she would do nothing. If Christopher Dove wanted the editorship, then she would let him have it. She needed neither the money—pitiful though the salary was—nor the work itself. There were other, more rewarding things to do, she had decided, than to sit in her study and read the manuscripts of obscure philosophers at remote universities. There was Charlie to be looked after; there were friendships to be cultivated; there were trips to be made to places that she had long wanted to visit. She could take Charlie—small babies were easy to travel with, she had been told, by comparison with older children. She could make that long-awaited trip to her cousin Mimi McKnight in Dallas. It had been years since she had been to Texas, and when Mimi had come to Scotland the previous year she had pressed an invitation on her, as she always did.

These thoughts occupied her all the way down the Mound and over the brow of George Street. Then, after a brisk walk down Queen Street, during which she thought of quite other matters, she found herself outside the auction rooms of Lyon & Turnbull. The rooms were busier than they had been the previous day, and now, on the final day of viewing, were crowded with those who had left it to the last minute. There would be more tomorrow—people who decided on the morning of the sale that they would go for something after all, who might just have stumbled across the catalogue and seen an item they wanted. Then there would be the impulse buyers, who decided to bid without even inspecting in advance the item under the hammer, and who would crane their necks to get a better view of the lot from over the heads of the seated bidders.

The McInnes picture had been moved, and for a moment Isabel wondered whether it had been withdrawn. That sometimes happened; impulsive sellers had their regrets as much as impulsive buyers did. But then she saw it, in the more prominent place that had been found for it, alongside a large William Gillies landscape, a picture of lowland hills in the attenuated colours of late summer. Scotland was a country of just those shades, thought Isabel, looking at the Gillies; faded blues, patches of red and purple where the heather grew, the grey of scree on exposed hillsides.

She looked at the McInnes and knew immediately that she

had to bid for it. It might have been different if she had not owned the smaller painting, the inspiration, perhaps, for this one. But now this picture spoke to her directly and she would bid for it. She swallowed hard. Isabel was used to giving large sums of money away, but not to spending them on herself. Now she was going to spend a considerable sum which could do so much good elsewhere. Scottish Opera had written to her recently about money, and the Meningitis Research Trust, and the University of Edinburgh . . . There were so many good causes, and she was about to spend money on a painting.

"Very interesting. Very nice."

She turned round sharply.

"Guy!"

The man standing behind Isabel bowed his head in greeting, a rather old-fashioned gesture, she thought, but exactly right. Guy Peploe ran the Scottish Gallery in Dundas Street together with Robin McClure, and Isabel knew them both. Both were the sons of painters, and Isabel had examples of both fathers' work in the house.

She smiled at Guy. He reminded her in a way of Jamie, of whom he could have been an older version; the same dark hair, kept short, the same strong features, the same good looks unconscious of themselves. And did he know? she wondered. Word had got round Edinburgh quickly enough about her pregnancy and Charlie, but there were still people who had not heard, who would be taken aback even if they did not disapprove.

"I take it that you . . . that everybody's well?" enquired Guy. And Isabel knew that he knew.

"Charlie's doing very well," she said. "Getting bigger."

"That's what happens," said Guy. "My children did too."

"And . . ." He searched for a name. He had seen him, that young man of hers; what was his name?

"Jamie is busy," Isabel said. "And Charlie is making him busier."

That settled that, thought Isabel. It was understandable that people should speculate as to whether Jamie had stood by her, but it still caused her minor irritation that they should. Of course, that was one of the uses of marriage; it made it clear that the father intended to honour his commitments.

She pointed at the painting. "Are you . . . ?" She paused. It was always awkward in the saleroom when one encountered a friend looking at the same item. One would not want to bid against a friend, but at the same time one hoped that the friend would feel the same compunction.

Guy shook his head. "Don't worry," he said. "We're not going to go for this. Are you?"

Isabel looked at the painting again. She wanted it.

"I think so."

Guy paged through his catalogue. "The estimate is a bit low," he said. "But it's difficult to tell. His works don't come up very often these days. In fact, I can't remember when I last saw one in the sales. It must have been years ago. Shortly after he died."

He moved forward to examine the painting more closely. "Interesting. I think this is Jura, which is where he died. It's rather poignant to think of him sitting there painting that bit of sea over there and not knowing that it was more or less where he was going to drown. It's rather like painting one's deathbed."

Isabel thought about this for a moment. How many of us knew the bed in which we would die, or even wanted to know? Did it help to have that sort of knowledge? She stared at the painting. In the past she had never worried about her own death—whenever it would be—but now, with Charlie to think about, she felt rather differently about it. She wanted to be there for Charlie; she wanted at least to see him grow up. That must be the hardest thing about having children much later in life—as happened sometimes when a man remarried at, say, sixty-five and fathered a child by a younger wife. He might make it to eighty-five and see his child grow to adulthood, but the odds were rather against it.

"He was quite young when he died, wasn't he?" she asked.

"McInnes? Yes. Forty, forty-one, I think."

Just about what I am now, thought Isabel. More or less my age, and then it was over.

"Why is it that it seems particularly tragic when an artist dies young?" Isabel mused. "Think of all those writers who went early. Wilfred Owen. Bruce Chatwin. Rupert Brooke. Byron. And musicians too. Look at Mozart."

"It's because of what we all lose when that happens," said Guy. "Owen could have written so much more. He'd just started. Brooke, too, I suppose, although I was never wild about him."

"He wrote for women," said Isabel, firmly. "Women like poets who look like Brooke and who go and die on them. It breaks every female heart." She paused. "But the biggest tragedy of all was Mozart. Think of what we didn't get. All that beauty stopped in its tracks. Just like that. And the burial in the rain, wasn't it? In a pauper's grave?"

Guy shrugged. "Everything comes to an end, Isabel. You. Me. The Roman Empire. But I'm sorry that McInnes didn't get more time. I think that he might have developed into somebody really important. In the league of Cadell, perhaps. Everything was pointing that way. Until . . . well, until it all went wrong."

"And he drowned?"

"No," said Guy. "Before that. Just before that. Everything collapsed for him before he went up to that island for the last time, to Jura. I can tell you, if you like."

Isabel was intrigued. "There's a place round the corner," she said. "We could have sandwiches. I'm hungry. It's something to do with having a baby. One begins to need feeding at very particular times."

Guy smiled at the thought. "A good idea." He leaned forward again and peered at the painting. "Odd," he said. "Odd."

Isabel looked at him quizzically. "What's odd?"

"It's unvarnished," Guy said, straightening up. "I seem to remember that McInnes always varnished his paintings. He was obsessive about things like that—framing, varnishing, signatures, and so on. This isn't varnished at all."

Isabel frowned. "Does that mean that it might not be—"

Guy cut her short. "No, certainly not. This is a McInnes all right. But it's just a bit odd that he didn't varnish this one. Maybe it's a very late painting and he died before he got it back for varnishing. Some painters sell their work before they varnish it, you know, and of course they can't varnish it until the paint is dry. That might mean six months, or even more, depending on how thickly the paint is applied. So they sell it to somebody and suggest that they bring it back for varnishing later on. Sometimes people don't bother."

"So that's all?" said Isabel.

"That's all," said Guy. "Nothing very significant. Just a bit odd."

JAMIE CAME to Isabel's house most evenings, round about the time that Charlie was due to have his evening feed and bath.

Isabel was pleased that he did this, although she found that he tended to take over, leaving her little, if anything, to do; and what with Grace assuming so much responsibility for him during the day, Isabel sometimes wondered whether she would end up playing no more than a marginal role in the care of her own child. But she was generous about this, and stood back while Jamie performed his fatherly tasks.

"He'll be ready for solid food any day now," said Jamie that evening. "Look. If I put this spoon there he seems to want to take it into his mouth."

"If you put anything there, he'd do that," said Isabel. "He latched onto the tip of my nose the other day. It was very disconcerting."

Jamie took the spoon away. "I've been reading a book," he said. "All about feeding babies."

Isabel said nothing.

"It says, of course, that breast-feeding is by far the best thing to do," Jamie continued. "Apparently the immune system needs . . ." He stopped himself and looked up.

"I'm sorry," he said. "That was tactless. I just wasn't thinking."

Isabel tried to smile. "Don't worry. I know that you didn't mean . . . didn't mean to criticise."

Unlike some, she thought. She had been a member—briefly—of a mother and baby group in Bruntsfield and she had been given looks of disapproval by one or two of the mothers when she had revealed that she was not feeding Charlie herself. Those women knew, she thought; they knew that there could be a very good reason for it, but they could not help their zeal. And she had felt guilty, although she knew that it was irrational to feel guilt for something that one could not help. Somebody had once said to her that people with physical handicaps could feel guilty, as if the failure of a limb to work was the result of some fault of theirs. It had been a salutary experience for her, because she had never before experienced social opprobrium. She had never been a smoker and been frowned at disapprovingly by nonsmokers; she had never been in a minority of colour, and made to feel different, looked down upon unjustly. She had, of course, tried to imagine it, how it felt to be disliked for something one could not help, and had succeeded to an extent; now, in that petty moment of judgement, she had actually felt it.

She stole a glance at Jamie; stole: she did not like him to see her staring at him. There was something particularly appealing in the sight of this young man engaged in the tasks of fatherhood. He held Charlie so gently, as if he were cosseting something infinitely fragile, and when he looked down at his son his face broke into a look of tenderness that became, after a second or two, an involuntary smile. It was difficult to explain precisely why this quality of male gentleness—a juxtaposition of strength and tenderness—was so appealing; yet every so often it was caught by a painter or a poet and laid bare.

After Jamie had finished feeding Charlie, they carried him to the bathroom, where his tiny bath had been placed on a table. The infant loved the water and waved his arms in excitement, kicked his legs.

"He's so long," said Jamie. "Look how his legs stretch out. And his little body, with its tummy." He reached out and placed a finger gently against Charlie's abdomen, and when he took it away again there was a tiny white mark, which faded quickly. "And here's his heart," he said, placing his finger where he might feel the beating within. "Little ticker. Like a little Swiss watch."

Isabel laughed. "The naming of parts."

"Naming of parts?"

"A poem," she said. "I remember reading it at school. We did war poetry for a few weeks and read an awful lot. There was a poem called 'Naming of Parts.' A group of recruits are being told the names of the various bits of the rifle. But what the poet sees is the japonica blossoming in neighbouring gardens, two lovers embracing in the distance, and so on. I thought it a very sad poem."

Jamie listened. And Isabel thought of Auden, too, or WHA, as she called him, *her* poet. He had written "Musée des Beaux Arts" about much the same thing; how human suffering always took place against a background of the ordinary—the torturer's horse scratching itself against a tree, a ship carrying on with its journey, all happening while Icarus plunged into the sea.

Isabel unfolded a towel, ready to wrap around Charlie. "So ordinary life continues," she said, "while remarkable things happen. Such as angels appearing in the sky."

Jamie reached carefully under Charlie and lifted him out of the shallow water. "Angels?"

"Yes. There's a poet called Alvarez who wrote a lovely poem about angels appearing overhead. The angels suddenly appear in the sky and are unnoticed by a man cutting wood with a buzz saw. But then it was in Tuscany, where one might expect to see angels at any time."

"Poetry," said Jamie. "Even at bath time."

He handed Charlie over to Isabel, and the baby was embraced in a voluminous towel. Jamie dried his hands and rolled his sleeves back down. Isabel noticed that his forearms were tanned brown, as if he had been out in the open. If I took him to Italy, she thought, he would be as brown as a nut.

Charlie settled quickly, and the two of them returned to the kitchen. Isabel poured Jamie a glass of wine and began to cook their dinner. This had become a comfortable domestic ritual, which both appreciated, and it occurred to her that it would be simpler, and more satisfactory, if Jamie moved in altogether. As it was, he stayed some nights, and not others, and on the nights that he was not there she had begun to feel alone, even with Charlie snuffling and occasionally crying in his cot. But they had decided, each separately and without discussing it with the other, that it would be best to keep their own places. It was something to do with independence, Isabel thought, but neither of them used that word.

"Your day?" she asked as she took a saucepan out of the cupboard.

"Uneventful."

"Nothing at all?"

"A rehearsal for Richard Neville-Towle's concert. Ludus Baroque. I told you about it. At the Canongate Kirk. Are you going to come?"

Isabel put the saucepan on the stove. "Yes. It's in my diary."

Jamie picked up that day's *Scotsman* newspaper and folded it neatly. He noticed that the crossword had been completed. "And your day?" he enquired. Isabel hesitated for a moment, and Jamie noticed. Concern crept into his voice. "Something happened?"

Isabel looked blankly at the saucepan. She had started to make a roux and the butter had almost melted; only a tiny mountain showed in a yellow sea. "Fired," she said. "Dismissed." She stirred the molten butter briefly, causing the last part of the mountain to fall into the sea.

"I don't understand."

"From my post," she said. And then she turned to him and

smiled. "You're having dinner, you see, with the *ex*-editor of the *Review of Applied Ethics*. Or soon to be ex. My post is to be taken away and given to somebody else. To a certain Professor Christopher Dove, professor of philosophy at the University of . . . someplace in London." She felt immediately guilty about that description. Isabel did not approve of snobbery and it was rife in academic circles, where older and richer institutions looked down on their newer and poorer brethren; rife and pervasive—with published lists which established the pecking order: Harvard, Oxford, Stanford, Cambridge, jostling one another in rivalry, while below them, almost beneath their notice, the struggling local universities with their overworked staffs and their earnest students. She should not have said *someplace in London* because that was precisely what some people would say from higher up the tree. "I mean the University of—"

Jamie interrupted her. He had been staring at her, open-mouthed. Now he said, "They can't."

"They can, and they have." She told him about Professor Lettuce and his letter. She mentioned the inept attempt at the friendly postscript; Jamie winced. She tried to remain even-voiced—she did not want him to know how much she had been hurt—but he could tell. He rose to his feet and came to her, putting his arm about her shoulder.

"Isabel . . ."

She put a finger to his lips. "I'm all right. I really am. I don't mind."

"You're playing the glad game."

She looked at him and shook her head. "The best of all possible worlds . . ."

"Yes. Pretending that everything is fine, when it isn't." He paused. "How dare they? You work and work for that stupid journal of theirs . . ."

"Not stupid."

"For that stupid journal of theirs. For nothing, or almost nothing. And this is the thanks you get."

She returned to her roux, moving the saucepan slightly off the heat and beginning to sift flour into the mixture. "But that's the way of the world, Jamie. It happens to just about everybody. You work all your life for some company and at the end of the day you find somebody breathing down your neck, itching to get into your office and sit at your desk. And any thanks that you get are not really meant. Not really."

Jamie sat down again. He was thinking of a brass player of his acquaintance whose lip had gone with the onset of middle age. The world of music could be cruel too; one either reached the high notes or one did not. "So you're not going to fight back? You're not going to write to . . . to whoever it is who owns it? Didn't you say that there was a publishing company some-where? Surely you could write to them, to the managing director or whatever?"

Isabel stirred the roux. There were people who never got lumps in their roux; she was not one of them. "The publishers have very little interest in the *Review*," she said. "They acquired it with a building. They tried to sell it once and would probably do the same again, if somebody came along with a large enough offer. No, they've got no desire to interfere."

"So they don't care?"

Isabel thought about this. It would not be correct to say that they did not care—they would care if the journal started to make a loss. But as long as it ticked over and made even a minuscule profit, they were content to let the board get on with it. She explained this to Jamie.

For a few minutes after that, neither spoke. Isabel stirred her roux, which was coming together well now; Jamie fiddled with *The Scotsman,* folding and unfolding a corner, the obituary page. "He had a profound knowledge of aviation," he read. "And his sense of the dramatic was legendary. Once, while speaking at a dinner, he announced that he proposed to buy an airline that . . ." There were such colourful lives in obituaries that the lives of the living seemed so much tamer, as did their names. Who would announce the intention of buying an airline? Presumably somebody did. People—individuals—owned airlines, just as they owned ships and tall buildings and vast tracts of land; or nothing at all, as Gandhi had done at his death. As a boy, Jamie had been given a book about Gandhi by an idealistic aunt, who had shown him the picture of Gandhi's possessions at his death: a pair of spectacles, a white dhoti, a modest pair of sandals . . . But when you leave this world you don't even take that, Jamie, she had said; remember that. And he had stared at the picture, and stared at it, and had wanted, for some reason, to cry, because he felt sorry for Gandhi, who had owned only those few things and was now dead.

"Why don't you sue them?" he asked.

Isabel was about to sample a small quantity of roux. She paused, the spoon halfway to her mouth. "Sue them for what? For unfair dismissal?"

"Yes," said Jamie. "Make them pay for getting rid of you. Make them pay for it."

"It's not all that simple," said Isabel. "And I'm not even sure whether I'm a proper employee. It's very much a part-time job."

Jamie was not convinced. "You could try at least."

Isabel shook her head. "It would be demeaning. And I don't like the thought of litigation. I just don't."

"Go on, Isabel," he said. "Do it. Don't just let yourself be walked over. Do it. Stick up for yourself."

"I couldn't."

Jamie shrugged. "Well, think about it. Please just think about it."

"All right," she said. "I will."

And she did, later that night, with Jamie beside her in her darkened room, she thought about it; and watched him, his arm across the pillow, so beautiful, she felt. If she did what he suggested, she could engage the most expensive, eloquent advocates to act for her, the cream of the Scottish bar. She could pay to have a spectacular day in court, in which her expensive lawyers would run rings around an inadequately represented *Review*. But she put the thought out of her mind because it was not her intention that she should ever, not even once, misuse the financial power which she had acquired through the laws of inheritance. If she had been wealthy through her own efforts it might be different; but she was not, and she would not depart from the code she had set for herself. It was hard, very hard sometimes; like the rule that a mountaineer makes that he should climb a certain distance each day, although the air is so thin and it is hard, so hard, to make the muscles do what one wants them to do.

❖

CHAPTER FIVE

DO YOU KNOW, I've never been to one of these before? My first time. I feel a bit like a schoolboy going into a bar."

Jamie, seated beside Isabel, looked about the saleroom. A large number of people had turned up, thanks in part to the publicity attached to the sale of a private collection of Scots Colourists. This collection had been put together by a business-man who had done well with a small oil company and who had attracted attention by his colourful—and tactless—remarks. The oil wells were on the shores of the Caspian, in one of those republics that people are not quite sure about—where it is and who runs it—and had suddenly dried up. There had been mutterings about geological reports and their manipulation at the other end, and the share price had plummeted. The sale of the Colourists was the result, along with the sale of a Highland sporting estate and a small fleet of expensive vintage cars. Of course people were sympathetic, but secretly delighted, as they are whenever those who boast of their wealth take a tumble.

The Colourists were prominently illustrated in the first few pages of the catalogue—landscapes, still lifes, a portrait of a woman with an elaborate feathered hat—and there they were, in the expensive flesh, hanging on either side of the auctioneer's podium. For the handful of saleroom voyeurs who came to auctions for the excitement of the high prices, this was the highlight of the day; these were the people who had taken the front row of seats although they had no intention of bidding for anything. They liked to watch the saleroom staff take telephone bids, connected to distant purchasers in exotic places, nodding to the auctioneer as the bidding went higher.

"Don't wave to friends," said Isabel. "Unless you want a painting."

Jamie folded his hands on his lap. "Surely not?"

"It's happened," said Isabel, adding, "I think."

The auction started. Isabel noticed Guy Peploe seated a few rows behind them; she smiled at him, and Guy made a thumbs-up sign for good luck. Now the Colourists started to fall: three hundred and twenty thousand pounds, two hundred and eighty thousand . . . Jamie let out a little whistle and nudged Isabel.

"Who's got that sort of money?" he asked. "Galleries?"

"Even if it's a gallery it will be for a private individual in the long run," Isabel whispered. "Rich collectors."

"Honest?"

"Probably. People with dishonest money tend to go for different things, don't they?" She realised, as she spoke, that she did not really know what happened to dishonest money. She was a philosopher, who thought about what we should do and what we should not do, and yet what personal experience enabled her to speak with authority on these matters? She led a very sheltered life in Edinburgh. How many wicked people did she actually know? Professor Christopher Dove? Professor Lettuce? She smiled at the thought. If Dove was wicked, and she really should give him the benefit of the doubt on that, then his wickedness was surely of a very tame nature, confined to academic machinations, jockeying for position on committees and the like. And yet wickedness like that appeared mild only because it occurred in a rarefied context; Trollope's scheming clergymen may not have resorted to guns and knives—those were not the weapons of their milieu—yet, as people, they were probably just as bad as any Sicilian mafioso for whom the gun, rather than the snide remark, was the immediate weapon to hand.

After the Colourists had all been sold, a number of people rose and made their way out of the saleroom. That was the end of the excitement for them; there would be no more sums like that bandied about. Isabel and Jamie watched the paintings disposed of, and there were one or two highlights. An unflattering portrait of a dancer, painted in the style of Botero by a Russian artist, went for forty-five pounds to a small man in an overcoat; a picture of a stag in the Scottish Highlands, by an unknown nineteenth-century hand, made the auctioneer wince—a momentary lapse which drew laughter from the crowd. It was an unfortunate slip, even if entirely understandable, but it did nothing to inhibit two telephone bidders who of course had not seen the wince and who bid against each other to drive the price up well above the estimate.

Then the McInnes came up, and Jamie reached over and touched Isabel lightly on the arm. She took his hand and gave it a squeeze. Her palm was slightly moist. But if I were bidding, I would be shaking, he thought.

"Nervous?" he whispered.

"No," she said. And then a moment later, "Yes, of course."

The bidding started low. The house had a bid in hand which had been put in for a client, and then it climbed. Isabel came in after the fourth bid, with a bid of ten thousand pounds, but that was immediately raised by a telephone bidder. Then somebody from the back of the hall put in a bid and the price went up another thousand. Jamie turned in his seat to see who it was, but there were heads in the way. Isabel now raised her card again and a thousand pounds was added. There were consultations on the telephone and a nod—another thousand.

At twenty thousand, Isabel was the highest bidder. The auctioneer looked up from his desk and surveyed the room.

"It's going to be you," whispered Jamie. "You're going to win."

"I'm not sure . . ." she began.

Jamie was alarmed. "Not sure you want it?"

The auctioneer glanced at Isabel and then looked over her head towards the back. He nodded at the bidder. "Twenty-one thousand pounds."

"No," said Isabel, slipping her numbered bidding card into her pocket.

The auctioneer looked at her enquiringly and she shook her head. Then he looked at his two colleagues with the telephones: both indicated that they were going no further. The auctioneer repeated the bid from the back and then dropped his hammer, a short tap, his hand covering the small wooden head.

Jamie looked at Isabel, who was reaching for the bag at her feet. "Bad luck," he whispered.

Isabel shrugged. "That's what auctions are about. They tell us something rather important, don't you think?"

"That what matters—"

Isabel completed the sentence for him. "Is money. Yes. It doesn't matter how much somebody likes something or deserves to get it—it's money that decides things. A simple lesson." She stuffed her catalogue into the bag.

Bidding had started on the next item, and they waited until

this had finished before they rose to their feet and began to make their way towards the back of the room. A couple who had been standing at the end of the row quickly took their vacant seats, smiling thankfully at Jamie, who had looked back at them.

Isabel turned to Jamie. "Did you see who got it?" she asked.

"There were heads in the way," he said. "But it was somebody over there." He pointed to the back, which was lined with thirty or forty people who had not managed to find a seat. "One of them, I think."

Isabel looked at the crowd of people: any one of them could have been the bidder.

"Why do you want to know?" asked Jamie, from beside her.

"Pure curiosity," she said. And she realised that there was no reason for her to know who had outbid her.

She stopped. There was a familiar face in the crowd, a man standing on the edge, examining his catalogue.

"Peter?"

Her friend, Peter Stevenson, looked up from his catalogue and smiled at Isabel. "I saw you," he said quietly—the bidding had begun on another painting. "I saw you bidding for that McInnes. You must have wanted it an awful lot."

Isabel made a gesture of acceptance. "All's fair in love and auctions."

Love. Peter glanced at Jamie, who was standing behind her: he thoroughly approved of the relationship between Isabel and Jamie and had once, at a dinner party, spoken up when somebody had made a pointed remark about the disparity in age between Isabel and her new boyfriend. *Envy,* he had muttered, sotto voce but just loud enough to be heard by the entire table and to bring a blush of shame to the countenance of Isabel's detractor. Peter's wife, Susie, had looked at him sharply, but she, like most others at the table, thought his comment well placed.

"Well, I'm sorry," whispered Peter. "Walter Buie obviously wanted it more than you did."

Isabel was interested. "He was the other bidder?"

"Yes," said Peter. "He left immediately afterwards. But he was standing quite close to me. Just over there." He looked at Isabel enquiringly. "Do you know him?"

Isabel thought. The name was vaguely familiar, but probably just because it was a rather unusual Scottish name. She had met Buies before, but not this one.

"He's a lawyer," said Peter. "He was with one of the large firms, but got fed up and set up by himself doing little bits and pieces for a few private clients. Modest stuff. I don't think he liked the pace in the firm—you know what those legal firms can be like these days. He lives quite close to us in the Grange. I often see him taking his dog for a walk. Nice man. Not such a nice dog."

"Well, he wanted it, obviously," said Isabel. "Is he a collector?"

Peter put a finger to his lips. "We're making a bit of a noise," he whispered. "I'm getting one or two looks." He leaned over and whispered in Isabel's ear. "Buie is a Jura name. His father probably came from there, or somewhere nearby. There are lots of Buies on the island. McInnes painted on Jura, didn't he?"

Isabel indicated that she was going to leave. "Come and see us," she whispered to Peter. "Bring Susie to have a look at Charlie. Any time." She paused. "Why are you here, Peter?"

"Susie's birthday is coming up," he said. "There's a little watercolour coming up a bit later on. Tiny one—this big. I might go up to eighty pounds!"

Isabel smiled. "Be careful."

Jamie followed her out of the saleroom and out onto Broughton Street. He looked at his watch; he had to be at the

Edinburgh Academy in half an hour to give a lesson. Isabel could not linger either; Charlie would need feeding soon and although Grace was looking after him, she wanted to see him. It was strange; a separation of just a few hours made her anxious. Was this what being a parent was going to be like? A life of anxiety, of fretting about little things? Have a child and give a hostage to fortune; yes, but have any human link, any friendship, and a hostage was given.

Jamie explained that he would have to go; it would take him fifteen minutes to walk to the school and he liked to have a few minutes in hand. Then he inclined his head back in the direction of the saleroom. "You could have gone higher, you know."

"Yes," said Isabel. "I could have. But I didn't."

Jamie looked into Isabel's eyes. "Just how well-off are you, Isabel?"

The question took Isabel by surprise. He had not spoken in a hostile manner, but it was a potentially hostile question.

"I've got enough to get by," she said. "That should perhaps be obvious—not that I want it to be."

Jamie continued to look into her eyes. He was experiencing a strange feeling: a feeling that she was his but not his. And at the root of it, he suspected, was the fact that their positions were so different. Everything about their relationship, in fact, involved contrasts; she was older than he was; she had so much more money; she lived on the south side of the city and he on the north; he was dark and she tended to the fairer. Jack Spratt and his wife.

Nothing was said for a while. "You're not answering me," he said eventually.

She remained patient. "Well, it's a question that I don't have to answer." She spoke quietly. "And why do you want to know, anyway? I don't ask you what you earn, do I?"

"I'm quite happy to tell you," he said. "But, anyway, you're right. It's none of my business. I shouldn't have asked."

She looked at him. She might have been cross, but could not find it within her. She could not be cross with him; she could not. You can say anything to me, she said to herself; anything at all. Because we're lovers. And I love you, Jamie, every bit of you; I love you so much.

She reached out and touched him. She swept the hair back off his forehead and then she slipped her hand down to the back of his neck. "There are shares in a company," she said. "They came from my mother. The company had land and buildings in Louisiana, and in Mobile too. It did well."

"You don't have to tell me this," said Jamie. "I'm sorry—"

"Eleven million pounds," said Isabel. "Depending on the value of the dollar."

Jamie was silent. He stared at her in astonishment.

"Is your curiosity satisfied?" she asked.

Jamie seemed flustered. "Sorry, I shouldn't have asked. I don't know why I did. I really don't."

Isabel took his hand. "Could you telephone the school and tell them that you can't come in?" she said on impulse. "We could go home."

He shook his head.

"Go on," she urged him.

He shook his head again. "Siren," he said.

They kissed, and she watched him for a few moments as he walked down Broughton Street. He must have sensed her gaze, as he turned round and waved to her before continuing. She blew him a kiss, which he did not return.

Isabel turned away and began to walk along Queen Street. The late-morning air was bright, the air warm for the east of Scotland. She was worried that she had divulged something that she should have kept private. A few minutes earlier she had thought of the giving of hostages. Well, she said to herself, I've just given another one.

ISABEL ARRIVED HOME to find that Grace had taken Charlie out into the garden in his pram, and was sitting under the sycamore tree at the back. Isabel peered down at Charlie, who was sleeping on his back, his head shaded by the pram's retractable hood. His mouth was slightly open and his right hand was holding the silk-lined edge of the blanket, the fingers where they were when he had fallen asleep.

"Something seemed to be bothering him this morning," said Grace. "He was all niggly and he wouldn't settle. Girned a lot. Then he became a bit better. I gave him some gripe water."

Isabel stayed where she was, bent over the pram, her face just above Charlie, but she looked sharply at Grace. "You gave him gripe water," she said evenly. "And?"

"And it did the trick," said Grace. "No more girning. Well, no more after about ten, fifteen minutes."

Grace used the Scots word *girn,* which Isabel always thought so accurately described the sound of a child's crying. But it was gripe water that concerned her. "I didn't know we had any gripe water," she said. And then, straightening up, she continued, "We don't, do we? We don't have it."

"I bought some," said Grace. "A few weeks ago."

Isabel walked round the side of the pram. "And he's had it before?" she asked.

"Yes," said Grace. "Quite a few times. It really is effective."

Isabel took a breath. She rarely felt angry, but now she did, aware of the emotion welling up within her—a hot, raw feeling. "But gripe water contains gin, doesn't it? For God's sake. Gin!"

Grace looked at her in astonishment. "Not anymore! It used to, I believe. I had it when I was a child, my mother told me. She said that she would take a swig or two herself as well. But that's years ago. You know how fussy people are these days."

"So what does it have in it now?" asked Isabel. "I like to know what medicines Charlie's taking, you know. As his mother I feel . . ." She knew that she sounded rude, but she could not help herself. And it did not help that Grace seemed so unapologetic.

"But it's not a medicine," said Grace. "It's herbal. I think that the one I bought has fennel and ginger and some other things. It soothes the stomach, which is what they niggle about." She looked up at Isabel. "You're not worried about it, are you?"

Isabel turned away. She struggled to control her voice, and when she spoke she felt that it sounded quite normal. "No, I'm not worried. It's just that I'd like to know if you give him anything unusual. I just feel that I should know."

Grace said nothing, and Isabel did not look at her to gauge her reaction. She did not want to argue with Grace because she felt that it would be wrong for her to do so when Grace was her employee. That gave her an advantage over the other woman which she should not use; Grace could not fight back on equal terms, and that was unfair. But at the same time, it was not unreasonable of her, she felt, to insist on being asked before Charlie was given things like gripe water. Fennel! Ginger! Unnamed herbs!

She began to move away, but Grace had something to say, and she stopped.

"Cat telephoned."

In the past, Cat had telephoned regularly. Then, with the breach in their relations, these calls had stopped; the significance of this was not lost on Grace, who said, "Yes. She actually telephoned."

Isabel turned round. "What about?"

"An invitation. She wants you to go to dinner with her." She paused, watching Isabel's reaction.

Isabel decided to be cool about this. "Oh? That's kind of her."

"Jamie too," said Grace. "She wants him to go too."

Isabel's manner remained cool, although this was a very unexpected development. "And Charlie?" she asked.

Grace shook her head. "I don't think so," she said. "She didn't mention him."

Isabel went into the house, into her study. For a few minutes she just stood there, inwardly seething. Grace had no right to take over Charlie like that. She was acting almost as if he were her baby, not Isabel's. And it irritated her, too, that the other woman should behave as if she knew more about babies than Isabel did; there had been many instances of that, sometimes subtle, sometimes not so subtle. Isabel knew that Grace had always thought of her as somebody who was otherworldly, somebody who did not really know how things worked. Isabel had ignored this in the past, but she found it hard to do that now.

She sat down. Things were going wrong: the job, her failure of nerve in the auction, that odd exchange with Jamie over money, Grace giving Charlie gripe water, and now this odd invitation from Cat. Why would Cat invite Jamie? To interfere? To try to get him back?

Isabel looked down at the floor. The carpet in her study was an old red Belouchi that had been in the house for as long as she could remember. She and her brother had played on it as a child. He had used it to make a tent from which he had shot rubber-tipped arrows in her direction. One had hit her in the eye and he had been punished by their father. He had blamed her for his punishment, for telling on him. *I'll hate you forever,* he had hissed at her. *Wait and see. I'll hate you forever.* And now, after all those years, she hardly ever saw him, and he never wrote. It was not the Belouchi, of course; it was something else, something private and nothing to do with Isabel herself. Children hated for a very short time; they forgot, sometimes after a few minutes, while adults could keep hatreds going indefinitely, across generations.

She thought of Jamie. It would have been so much simpler if he had been her own age and she could have accepted his proposal of marriage there and then. It was bad luck, just bad luck to fall in love with the wrong person. People did that all the time; they fell in love with somebody who for one reason or another could never be theirs. And then they served their sentence, the sentence of unrequited, impossible love, which could go on for years and years, with no remission for good behaviour, none at all.

She looked up at the white expanse of ceiling. In her mind the most worrying thing about Cat's invitation was this: Jamie had recovered from Cat—Isabel thought of it as a recovery— but if he were to spend any time in her company his feelings for her might be reignited. It could happen. So should she conveniently forget to mention the invitation to him? Or should she go further and tell Cat that he did not want to come? For a short time the dilemma which this posed made Isabel forget her worries. If she simply did not pass on the invitation, she was merely omitting to do something; if she went further and told Cat that he did not want to come then she was actually telling a lie. As to the omission, she was not sure what duty one had to pass on information to another. If A says to B please tell C something or other, does B have any obligation to do so? It would depend, thought Isabel, on whether B had agreed to take on the duty of passing on the message. If he had not, then a liberal individualistic philosopher would probably say that he did not have to exert himself. That was liberal individualism, of course, with which Isabel did not always agree. Don't go swimming with a liberal individualist, she told herself; he might not save you if you started to drown. No, liberal individualism was not an attractive philosophy. Except now. Now it offered a very attractive solution to her problem.

I'll discuss the question with Jamie, she decided. And then she thought: How can I be so stupid? Oh, Christopher Dove, if only you could hear this interior monologue. If only. And you too, Professor Lettuce, you great slug!

She felt much better.

❖

CHAPTER SIX

TWO DAYS AFTER THE AUCTION, Isabel was seated at her desk, halfheartedly paging through a submission for the journal—*not* a good one, she thought, but she always read to the end, no matter how tedious. She had not done anything about Cat's invitation, and was still uncertain just what she would do about it; so when the telephone rang she looked at it for a few moments, uncertain whether to answer. It could be Cat, in which case she would be put in an immediate spot for having ignored the invitation.

She picked up the receiver and gave her number. Cat always interrupted her if she did that. "I know your number," she would say. "I've just dialled it." But, rather to her relief, it was not her niece, but Guy Peploe.

"I'm sorry that you didn't get your picture," he said. "I was crossing my fingers for you."

"That's what happens at auctions," Isabel said. "And there'll be another chance some day, no doubt."

Guy laughed. "True words," he said. "In fact, there's a chance right now, if you're interested. Not that picture, of course, but another McInnes. Interested?"

Isabel said that she was. But was it at auction?

"No," said Guy. "Somebody has brought it in to the gallery and wants us to sell it on commission."

Isabel thought for a moment. She was interested in seeing it, but she wondered whether she would want to buy it. The picture she had missed at auction had been a special one, as far as she was concerned, because of its link with the small study that she already owned; she had no particular desire to own a McInnes just because it was a McInnes.

"All right," she said. "I'll take a look at it some time over the next few days."

Guy hesitated at the other end of the line. "Sorry to press you," he said, "but I think that you should come down more or less immediately. I've got somebody coming in later this afternoon to look at a number of other things who may well go for this one too. He buys for a collector in Palm Beach. This is exactly the sort of thing that his man in Florida likes."

Isabel looked at her watch and then glanced down at the manuscript she was reading. "Look, Guy, I'm in the middle of something really tedious. It'll take me about forty minutes to finish and then I can come. And can I bring Charlie?"

Charlie, she was told, would be very welcome: one could never start them on art too young. Isabel then returned to the paper she was reading. She had lost the thread of the argument, which was all about individual autonomy within the family, and had to go back several paragraphs to regain it. There was something wrong with this paper, she thought; something odd that she could not quite put her finger on. Then it occurred to her: the author did not believe what he was writing. He was making all the right arguments, saying all the right things, but he simply did not believe it. She looked at the title page, where his name and institution were typed. Yes. It was just as she thought. That particular department of philosophy was known for its ideological position; one could not even get an interview for a job, let alone a job, unless one adopted a radical position. This poor man was uttering the shibboleths, but his heart was obviously not in them: he was a secret conservative! In this paper he had argued against the family, calling it a threat to individual autonomy, a repressive institution. That was the party line, but he probably loved his family and believed that the best way of growing up adjusted and happy was to have a mother and a father. But that was heresy in certain circles, and *very* unfashionable.

She finished the paper and wrote what she thought would be a quick note to the author.

I shall pass your article on to the editorial board for a verdict. I am about to give up the editorship of this journal, and so you will probably be dealing, in due course, with the new editor, who will be Christopher Dove, whom you may know. I am sure that he will be very sympathetic to the argument that you put forward in this paper, as he has often expressed views similar to your own. I think he believes them, but, and forgive me if I am wrong, I get the feeling that your heart is not behind the arguments you present. Not your heart. You see, there are occasions when a theoretically defensible position, based, say, on an argument of individual rights and equality, goes completely against what we see about us in the world. And what we see about us in the world is that the conventional family, where there is a loving mother and a loving father, provides by far the best environment for the raising of children. That's the way it has been for thousands of years. And should we not perhaps take into account what the wisdom of thousands of years teaches us? Or are we so clever that we can ignore it? That is not to say that there are all sorts of other homes in which children may grow up very secure and very happy. Very loved too. But the recognition of that should not lead us to condemn and thereby weaken the conventional family ideal, which is what you do here. Do you really mean that? Do you really think that we would be happier if we abandoned the conventional family? I'm sorry, but I don't think that you do; you're just saying that you do because it's the position to take.

She read what she had written, and then read it again. Did she herself believe this? What was she providing for Charlie? What did she *want* to provide for Charlie? She reached for her pen and crossed out the final sentence. But that made the letter useless; crossed-out words are still words. So she crumpled the letter up and tossed it into the bin. Then she reached for another sheet of letterhead and wrote: "Thank you. Interesting article. I'll pass it on to the editorial board. You'll hear from the new editor. I.D. ed."

Coward, she said to herself as she rose from her desk. Just like him.

ISABEL TOOK THE BUS from Bruntsfield. Charlie slept contentedly in his sling; he had been fed and had shown no signs of colic or any other discomfort. Isabel had found the bottle of gripe water which had been purchased by Grace. She had moved the bottle to the bathroom cupboard; Grace might find it there if she looked, but Isabel's act of reshelving it at least made her point. In fact, she thought Grace had picked up on her irritation at her taking Charlie over—that morning she had very pointedly asked Isabel if she minded if she took Charlie out into the garden to walk him round the flowers; previously she had done that without asking.

Charlie slept through the bus journey and was still fast asleep when they entered the Scottish Gallery. Guy Peploe and Robin McClure were in consultation with a client when Isabel went in, but Guy detached himself from the group and came over to greet her.

"It's downstairs," he said. "Come with me." He reached forward and tickled Charlie under the chin. "My own are growing up so quickly. One forgets one used to carry them all the time."

"Did you use gripe water?" asked Isabel.

Guy thought for a moment. "I think so," he said. "Doesn't everybody? It tastes rather nice, if I remember correctly. Very sweet."

Isabel smiled. "It used to contain gin."

"Mother's ruin."

They made their way downstairs. The lower floor housed three rooms, one given over to jewellery and glass and the other used for overflow exhibitions from the main gallery above. When they went into the back room, Isabel saw the painting immediately. It was propped up against a wall, directly below a small Blackadder watercolour of a bunch of purple irises.

"That's it," said Guy. "It's a stunner, isn't it?"

Isabel agreed. The painting was not quite as large as the one in the auction sale, but it was clearly the finer picture, she felt, and Guy, she could tell, agreed.

"It's—" she began.

"Even better," he said. "Yes, it is."

She moved forward to look more closely at the painting. It was a picture of a boy in a small rowboat, on the edge of a shore. It was clearly Scotland—and somewhere familiar in Scotland, she thought; behind the shore there were buildings of the sort that one sees in the Western Highlands, or on the islands, low, white-painted houses. And then a hillside rising up into low clouds.

"You can almost smell it," she said. "The peat smoke, the kelp . . ."

"And the whisky," said Guy, pointing to a small cluster of buildings portrayed on the left of the painting. "This is Jura, you know, as the other painting was. And those are some of the distillery buildings. See them? And there are some of the kegs outside."

Isabel bent down again and peered at the passage that Guy had indicated. Yes, it was Jura, and that was why it seemed familiar. She had been there on a number of occasions to stay with friends at Ardlussa. That was towards the north of the island; this was to the south, near Craighouse, where the island's only whisky distillery was.

She stood back from the painting. "What makes this so special?" she asked.

Guy stared at the painting. "Everything," he said after a while. "Everything comes together in it. And it captures the spirit of the place, doesn't it? I've been on Jura only once, but you know what those west coast islands are like. That light. That peaceful feeling. There's nowhere like them." He paused. "Not that one wants to romanticise . . ."

Isabel agreed. "And yet, and yet . . . We do live in a rather romantic country, don't we? For us, it's just home, but it's very dramatic, isn't it? Rather like living on an opera set."

They both stood and gazed at the painting for a while. Then Isabel shook her head. "I don't know, Guy. Or maybe I do. Maybe not." He was putting her under no pressure to buy the painting, but she felt that she should explain to him. "It's just that the other painting had that particular significance for me. I hope you understand."

Guy reassured her. The other prospective purchaser would almost certainly take the painting. It would leave Scotland, of course, but it was a good thing to share . . . "But again it's odd," he finished. "And getting a little bit odder."

Isabel frowned. "This one isn't varnished either?" She bent down again and peered at the painting at close quarters. Charlie, feeling himself being tilted, let out a little murmur, something that sounded like a mew.

"No, it isn't," said Guy. "There's that. But the other thing that puzzles me is that the two paintings should come onto the market one after the other, and within the space of a few days. That's a bit surprising, especially when the market has been starved of McInneses for a long time. People tend to hang on to them."

"Somebody has obviously decided to sell," said Isabel. "Or they've died and their family are disposing of them. You can imagine the scene. Young relatives with no interest in painting. Highland scenes. Sea. Hills. Not what we need. Let's sell and take the money."

"That happens," said Guy. "But these would appear to be from different sources."

"Who?"

Guy sighed. "I can't tell you, I'm afraid. I hope you don't

think I'm being unhelpful, but I can't really disclose who is offering this one. These things are confidential, you see—clients like it that way."

Isabel understood. People might not like others to know that they were having to raise money. "Of course." But how would Guy know that this painting came from a different source if he didn't know—and the same principle of confidentiality would preclude it—who had consigned the other painting to Lyon & Turnbull?

He saw the question coming. "You'll be wondering how I know they're from different places? Well, our client told us that he"—he corrected himself—"that she hadn't heard about the painting at Lyon & Turnbull. Unless she's misleading us, which I don't think she is. In fact, it's impossible. She's not the type."

"I wonder where she got it from?" asked Isabel.

"In this case, I believe she bought it from the artist himself. Shortly before his death, I think. Sometimes there's a gallery label," said Guy. He reached forward and tilted the painting away from the wall. "Look—nothing on the back, apart from that writing over there." He pointed to where somebody had written, in pencil, JURA, WITH MOUNTAINS. There was another handwritten line underneath: *The boy's called James.*

"That's McInnes's writing all right," said Guy. "I've seen our own labels that he scribbled on. Or sometimes he wrote instructions about where the painting was to be delivered. Or where he was staying when he painted it. Sometimes lines of poetry—he liked to put MacDiarmid in. Odd things."

"MacDiarmid liked that part of Scotland," said Isabel. " 'Island Funeral.' That was one of his better efforts, in spite of the flannel. He was a bit of a shocker, you know."

"But he could . . ."

"Yes, he could," said Isabel. "He could stop us in our tracks. That poem about the island funeral makes the hairs on the back of one's neck stand up." She paused and remembered. "I went to one once, you know. An island funeral. An aged cousin of my father's who had married into a family on South Uist. They were Free Presbyterians and there were no prayers. All those dark-suited men standing in a huddle, and the coffin left outside. They sang psalms, those strange Gaelic psalms, and then they went and buried her in silence with rain coming in from the Atlantic, nothing heavy, just soft rain. And that light. The same light that's in that painting over there."

Guy said nothing for a moment. He could see the scene that she was describing, and there was nothing that he could add.

Isabel broke the silence. "Are you sure that this is a McInnes? Are you absolutely sure?"

He was. "I'm pretty certain, Isabel. We wouldn't offer it as a McInnes if we weren't. All my colleagues are sure. Robin. Everybody."

Isabel wondered how anybody could be certain about anything in the art world. There were all those fake Dalí prints still in circulation—almost mass-produced fakes, like the reproduction paintings turned out to order from Russian studios. If they could do old masters for a couple hundred dollars, then surely with a bit more time they could do something considerably more convincing?

"I see you're still doubtful," said Guy. "And yes, there are forgers who will do a very careful job. But one develops an eye for particular painters, you know, and one can just tell. It's like hearing somebody's voice. Little things that all add up to an overall impression that this is it." He paused. "And provenance is pretty important. In this case, the person who brought this in knew him. Knew McInnes. We know that she did, and so it all makes sense."

"All right," said Isabel. "I was just thinking aloud."

Guy said that this was reasonable enough. Then, "Do you know much about McInnes? Do you know about what went wrong at the end?"

"He drowned, didn't he?"

"Yes. Off Jura. But it was very sad, even before that. He had a big exhibition here in Edinburgh—two years' work. It went on just before the Festival and a whole group of London critics traipsed up for it. They decided to slaughter McInnes because he had given a lecture at the Tate in which he pointed out how the London critics had ignored Scottish artists. He did it quite politely, but he did accuse them of metropolitanism, and that's the one thing you mustn't accuse metropolitans of. So they decided to get their own back—in spades. They called him an overrated minor landscape painter. One of them headed his crit 'Provincial Painting by Numbers.' They egged one another on."

Isabel felt outraged. But her outrage had nothing to do with painting by numbers; it was the word *provincial*. "Provincial!"

"Yes. Exactly. And the effect on McInnes was pretty disastrous. I saw him the day after the first of these notices was published. He was sitting in the Arts Club all by himself, a drink in front of him. I went and had a word with him, but I don't think that he was taking much in. His hands were shaking. He looked awful."

Isabel winced. "Poor man. I had a friend who made the mistake of being both an author and thin-skinned. Journalists toss off their cutting remarks without realising the effect they have on the people they're talking about."

"There are plenty of people like that," said Guy. "But it wasn't just the bad reviews in McInnes's case. It was the timing. On virtually the same day that things went wrong with the show, he found out that his wife was having an affair. It all came at once. He was devastated."

Isabel suddenly thought of Cat. Sexual jealousy was powerful, and that's what Cat felt about Jamie; she must, even if she had got rid of him in the first place; it was still there, cutting and cutting away.

"So . . . the drowning . . ."

She left the question unfinished. Had it been a suicide? If one wanted to make a death appear like an accident, drowning was probably the best way of doing that. There were seldom any witnesses; it was easy to arrange, especially in a place like the west of Scotland with its tides and currents. But what a lonely death it must be; out in those cold waters, on the edge of the Atlantic, like a burial at sea.

"No," said Guy. "I don't think that he killed himself. He went off to Jura after things came apart down here. He left his wife more or less immediately and hid away in a cottage he used to rent up there. Rather like Orwell, in a way, who went off to Jura to write *1984*. Anyway, he went up there and a month later it happened. He had a boat which he often took out. That's why I don't think it was suicide. It was consistent with the normal pattern of his life up there."

Charlie was now quite awake and was staring up at Isabel with that intense, slightly puzzled stare that babies fix on their parents. "I'm going to have to feed him," she said. "I've got his bottle here."

"I'll get you a chair," said Guy. "Then, if you don't mind, I'd better go and speak to those people upstairs again."

"Of course."

He fetched a chair and she sat down in a shaft of sunlight that came in from the back window. Like a woman in a Vermeer painting, she thought. Woman with child.

"One last observation," said Guy. "McInnes's death wasn't suicide, as I said. In my view it was something worse. I think of it as murder."

Isabel looked up sharply; an unfamiliar word in Edinburgh. "Murder?"

"Yes," said Guy. "A form of murder. By the critics. They killed him."

She was relieved; nothing nasty—there was real murder and metaphorical murder. The first of these was a sordid, banal business; the second was considerably more interesting.

❖

CHAPTER SEVEN

S HE LET JAMIE in the front door.

"I left my key at home," he said. "Sorry."

She had presented him with a key shortly after Charlie's birth, or slipped it into his hand; a presentation would have been more ceremonial. At first he had kept it on his main key ring, but then, for some reason, he had moved it onto another one, by itself. She had wondered about this—whether the separation of keys meant anything, but dismissed the thought; one could read too much into little things.

"You should keep all your . . ."

He bent down and kissed her, and her question trailed off. "Yes, of course. Of course. Where's Charlie?"

Charlie was lying on his back, on a blanket in the morning room, staring up at the ceiling. He appeared to be fascinated by the ornamental plaster rose in the centre and would gaze at it for long periods. "He must think that's the sky," said Isabel. "And the plaster rose is a cloud."

Jamie laughed and went down on his hands and knees beside Charlie, who lifted his arms up and gurgled with plea-sure. Isabel left them playing with one another and went through to the kitchen to prepare dinner. Charlie would be attended to and put to bed by Jamie while she cooked. Jamie liked to sing to him when he put him down, and Charlie seemed to like this, staring wide-eyed at his father, watching his lips, calmed by the sound of the voice.

> *Dreams to sell, fine dreams to sell,*
> *Angus is here with dreams to sell.*
> *Hush now wee bairnie and sleep without fear,*
> *For Angus will bring you a dream, my dear.*

She had stood transfixed when she first heard him singing that to Charlie, and had even found herself weeping. "Why?" he had said, turning round and seeing her. "Why are you crying?" And she had shaken her head and muttered something rambling, something about lullabies being the saddest of songs, for some reason. "They always do this to me. The lullaby in *Hansel and Gretel*—you must know it: 'When at night I go to sleep, Fourteen angels watch do keep. Two my head are guarding, Two my feet are guiding . . .'" He had put his arms around her and said, "Yes. Why not? All those angels. And Dream Angus too, with his dreams."

Now she stood at the cutting board and asked herself: Is this complete happiness? Am I happier now than I have ever been before? The answer, she thought, was yes, she was. There had been periods of unhappiness in her life—the John Liamor episode being one of those—but she thought of herself as having been, for the most part, reasonably happy. But since the beginning of her affair with Jamie she had been conscious of being in a state of heightened happiness, a state of . . . well, she had to resort to the concept of blessedness. I am blessed, and being blessed is something more than just having something; it is a state of mind in which the good of the world is illuminated, is understood. It is as if one is vouchsafed a vision of some sort, she thought, a vision of love, of agape, of the essential value of each and every living thing.

For a moment, Isabel stood stock-still. There were vegetables on the board before her, ready for the knife, but she did not move; her hand was arrested in its movement, motionless. She was aware of a physical sensation, a sort of rushing within her and around her, a current, which seemed to fill her with warmth. She closed her eyes and, oddly, there was no darkness, just light; it was as if she were bathed in light both within and without.

She opened her eyes again. The ordinary material world was there, the vegetables, the sink, the unopened bottle of wine, the recipe book lying open at the page to which she had turned, the pen-and-ink drawing on that page, everything. She breathed. The warmth, the feeling of suffusion had gone, and she felt that she was back in the same place. She moved her arm and felt the coldness of the granite worktop under her skin, all quite normal. But she felt different; she felt that the world had suddenly become infinitely more precious to her, and that there was more love within her. It was that simple, perhaps; there was just more love within her.

Later, with Charlie asleep, she and Jamie sat at the kitchen table. She had prepared scallops for them, to be followed by a risotto, which she knew he liked. They had chilled white wine with the scallops, and he raised his glass to her. *To Charlie's mother.* She had laughed, and replied, *To his father.* She looked down at her plate. She wanted to tell him what had happened, there in the kitchen, while he was attending to Charlie, but how could she put it? *I had a mystical experience in the kitchen this evening?* Hardly. I am not the sort who has mystical experiences in the kitchen, she said to herself; the world is divided between those who have mystical experiences in their kitchens and those who do not.

He said, "You're smiling to yourself about something."

"I suppose I am. Just a silly thought."

He took a sip of his wine. "About?"

"About something that happened to me. I had a moment of . . . well, I suppose I might call it a moment of inspiration, while I was preparing dinner."

He did not seem surprised. "I had one of those the other day," he said. "I was waiting for one of my pupils and I had a moment of inspiration. A musical idea. I wrote it down as quickly as I could but when I played it later on . . . A great disappointment."

She thought that they were not talking about the same thing. She had been wrong to call it a moment of inspiration; no ideas had come to her, rather an insight, and that was different. But it was difficult to define it, because language was not suited to describing such things; one ended up talking at great length about what seemed ultimately to be something very small, as happens in the writings of mystics, where a cloud of words surrounds the brief light about which they write.

No, she did not want to appear foolish, and this was a subject on which she realised she knew very little about Jamie's views. Did he believe in anything beyond the material? They had never talked about that, and she had no idea. But that was probably not unusual amongst couples—how many people these days, in her sort of society, talked to one another about *that*? She thought of her friends, and wondered which of them believed in the existence of God. She knew one or two of them went to church, and they, she assumed, either believed in God or wanted to believe. That was probably true of many people in any congregation, of course: they were there not because they believed but because they felt the need for religion, for something beyond themselves. So what did Jamie believe in, if anything? Did he think that he had a soul? She watched him pick up his glass. He was looking at her, his eyes smiling. Of course he had a soul, she said to herself; that gentle, kind, loving part of him. That was there, and she could see it.

"We've had an invitation," she said. And immediately she wondered why she had said this. She had not been thinking about it, and even if she had, she would not have thought about bringing it up right now. But it came out, unanticipated.

"Oh?"

She swallowed hard. She had just had a vision of love, or something to do with love, and she had to go on in that spirit. "Cat has asked us to dinner."

She watched him closely. Sometimes words can be seen, she thought; one sees them travelling through the air and reaching their target as if an invisible wave had moved through the room. Isabel remembered how, as a young woman, she had once gone to sit through a trial in the High Court. She had a friend who was a junior advocate in the trial and she wanted to see her in action. It had been dramatic; she had seen the jury return its verdict and the judge had shifted in his seat to face the accused. Then he simply said, "Six years," and she saw the man in the dock reel backwards as if he had been hit by an unseen hand, pushing him back.

Jamie put down his glass and looked at her. The light that had been in his eyes, the smile, was no longer there; it had been replaced by something flat, something guarded. "That's kind of her," he said. "When?"

"She didn't say. It was a message, actually. She left it with Grace."

"I see."

She toyed with her fork. "Do you want to go? We don't have to." She thought that Cat would understand; they had kept off the subject of Cat, by unspoken agreement, because they both knew it was a wound that should not be breathed into.

He did not reply for a moment. "I'm over her," he said, but he did not look at Isabel as he spoke, and she knew it could not be true. If Cat meant nothing to him anymore, then he would have looked at her; Jamie always engaged with people directly, looked them in the eye. But not now.

Isabel stared at him. This hurt her. "I don't think you are, Jamie. I really don't think you are."

Now he looked up at her. "No. You're right."

"So do you still love her?"

His voice was low. "Maybe I do. Maybe. You know how it is."

"Of course. I was in love for years and years. Even after John had left me I still loved him, went on loving him, so foolishly, pointlessly. But we can't help ourselves, can we?"

He suddenly pushed his chair back and rose to his feet. Something—his glass of water—toppled and was spilled, and made a long dark stain down the leg of his jeans. He came round to her and crouched down. He put his arm about her. His voice sounded hoarse; that was from emotion, she thought. "Don't you think that it's possible that we can . . . that we can end up loving lots of people? People we used to love, still love. Them. But they're just there in the background, and we get on with loving other people, people from our present rather than our past. Don't you think that?"

She reached for his hand and pressed it. Blessedness: she could not believe her state of blessedness; this young man, with all his beauty and gentleness, in her arms, hers. "Of course I believe that," she said.

"So do we go, or not?"

"I think we should go. Cat and I are family. I don't want her cut out of my life with you."

He kissed her on the brow, then on the lips. "All right."

THE MAIL THE NEXT DAY brought two manuscripts that Isabel knew were coming and which she had been looking forward to receiving, and she read these in preference to the items immediately below them in the pile, some of which looked like bills. The manuscripts were as interesting as she had hoped, and she started to write grateful letters to their authors. Both were solicited contributions to a special issue on the philosophy of taxation, a subject that proved to be considerably more thought-provoking than Isabel had imagined. Why should the wealthy pay more tax than the poor? They did, or at least they did in most systems, but on what grounds was this defensible? Should taxation be used as a tool to redistribute wealth? She thought it should, and many others thought so as well, but it was not so clear that taxation was the most appropriate way to achieve that. Should governments perhaps be honest and say that they intended simply to confiscate assets over a certain level? She gave some thought to that, wondering how she would feel if the government started to take her capital away, beginning right now, appropriating her funds, turning them into military equipment and welfare payments and new roads, as governments tended to do. I don't have a very strong right to have what I have, she thought. All of it comes to me simply because a member of my family had it, and then died. What sort of moral right did that give? Not a very convincing one, she felt. But so much of life turned out that way—things were gained and then handed on; not just physical things but tastes, qualities, insights. Would Mozart have written what he did had it not been for Leopold Mozart, who had placed his tiny son on the piano stool? Presumably not; the genius, the particular capacities of the brain might have been there but could well have remained locked away, had there been no musical father to bring them out. And Mr. Getty, a rich man—and a very generous one too—had received his oil fields from Mr. Getty before him; he might never have found oil by himself. She smiled at the thought; of course he might not have *looked* for oil—it does not occur to everybody to go looking for oil.

Her train of thought was interrupted by a noise from within the house. Grace was not there that morning—she had a dental appointment and Isabel had told her not to bother coming in. That was more than just concern for Grace's welfare on Isabel's part; Grace was undergoing root canal treatment on a tooth, and Isabel knew from experience how miserable this made her feel. Grace did not like dental anaesthetics, and preferred to endure the pain rather than to experience the lingering numbness that went with the local anaesthetic, a bizarre preference, in Isabel's view, but one which was firmly held. Isabel thought that this might be understandable, just, when it came to minor treatment, but root canal treatment, with its deliberate engagement with the nerve, could be an exquisite agony. She had found out that Grace loved to give a blow-by-blow account of her visits to the dentist and she did not feel in the mood to listen to a long story about root canals punctuated by the sort of grumpiness that Grace could, on occasion, muster. By tomorrow the memory of the pain might be less vivid, and Grace's mood might be restored.

So Isabel was now in sole charge of Charlie, and the sound

from within the house was of Charlie waking up and crying. She put the papers on the philosophy of taxation to one side and went through to the room at the back of the house where Charlie had his afternoon naps. He stopped crying when he saw her and looked up with that strange expression of astonishment that makes parents feel that their child has forgotten them entirely and is seeing them now for the first time.

She picked him up and cuddled him. He felt warm, his skin slightly damp. He started to niggle again.

"You're hungry, aren't you?" she asked. And answered on his behalf, "Of course. Of course. Feeding time."

He took his formula hungrily, sucking strongly at the bottle. Then she winded him, holding him over her shoulder, patting his back gently. This usually comforted him and brought up the wind in an audible burp, but today he seemed to resist her ministrations, squirming in her hold, as if wanting to escape.

"Not right?" she muttered. "You're not feeling right?"

Charlie answered with a wail, screwing up his features into an expression of minor rage, his face colouring from the exertion. He did not need changing, and Isabel felt a momentary twinge of alarm. She knew that she should not imagine things, that the flushed expression was not normally a sign of meningitis, that diarrhoea was not typhoid, but all parents had their anxieties and would think just that, even if only until reassured by somebody else. It's normal, she thought. He's been feeling a little hot—and that room was a bit warm when I went in—so he's registering his displeasure. All quite normal.

She took Charlie through to the kitchen. He liked it there, picking up, she thought, the bright colours—the red of the Aga stove, the glowing yellows of a large print of flowers framed above the refrigerator, the chequered blues of the tea towels; but now he continued to whine, ignoring the distractions of colour.

"Come on, Charlie," she said. "It's not all that bad! Surely not."

But it was, and he began to cry again, at full lung. Once again she put him over her shoulder and patted his back, hoping to dislodge the wind that she suspected was causing his discomfort. This appeared only to add to his unhappiness and she stopped. Gripe water.

She laid Charlie down on the floor of the small playpen that she kept in the corner of the kitchen. He protested, screaming at the outrage, and was unconsoled by Isabel's placatory cooing. Then she went upstairs, momentarily leaving Charlie to his anger, and opened the door of the bathroom cabinet.

The bottle of cough syrup was there, as was the tin of sticking plasters, the aspirin, and the thermometer, but there was no gripe water. Isabel was puzzled. She had put it there, behind the cough syrup; she was sure of that. But it was definitely not there, which meant that Grace had discovered it and moved it.

Isabel felt angry. Grace must have searched for the gripe water and taken it upon herself to move it. She had no right to do that, she thought, no right. This was her cabinet, not Grace's, and she and she alone would decide what it contained.

She went downstairs. Charlie was still protesting, his wail drifting up from the kitchen. "I'm coming, Charlie," she called out as she made her way down the stairs. "I'm coming."

The sound of her voice seemed to calm Charlie, and he fell silent. Or had he choked? Isabel asked herself, and began to run, taking the steps two at a time. He had not, and when she reached the kitchen he started crying again, waving his arms in impotent fury, his face flushed red with the force of his tears. He calmed down a bit when she picked him up but was still obviously uncomfortable.

"What's wrong, my darling? What's wrong?"

Charlie seemed to listen to her, paused briefly, and then continued with his sobbing. There was so much wrong, he seemed to be saying; and it is all your fault, all of it.

Isabel decided that what was needed was a dose of infant aspirin. She had a bottle of the suspension in one of the kitchen cupboards, where Charlie's formula and spare bottles were kept, and she cradled the baby gently as she opened the door with her free hand. There, beside the bottles, was the gripe water, with its characteristic old-fashioned label. Isabel smiled grimly. So it was Grace's doing after all, just as she had suspected; she had been right.

She reached for the bottle of aspirin suspension and then stopped and took out the bottle of gripe water instead. Twisting off the cap, she sniffed at the colourless, slightly viscous liquid within; it had a sweet smell, exaggeratedly floral, like an overstated, cheap perfume. It was not unpleasant, she decided, and on impulse she held the open bottle under Charlie's nose. The effect was immediate and dramatic, as if she had applied smelling salts of the sort resorted to by Victorian ladies for their swooning. The crying stopped immediately, and Charlie made an inept attempt to seize the bottle.

Isabel extracted a teaspoon from a kitchen drawer and set it down on a surface at the side of the sink. It was difficult to pour the gripe water using only one hand—Charlie was still cradled in the other—and she spilled a bit of the liquid in the process. But she succeeded by dint of a steady hand, then picked up the spoon without spilling any more and manoeuvred it into Charlie's mouth. His expression of contentment was immediate; the crying stopped.

"Darling addict," she whispered.

She looked again at the bottle. The contents were listed. Common herbs, she read: ginger, fennel, and dill, all of which one might see on the open shelves of a supermarket. She searched for the offending word, *sugar,* but she did not see it. Nor did she see any reference to alcohol. It was perfectly harmless.

Charlie settled, and after some time in the garden with Isabel, he dropped off to sleep again. Isabel put him in his cradle and returned to her study to deal with the rest of the morning's mail. She had been distracted by the arrival of the papers on the philosophy of taxation, and then by Charlie, and so she had not seen the letter from Professor Christopher Dove. Now she opened it, knowing immediately from the printed letterhead within that it had come from him. You write to me, Dove, she thought. Not content with displacing me, you write to me.

She sat down to read the letter.

Dear Ms. Dalhousie *[I have a doctorate, Dove, not that I use the title, but you might at least have shown the courtesy],*

I believe that you may have heard from Professor Lettuce about changes that have been proposed at the *Review. [You proposed them, Dove.]* I have been asked by the board to assume the editorship, and although I am hesitant to take over a post which has been so admirably filled by another *[Pass the gripe water!],* I have nonetheless indicated that I am prepared to do this.

I am aware of the fact that we have a number of special issues planned, including one on the philosophy of taxation. I would not like to interfere prematurely, but I am a bit doubtful about the value of our doing too many of these, especially in areas as specialised as the philosophy of taxation. My own view is that we should not lose sight of the fact *[In other words, I think,* muttered Isabel] that we are primarily a generalist journal.

There are, as you know, numerous more specialised journals, including several that deal with business ethics, and I think that the philosophy of taxation would be more appropriately covered by them, rather than by us. *[Come to the point, Dove.]* For this reason, I think we should revisit our plans for that issue.

I think that this is just one of the matters which would be much better discussed in a meeting between the two of us. I believe that you now have a baby—Congratulations!—and therefore it would be easier for me to come to Edinburgh than for you to come to London. If you would let me know what dates you are free, I shall come up for a meeting. We can then sort out the details of the handover, and I can look at the editorial archive. We will need to make arrangements for that to be sent down at some stage. I have quite a bit of storage space in my department—we *do* have empty cupboards, believe it or not, not that I advertise the fact, in case the university authorities convert them into offices (for junior academics!). *[That was a joke.]*

The letter ended with a few additional pleasantries. After she had finished reading it, Isabel stared at it for a moment and then rolled it up into a ball and tossed it towards her wastepaper basket. She had not expected it to go in, but it did just that, like a skilfully placed basketball. But then, almost immediately, she felt guilty and walked over to the bin, retrieved the ball of paper, and uncrumpled it. *I shall not descend to the level of Dove,* she said to herself. *I shall not.*

She sat down at her desk and took out a fresh piece of writing paper.

Dear Professor Dove,

It was good to hear from you. Of course I shall be happy to see you in Edinburgh, and here is a list of dates on which I am free and on which we could certainly have a meeting. I must warn you that the editorial archives are quite large and need considerable space to be stored.

She paused and looked out the window. Should she? She resumed her writing.

And perhaps I should also warn you that I do not consider these archives to be anybody's property but my own.

She read over what she had written. What she had said about the ownership of the archive was probably wrong. Some of it belonged to her—the letters written to her as editor were often of a personal nature and the copies of the letters which she had written, on paper which she had provided—those, she thought, were surely hers. But it was a warning shot, which she felt was worth firing.

She signed the letter, slipped it into an envelope, and stuck a stamp on the top right-hand corner. The stamp was simple in its design, almost stark, and bore, as always, the monarch's head. To what correspondence, she thought, has Your Majesty been made an unwilling party, with your head, and all its gentle authority, attached to all sorts of unhappy and shameful letters—letters of rejection, threatening letters, letters from lawyers, anonymous letters . . . She stopped the list there. Her letter was to the point and dignified, the sort of letter which the Queen herself would undoubtedly write to a prime minister attempting to usurp her authority. No, the letter needed no further justification: it would be posted, received by Dove himself in his obscure headquarters, and, she hoped, duly digested.

Be very careful, Dove, she thought. You may take one step too far. Be very careful when you come to Edinburgh.

She stood up and crossed to the window. She looked outside, at the large rhododendron bush, which was quite still; there were no birds, or so it seemed, no fox lurking below. What if Dove came to Edinburgh *and something happened to him*? What then?

Within each of us, she thought, there is evil. It lurks in the deep recesses of the mind, those depths in which the atavistic clutter of our distant past still lodges. We should not delude ourselves that it is not there; it is there, but it is covered, thank heavens, by the veneer of civilisation, of morality. First came the early *I*, red in tooth and claw, then came Mozart, David Hume, Auden.

With a shock she remembered something—something that she did not like to think about. Auden had once almost killed somebody; had put his hands around the neck of his lover and had been on the point of strangling him, driven to this shocking extreme by jealousy. And then he had written about it, had confessed that he had almost become a murderer. If that could happen to him, to that great, humane intelligence, then how easily could it happen to the rest of us, who are weak, and subject to all the passions of our weakness.

No, Professor Dove; you are in no danger from me. By the time you arrive in Edinburgh I shall have mastered my anger. I shall love you, Professor Dove, as I am commanded to do. Or that is what I hope, most fervently hope.

CHAPTER EIGHT

DON'T TALK TO ME about it," said Grace the next morning. "Just don't talk to me about it!"

Isabel was on the point of agreeing. She did not wish to discuss dentists and would be quite happy not to go into the details of Grace's dental trauma of the previous day. But then she realised that although Grace said that she did not want to discuss the matter, that is exactly what she intended to do.

"Yes," said Grace, removing the headscarf she had worn on the journey to work. "The least said about yesterday the better."

Isabel looked up from *The Scotsman* crossword. She had been constructing her own clue. Three words: four, five, and nine letters. *A plant's base beside a waterway precedes intervention.* Root canal treatment.

"Uncomfortable?"

"Extremely," said Grace. "He tried to persuade me to have one of those injections, but I said no. He told me that it would be very painful, but I stuck to my guns. I can't stand that stuff, that . . ."

"Novocaine," said Isabel. How might one express that in a crossword? *Sounds like a new rod with which to beat another until numb?* Not a very good clue, but it would have to do.

"Yes, that stuff," said Grace. "I can't bear it, you know. That awful feeling of being all puffed up, as if somebody had just hit you in the jaw. No thank you!"

"But if you don't—"

Grace cut Isabel off. "I can take pain. I've never been one to dodge that. But this was really, really sore. He had to guddle about inside the tooth and it felt as if somebody was putting an electric wire down there. It was terrible."

They were both silent for a moment, Grace remembering the pain, Isabel thinking about how much pain there was, that life itself floated in a vast sea of pain, numbed here and there for brief moments, but coming back in great waves.

"You see what he had to do," Grace went on, "was to take out the nerve from the root of the tooth. Can you imagine that? I kept thinking of it as a long piece of elastic being dragged out of me. Do you remember knicker elastic? Like that."

"I don't think nerves are like that," said Isabel. "I don't think that you can actually see them. They don't look like elastic, or wires for that matter."

Grace stared at her. "Well, what do they look like?" she asked.

"I think they must be tissue of some sort," said Isabel. "A bit like . . ."

She shrugged. She had never seen a nerve.

"Well, whatever it looked like," said Grace, "I felt it all right. But now . . . nothing! I can chew on that side and I feel nothing."

"They are a very great boon to mankind, dentists," said Isabel. "And I'm not sure that we are grateful enough to them. I'm not sure that we even bother to thank them." She paused. Were there any *statues* of dentists? She thought not. And yet there should be. We had so many statues of generals and politi-

cians and the like, who made wars and took life, and none of
dentists, who battled pain. It was all wrong.

And yet, would anybody be able to take a statue of a dentist
seriously? What if one were to go into some small town somewhere and find a bronze equestrian statue of a great dentist?
Would one be able to do anything but laugh? Of course there
was St. Apollonia, the patron saint of toothache, and she had
read somewhere that the British Dental Association had a small
statue of her in their headquarters.

"Why are you smiling?" asked Grace.

"Just thinking of something odd. It suddenly occurred to me
that there are no statues of dentists—anywhere in Scotland, as
far as I know. Maybe they have them elsewhere—I don't know.
But it does seem rather unfair, don't you think?"

"Very," said Grace. "Mind you, root canal treatment—"

The telephone went, and Isabel rose to her feet to answer.

"Isabel?"

"Peter."

"I know that you sit there doing the crossword," said Peter
Stevenson, "and I would not want to disturb that. But I have some
interesting news for you. Are you in a mood for interesting news?"

Isabel, who had kept the copy of *The Scotsman* in her hand,
now put it down on one of the kitchen work surfaces. It was not
a difficult crossword that day, and it could keep until later. "I'm
always ready for interesting news." She was intrigued. Peter was
not one for idle gossip, and interesting news from him would
probably be worth listening to.

"Your painting," he said. "The one that I saw you trying to
buy at Lyon & Turnbull—that painting of the island, somewhere over in the west. Remember that?"

She wondered whether he had found out something more

about the painting; would that really be all that interesting, or even interesting enough to warrant a telephone call? "Of course. The McInnes."

"Yes," said Peter. "Well, do you want it?"

She was puzzled. Of course she had wanted it—that was why she had tried to buy it. "Well, I did want it. I bid for it, as you may remember."

"Of course I remember that," said Peter quickly. "But the point is this: Do you *still* want it? Because if you do, then it's yours. For the price the purchaser paid for it. Not a penny more."

She was not sure what to say. Did she still want it, or had her enthusiasm for the picture waned after she had seen it go to somebody else?

"I know that you'll probably want to think about it," said Peter. "So why don't you do so and then come over this afternoon for tea with Susie and me? We can talk more about it, and Susie wants to see you anyway. She says that she hasn't seen you since . . . since Charlie, and she'd like to see him, and you of course."

She accepted the invitation. She would drive round in her green Swedish car, or they would walk, which would be more responsible. Talk of global warming had made her feel guilty about her green Swedish car, although for many people the possession of a Swedish car was almost a statement about the world. Swedish cars came with no baggage; they had never been used as staff cars by the officers of invading forces, they were built by well-paid labour that enjoyed full social welfare benefits, they were neither ostentatious nor greedy in their fuel consumption. But they were still cars, and it was cars that were ruining our planet. So that afternoon she would push Charlie round to the Stevenson house in his baby buggy and push him back afterwards, leaving little or no carbon footprint behind them.

PETER MET HER at the door of West Grange House.

"I didn't hear you arriving," he said. "Did you drive?"

"Yes, I drove," said Isabel, pointing to the road, where she had parked her car. "I didn't intend to, but I drove."

"I see," said Peter, smiling. "The road to our house is paved with good intentions."

"And copies of unsold romantic novels," said Isabel, as they went in. "Did you know that unsold paperback novels make an ideal base for roads? Apparently they chop them up and compress them and there you have it—a very good material for putting under tarmac."

Peter had not heard this. "But why just romantic novels?" he asked. "Why not copies of . . . I don't know, literary novels perhaps. Proust even . . ."

Isabel thought for a moment. There were some literary novels that would have been good candidates for such treatment, and the work of one author in particular, now that she came to think of it. There was something about his prose, she thought, that made him ideal for such a purpose. But she did not feel that she should reveal this to Peter, who was a fair-minded man who might feel her comment less than kind. And he would have been right; the thought had not been a charitable one and she made an effort to put it out of her mind—easier said than done, as the image came to her of quantities of that author's latest novel being spread before an advancing steamroller. "Anything will do," she said. "Even copies of the *Review of Applied Ethics,* I suppose. People could then drive roughshod over my editorials, as I expect they have wanted to do for a long time." But then she wondered: How many people actually read her editorials? Fifty? One hundred?

"I wouldn't," said Peter. "I would feel very bad about driving over you."

They went into the hall, to meet Susie coming down the stairs. Susie smiled warmly and held out a finger for Charlie to grip. He accepted firmly and, cross-eyed, stared at the new person.

"He likes you," said Isabel. "Look, he's smiling."

"A secret joke," said Susie.

"Which he probably won't share with us for a few years yet," added Peter.

They went into the kitchen, a comfortable, long room at the back of the house. It was a warm day, and the windows were all open, letting in the smell of newly mown grass from outside. The usual faded green tea cups and plates were laid out on the kitchen table, the surface of which was marked with numerous dents and scratches from years of children's homework. Susie took Charlie and perched him, supported, on her knee, while Peter attended to the tea.

"You're so lucky," said Susie.

Isabel wondered what aspect of her luck was being singled out, and realised that it was Charlie, the sheer fact of Charlie. Yes, she was lucky, doubly so. She had been blessed with Jamie, and following upon that she had been blessed with Charlie.

"I am," she said simply. "And I know it."

Peter poured the tea. "Now, the painting," he said, as he handed Isabel her cup. "It was bought by Walter Buie—I did tell you that, didn't I? I was standing near him during the auction."

"Yes, you did tell me," she replied. "I had forgotten the

name, but you did tell me something about him. He's a lawyer, isn't he?"

Peter nodded. "Yes he is. He lives just round the corner in Hope Terrace. He has a rather nice house which belonged to his parents before him. Walter is one of those people who's destined to die in the house in which he was born. Or that's what he says."

"Not a bad idea," said Isabel. The thought occurred to her that she was one of them too. She had been away, of course, but she had come back to the house in which she had lived as a child. Would Charlie do the same? It seemed unlikely, now that the world was so fluid, so open. She glanced at her son and thought, For the first time in my life it matters to me, really matters, that the world should not change too much.

Peter smiled at Charlie, who was throwing his hands about enthusiastically. "Anyway," he continued, "I met Walter Buie in the street yesterday. I was taking our dog, Murphy, for a walk when I saw him coming along on the other side of the road. Walter has a horrible dog, a scruffy brown creature that has a criminal record with the local cats. I've always kept Murphy away from him but, surprisingly, Murphy and Basil, this dog of Walter's, started wagging their tails as if they were old friends. So I could stop and have a word with Walter while the dogs exchanged news with each other. I told him that I had seen him at Lyon & Turnbull and asked him how he was enjoying his new picture.

"Walter made some remark about not having put it up yet, and I then happened to mention that you had been after it too. I told him that I thought it interesting that there were two people I knew who were going so strongly for the same thing."

Peter paused as Susie handed Charlie back to Isabel so that she could refill the teapot.

"A happy baby," said Peter, looking at Charlie. "You must be thrilled."

Isabel settled Charlie on her lap. "Thank you. He is. And I am."

"But back to Walter," said Peter. "When I told him that you had been after that painting, he went quiet for a moment. He was obviously going over something in his mind and it took him a minute or so before he came up with his response. And what he said was this: 'She can have it, if she wants it. She can have it for what I paid, which is not very much above her last bid.' That's what he said. So I told him that I would pass on his offer."

Isabel frowned. What intrigued her about this was the question of why Walter Buie should want to get rid of something which he had just made some effort to obtain. That seemed strange, and again the thought occurred to her that there might be something wrong with the painting. Or could it be that once he saw it in his house, he decided that he didn't like it for some reason, possibly because it clashed with something else, the wallpaper perhaps?

"I can see what you're thinking," said Peter. "I also wondered why he should want to get rid of it so quickly. So I asked him whether he had gone off it, and he simply shook his head and said no, not really. But he had realised that he didn't have the great passion for it that he had felt at the auction. That's what he said, anyway."

"In other words, altruism," said Isabel.

"Precisely," said Peter.

Susie had said nothing about this; now she joined in. "But if that's the way he thought about it, then why would he have bid against Isabel at the auction? It must have been apparent then that she wanted it quite badly."

"Perhaps altruism takes time to emerge," said Isabel. "We

often think differently about things some time after the event. I certainly find that—don't you?"

Susie was not convinced. "That may happen sometimes," she said. "But I don't have that feeling about this. I think that there's something wrong."

"Well, I don't," said Peter. "Walter Buie is very straight-forward. He's exactly the sort of person who would do this. He's . . ."

"A bit old-fashioned," said Susie. "I don't mean to be unkind, but he's what some people would call old Edinburgh. Just a bit old-fashioned."

Old Edinburgh: Isabel knew exactly what that meant. And she used to laugh at it, or feel irritated by it, but now that the world was so different she was not so sure. Old Edinburgh had been so sedate, prissy even—like a maiden aunt—and it had been an easy target. But had the correction gone too far? Old-fashioned manners, courtesies, had been swept away every-where, it seemed, to be replaced by indifference, by coolness. And yet that had not made people any more free; in fact, the opposite, surely, had happened, as the public space became more frightening, more dangerous.

"It's kind of him," she said. It was the charitable interpreta-tion of his gesture and it made Peter nod his head in agreement.

"I think you're right," he said. "And I also think that you need to accept—if you still want the painting. I think that it's very important to be able to accept things. People often know how to give, but they often don't know how to accept graciously."

Isabel looked at him, and Peter blushed. "I didn't mean you, of course," he said hurriedly. "I'm sure you know how to accept."

Isabel was not so sure about that; now that she thought of what Peter said about accepting, she realised that she probably was not very good at it. She felt guilty when people gave her presents, because she did not like the thought that somebody had spent money on her. Where did that come from? She thought that perhaps it was a result of not wanting others to be put out on her behalf, which was ridiculous. And it made her remember the story of a Scottish government minister who had been so well-mannered that, when allocated a female driver, he had insisted on opening the car door for her. People had laughed, but it said a lot for the moral quality of the minister himself; it was the opposite of the sort of arrogance that one sometimes saw in people who had found themselves in positions of power.

She should accept Walter Buie's offer, but did she still want the painting? Peter noticed her hesitation.

"Don't take it if you don't want it," he said. "People change their minds. You can change yours."

"I don't know," said Isabel. "I really don't know."

"Do you want to look at it?" asked Peter. "Walter said that he'd be very happy for you to take a look at it. We could go round and see him now."

"But it would be awkward if I wanted to say no."

"Not at all. You can turn him down if you don't want it anymore. Just tell him that you've changed your mind."

She was not certain, but Susie said that she would look after Charlie if they wanted to walk round to Walter's house. Isabel thought for a moment and then said yes. She was intrigued by Walter Buie and wanted to know a bit more about him; a guilty feeling, because she knew that she should not be so inquisitive. But I can't help it, she thought; I just can't.

IT WAS NOT a long walk, and the road was quite empty. "We'll be at his gate in a moment," said Peter, pointing down Hope Terrace. "That drive off to the right—that's him. Walter has an old Bentley—a really old one. Sometimes you see its nose sticking out of the driveway and then the whole car emerges—it's a wonderful sight. He goes on rallies, apparently. He tried to invite me along once but I didn't see the point. Why go and sit around in a field with lots of other people who happen to own old Bentleys?"

It was not something that appealed to Isabel either, but she understood why people would want to be with others who share their interest. "Presumably they talk about Bentleys," she said, "which is fair enough. I go to conferences of philosophers. We sit around, not in fields, admittedly, but we do sit around together."

"Very odd," said Peter.

They reached the driveway. A large pair of wooden gates, set in a high stone wall, prevented any access from the road, but there was a small door to the side which Peter pushed open. Inside was a walled garden, with a greenhouse and, at the far end, an attractive Georgian house in the style of that part of town. It was built of honey-coloured stone which had weathered dark in uneven patches, giving it a not unpleasing mottled appearance. The windows at the front, with their white-painted astragals, had that pleasant, harmonious feeling of Georgian design, and the sun was on the glass, making it flash silver and gold.

Isabel took to the house immediately—at least to that part of it she could see. "It's beautiful," she said. "One to one point six one eight."

Peter looked at her sideways.

"The golden mean," Isabel said. "If we measured the height of those windows and then their width, the ratio between the two would be that: one to one point six one eight, or near enough."

"Ah," said Peter. "Of course."

"Most of classical Edinburgh observes that ratio," Isabel said. "And then the Victorians came along and got all Gothic."

"But your house is pretty," said Peter. "And it's Victorian."

"Yes," said Isabel. "I'm not being disloyal to my house. It was a child of its time. But the ceilings are just a little bit too high for the width of the rooms. Not that I sit there and fret about it, but it's true."

They walked up the drive. Peter had telephoned Walter, so they knew that he was in. They stood at the front door; Peter pressed the small white button in the middle of a brass fitting to the right; PLEASE PUSH was written on the porcelain; old Edinburgh—modern buttons just said PUSH, the simple imperative, not the polite cousin.

Walter Buie answered the door. He was younger than Isabel had thought he would be; she had imagined a man in his fifties or sixties, whereas the person who stood before them looked to be in his late thirties at the most. He was a tall man, with a thick head of sand-coloured curly hair. He had a strong face and piercing blue eyes; Nordic, thought Isabel, a type that one still encountered in the north and west of Scotland.

Walter held out a hand to Isabel. "We've almost met in the past," he said, and named a mutual friend.

They shook hands and Walter gestured for them to come in. There was a formality about the way he spoke, and in his movements—old Edinburgh, as Peter had described it. And he was right, thought Isabel, as they went into a large, airy hall. But there was something contemporary about Walter too: a freshness, an athleticism, which seemed at odds with the formal manner. It was difficult to see him as a lawyer who had dropped out of private practice, even if one could see him behind the wheel of a vintage Bentley.

Walter led them through to the drawing room, a perfectly proportioned room at the end of which three windows descended from the ceiling almost to floor level. On one wall there was a large, white marble mantelpiece on which a matching pair of famille rose vases stood on either side of a Tang horse. In front of a further expanse of marble, serving as a hearth, there was a low gilt table on which there stood piles of books and magazines. Isabel's eye ran discreetly to the magazine titles—*The Burlington Magazine, Art Quarterly,* and one she could not make out.

She glanced at the walls. Opposite the fireplace a very large Philipson nude gazed out of a wide black frame; to either side of it were what looked like two Ferguson portraits of women in extravagant, ostrich-feathered hats. And then, on another wall, above a long, white-painted bookcase, were two medium-sized paintings which Isabel immediately recognised.

Walter saw her eyes move to them. "Yes," he said. "Those are McInnes, too. They're quite early ones, actually. I think that he did those when he first started going to Jura. That was before he married. He was fresh out of art college, but already he had that very mature style. That's what got him noticed."

Now that he had drawn attention to them, Isabel felt that she could move over and look more closely at the paintings. Other people's possessions were an awkward thing, she thought; one should not snoop too obviously when one went into a room—a close examination of one's host's books always seemed to be too much like an attempt to judge their tastes—but pictures were different. The reason for hanging them on the wall was for people to see them—and that included guests. Indeed, many collectors *wanted* one to see their paintings, which was why well-known painters fetched higher prices. They gave no greater enjoyment, necessarily, than others; but they were evidence of wealth. There were people for whom the whole point of having a Hockney was that those who did not have Hockneys could reflect on the fact that you had one and they did not. Isabel did not care for this; she had no desire that others should see what she had.

She approached the paintings to look at them more closely. One was of a group of people cutting and stacking peats: a man and a woman worked with the stacks of dark blocks, while behind them, seated on the edge of the cutting, a young woman unwrapped a packet of sandwiches. It was a compelling picture, with a certain sadness about it, although she could not understand why it should be sad. That, perhaps, was why McInnes was considered such a good painter: he captured the moment, in the way in which a great painter must; a moment when it feels that something is about to happen, but has not yet. And what was about to happen in this painting was sad, inexpressibly so.

She turned to the other painting. This was a landscape, with the unmistakeable mammary hills, the Paps of Jura in the background. There was nothing in the subject matter which made it exceptional—so many artists had painted the western isles—but again there was that quality of attenuation of light, of sadness, that made the painting stand out.

She became aware that Walter was standing directly behind

her. She heard his breathing and she straightened up. His physical presence was powerful in a way which she would not have been able to define; but it was there.

"That one of the peat cutters is one of my favourites," he said. "The tones are almost sepia, don't you think? Like an old photograph."

Isabel agreed. "When I look at old photographs," she said, "I often think of how the people in them are all dead and gone. It's a thought, isn't it? There they are in the photographs, going about their business without much thought to their mortality, but of course it was there all the time."

Walter was intrigued. "Yes, of course," he said. "There's a photograph which really affected me, you know, when I was sixteen or seventeen. We had a book of poetry of the First World War—Owen, Sassoon, people like that—and there was a photograph in it of five or six men in the uniform of a Highland regiment—kilts—standing in a circle in front of the local minister. They were about to leave the Highlands to go off to the war." He paused, and his eyes met Isabel's. "When I first saw it, I stared at it for quite some time. Half an hour or so. I just stared and wondered which of those men, if any, came back to Scotland. It was an infantry regiment, as the Highland regiments were, and their chances must have been pretty slim. They were slaughtered, those men. I remember looking at the faces, looking at the detail, thinking, *You? Did you come back? Did you?*"

They were both silent for a moment. Then Isabel said, "Rather like those pictures of the young men sitting on the grass around their Spitfires, waiting to be scrambled. How many of them lasted more than a few weeks?"

"Not many," he said. "No. Awful. But have you noticed how those young pilots seemed to be smiling in so many of the photographs? Whereas those Highlanders just looked sad, uncomprehending, I suppose. It seems somehow different."

Walter took a step back and looked at Peter. "You've explained to . . ."

"Isabel."

"Yes, of course. Well, perhaps you'd like to have another look at the painting. It's in the dining room."

They followed him into the adjoining room. The painting was propped against a wall, half in shadow, and Walter moved it out, leaning it against the back of a chair. "It's lovely, isn't it?"

Isabel looked at the painting. "I can understand why people were so sorry about his death," she said. "He would have been a very great painter. When did it happen, by the way?"

"About eight years ago," said Walter. "It was all over the papers at the time. It made the front page of *The Scotsman;* even *The Times* deigned to notice it. He fell foul of the Corryvreckan. It's a bad bit of sea off Jura. People call it a whirlpool, but it's more than that."

There was silence. Walter pointed to the painting. "Just round the corner from that point. He'd taken to putting out lobster pots and so he had a small boat which he took out in the wrong conditions. Exactly what happened to Orwell, or just about. Orwell survived, and finished *1984.* McInnes didn't."

Peter, who had been staring at the painting, looked up. "I've seen it. We were up on Islay once and went for a cruise round Jura. We stopped some way away from the Corryvreckan itself, but we could hear it. It was like a jet—a roaring sound. And there were amazing high waves rising and falling."

"If you get the tides right," said Walter, "you can sail right through it. It's like a millpond at slack water. Then, when the tide turns, it hits a submerged mountain of some sort under the surface and all hell breaks loose. That creates the whirlpool effect."

As Isabel listened, her eye wandered back to the painting. Perhaps that was what made these paintings sad for her—the knowledge that McInnes would die in the very place he painted so lovingly. But this, she thought, was not a McInnes. If one looked at the two paintings on the wall, and then at this one, it just felt different. They were not by the same hand.

"WELL?" SAID PETER as they walked back along Hope Terrace.

"That was interesting," said Isabel. "Thank you for arranging it."

Peter stared at her quizzically. "Is that all you're going to say?"

Isabel looked up, at the thin layer of high white cloud that was moving across the sky from the west. Cirrus. "No, I'll say more if you want, but I'm not sure where to start. Him? Walter himself? A surprise. The way you'd spoken I thought of him as being much older. And there he is, living in that rather museumish house . . ."

"With his mother," added Peter.

Isabel was surprised. "Really? I thought you said . . ."

"I thought that the parents were dead, but I was wrong. She's still with us, he told me. When you went out of the room to go to the loo, he said something about her. I was astonished. I've never seen her, but she's there apparently. She's only in her early seventies, but he says that she doesn't go out much."

Isabel thought for a moment. Did that change anything? The idea of Walter Buie living in that house by himself, with his ill-tempered dog—whom they did not meet—intrigued her simply because she wondered why he chose to live by himself. What did he do about sex, or was he one of those asexual people—there were some, she knew—who did not care one way or the other, for whom sex was nothing too important, a minor itch at most. Was he gay? She found it difficult to tell these things, and often misjudged, particularly in the case of feminine men who were also resolutely straight. Or, finally, was it simply nobody else's business, and therefore none of hers? That was true, but she decided to allow herself one final speculation. If his mother was still alive, was he there by choice, or because he was under pressure to stay? Some parents held on, and made it difficult for their offspring to leave. Walter Buie could be an emotional prisoner, the victim of a retentive—very retentive—mother. And in that case, it was just possible that he was being made to sell the picture by his mother, who might be refusing to come up with the money that he thought he would be able to get from her. In that case, her conclusion that there was something wrong with the painting might be unjustified, and it might simply be a case of Walter's needing to sell it.

"I don't know what to think," she muttered.

"You don't have to do anything," said Peter. "You're under no obligation to him—nor he to you."

Isabel smiled—not to Peter, but to herself. Peter was conscientious, but he was practical too. He made things work, whereas she could not help but be the philosopher. You and I are never going to agree on this, she thought. We are all under obligation to one another, deep obligation. I to you. You to me. Walter Buie to us, and we to Walter Buie. And we are even under obligation to the dead, whose serried ranks in this case include one Andrew McInnes, painter, husband, our fellow citizen, our brother.

But she said none of this. Instead, she said, "Look at that *cirrus uncinus* up there. Just look at it."

Peter looked up at the sky, at the wisps of cloud, and at first

WITH THE INTIMACY of a married couple—which they were not—but with the sense of novelty and awe of lovers—which they were—Isabel and Jamie prepared for their dinner with Cat. Isabel sat on the edge of her bed half dressed, examining a black cocktail dress and wondering whether it was the right thing for her to wear to Cat's; Jamie came out of the bathroom wearing only a white towel wrapped round his waist, his hair wet from the shower, tousled, small drops of water on his shoulders and forearms. She looked up at him and then looked away again because she did not want him to see her looking upon him. That was a wonderful expression, she thought; *looking upon* somebody suggested that one was devouring the other. One looked upon with lust, or with something akin to lust, and one would not want to be seen looking upon one's lover in the way in which a gourmet, sitting at the table, would look upon an enticing dish.

Jamie moved over to the dressing table and picked up a brush. Bending down to look into the mirror, he brushed his hair roughly, but it sprang back up, as it always tended to do.

"Don't worry," said Isabel. "It looks nice like that. Your hair sticks up naturally. Lots of women would commit murder for that."

"It annoys me," says Jamie. "Sometimes I think I'll go to that place in Bruntsfield, you know the barbers near the luggage shop, and get a crew cut or one of those totally shaved styles. What do they call them? A number one, I think."

"You couldn't," said Isabel flatly. "It would be a crime."

He turned to face her. "Why? It's my head."

She wanted to say, No, it's not, it's mine too, but she stopped herself. That was what she thought, though, and even as she thought it, she realised that Jamie was on loan to her, as we all are to one another, perhaps.

She picked at a loose thread on the cocktail dress. "I think it would be a pity to look shorn. And don't you think that deliberately shaved heads look aggressive?"

"I'm not serious." He paused. "Do you think I should get a tattoo?"

She laughed, and he did too, and the towel round his waist fell down. Isabel felt herself blushing involuntarily, but stood up and went to pick up the towel before he could do so himself. She dried his shoulders with it, and then his chest. Jamie was not hirsute; he was like a boy, she thought, still.

They dressed. He said, "Will Charlie wake up, do you think?"

She did not think it likely. Grace was babysitting for them, and ensconced in the morning room, where Isabel kept the television. Charlie had been fed for the evening, and Isabel thought he would sleep through until midnight at least. "I doubt if we'll be all that late," she said. She left the reasons for this unsaid, but Jamie guessed what she meant. He was beginning to wonder whether he should have accepted Cat's invitation. It might have seemed churlish to have refused, but now that he had accepted he felt a strong sense of anticipation over the meeting.

He decided to confide in Isabel. "I feel a bit jumpy about this," he said. "I'm sorry. I just have these butterflies in my stomach."

Isabel tried to reassure him. "The best way to deal with an old flame is to treat him or her as an old friend, or a cousin, maybe."

He thought about this for a moment. "That's all very well, but I don't feel like this when I'm going to see an old friend. This is a different feeling."

"Just don't worry," she said. "Just stop thinking about it." She reached out and took his hand. "Look, why don't we go downstairs and have something before we go? A . . . gin and tonic."

"For Dutch courage?"

"Yes," she said. "Although I must say that that expression has always seemed to me to be a bit unkind."

"Are the Dutch naturally brave?"

"I suspect that they're the same as anybody else. Some are brave, some aren't. But it's got nothing to do with the Dutch themselves. It's the gin they made." She squeezed his hand. "Don't let Cat intimidate you."

"Why has she asked us?" he asked. "Why?"

Isabel could not answer the question, and did not try to. They went downstairs and into the drawing room, where she started to prepare the drinks while Jamie went into the morning room to speak to Grace. When he came back he said, "I'm going to call a taxi for Grace. She has a migraine coming on."

Grace was prone to the occasional migraine, and would need to go to bed for twenty-four hours to ward it off. Isabel handed the preparation of the drinks over to Jamie. "You do this," she said. "I'll phone for a taxi and get her organised."

"Will we call off?" Jamie said. There was no disappointment in his voice.

Isabel, halfway out the door, gave him a look of mock surprise. "Why? Charlie can come in his carry-cot." And why shouldn't he? she thought. Cat could no longer pretend that Charlie did not exist; she had been cool towards him, barely acknowledging him, but that could not go on.

Grace kept a migraine pill at the house. She had taken it, and was feeling slightly better, but Isabel insisted that she should go home and bundled her into a taxi. Then she returned to the drawing room, where Jamie handed her her glass.

She raised it to him and took a sip. "Strong," she said, making a face.

Jamie grinned. "We've got a long evening ahead of us."

There was a frisson to the drinking of a strong gin and tonic, but Isabel felt that she needed this. Jamie felt the same, and by the time he had drained his glass he felt more confident about the encounter with Cat; but that feeling still lingered, that anticipation, which he realised now was sexual excitement. He looked away from Isabel, as if she might see it in his eyes.

CAT HAD RECENTLY moved to a flat in Fettes Row. It was on the third floor of a Georgian block, reached by a winding common stair that connected the landings of each flat. They had travelled across town by taxi, with Charlie obligingly asleep in his carry-cot on the floor of the cab, and now Jamie was carrying him up the last few steps to Cat's door. Isabel, standing behind

Jamie, bent down and looked at her son. "How can she dislike him?" she muttered.

Jamie reacted sharply. "Who?" he asked. "Who dislikes him?"

Having kept off the subject of Cat with Jamie, Isabel had never mentioned to him the animosity that she had picked up in Cat's reaction to Charlie; and she had not intended to do so now. Her muttered words, thoughts inadvertently expressed aloud, had not been meant for his ears, but they would not be easily retracted now. But she tried nonetheless.

"I don't know if she does," she said apologetically. "I sense something in her attitude, but perhaps I shouldn't go so far as to say that she dislikes him."

Jamie frowned. He cast a glance down the stairs. "We could go home, you know," he said, in a lowered voice. "We have a perfectly reasonable excuse, with Charlie. Babies and dinner parties don't mix."

Isabel thought that she saw anger in him, which surprised her. Jamie was normally of a markedly affable temperament, but this appeared to have riled him. Of course he was a father, she reminded herself, and any parent, especially a newly besotted one, resents the thought that somebody else might find fault with his child; our children are perfect, especially when they have just arrived and not disclosed their hand. But she and Jamie had come this far, and she thought it likely that Cat had even heard the front door being opened and the sound of their coming upstairs. For a few moments Isabel imagined how it would be to leave now, to begin sneaking downstairs again, and then for Cat to open the door and look down at their retreating heads. A hostess might have cause to reflect on such a scene and to wonder why it was that her guests should feel compelled to leave before arriving, but would Cat do that? Isabel thought not, and nor, to be honest, would she do so herself: the light from such incidents rarely fell on ourselves and our faults.

A tall, slender young woman opened the door. Her eyes went to Isabel first, then to Charlie, and finally to Jamie, where they lingered. Isabel glanced at Jamie, who, if he had looked at the young woman to begin with, had now looked away. Our eyes give us away, she thought; they move to the beautiful, to the attractive; they slide off the others; they flash out our emotional signals as clearly as if they were Aldis lamps. Jamie seemed irritated, almost flustered. We have barely arrived, Isabel thought, and the evening's becoming difficult.

The young woman gestured for them to enter. "I'm Claudia," she said. "Cat's flatmate."

"Of course." Isabel had heard that Cat had taken a flatmate when she moved into Fettes Row, but she knew nothing about her other than that she came from St. Andrews and that she played golf, which almost everyone in St. Andrews did. This information had come from Eddie, who had met Claudia when she came into the delicatessen. He had curled his lip around the word *golf,* and Isabel had scolded him. "You may not like it, but others . . ."

"Get their kicks from whacking a little white ball around," he said. "Yes, sure."

"Each of us has something," she said. She felt inclined to ask Eddie how he spent his spare time, but hesitated. Eddie was more confident now, but there was a fragility to him, a vulnerability, that was just below the surface. Yet he could not expect to make scornful remarks about golfers and get away with it. So she said, "So, what do you do, Eddie? In your spare time? What do you do?"

The question had taken him aback. He looked at her, almost in alarm. "Me?"

Isabel nodded. "Yes, you."

"I chill out."

She laughed and straightaway regretted it, as his face had immediately crumpled. He was still too weak; whatever had happened, that thing that Cat knew about—and it must be some time ago by now—had damaged him more than people might imagine. Quickly she reached out and touched his forearm. He pulled back. "I'm sorry," she said. "I didn't mean to be rude. It's just that chilling out—well, it doesn't tell us much. Maybe to you . . ." Absurdly, the thought came to her of people sitting in a cold place, scantily clad perhaps, chilling out, beginning to shiver . . .

Claudia led them into the hall. Like many flats in the New Town, this was a generous, classically proportioned space, in this case not very tidy—Cat had a tendency to disorganisation in her personal life, and Isabel noticed the pile of mail that lay unopened on the hall table, alongside a muddle of unsolicited advertisements for pizzerias and Indian restaurants. Claudia saw the direction of her gaze and laughed. "We meant to tidy it up for you," she said, "but you know how it is."

"I feel more comfortable with a bit of clutter," said Isabel. "And you do too, don't you Jamie?"

He tried to smile, but the result was halfhearted. Isabel noticed that Claudia was staring at him again. This made her wonder whether Cat had told her flatmate that Jamie was an ex-boyfriend. And would she then have gone on to explain that he was an ex-boyfriend *stolen* by an *aunt*? If she had, then Isabel might as well play the part of the brazen cradle snatcher, the ruthless man eater; which she could never do, she thought—or at least not with a straight face.

Claudia asked where they would like to put Charlie. He could have her bedroom, if Isabel thought that would be suitable. "It's at the back," she said. "It's quiet. It looks over towards Cumberland Street."

She took them into the room. There was a double bed with an Indian-print bedspread, a small bookcase, a writing table. Above the bed there was a print of a Hopper painting, a young woman at a table, the light upon her. They put Charlie's carry-cot on the bed and Jamie bent down to adjust his blanket.

"He's out for the count," Jamie said. It was his first remark of the evening, and Isabel noticed that Claudia seemed to listen to it with grave interest, as if Jamie had said something profound.

Then Cat came into the room. She was carrying a small piece of paper towel and she was wiping her hands with it. She looked at Isabel, but while she was looking at her she said, "Hello, Jamie." Then, "Hello, Isabel."

Isabel gave Cat a kiss, a peck on the cheek. As she did so, she felt the tension in the other woman, a tightness of muscle. "And there's Charlie," said Isabel. "Fast asleep."

Cat glanced down at the carry-cot. She did not bend down to kiss him, nor did she touch him; she just looked. "Hello, Charlie," she said.

Isabel watched her. She had not looked at Jamie, not once, and that hardly boded well for the evening. The recipes for social disaster were varied and colourful; within the small compass of Edinburgh dinner-party lore, they included the going to sleep of the host—at the table—during the soup course, the soup on the same occasion being so heavily salted that it was inedible and had to be left in the bowl by the guests; an argument between guests leading to the early departure of the offended party; and, of course, inadvertent guest-list solecisms, such as the placing, on one famous occasion, of the survivors of acrimonious divorces next to one another. Her own worst experience had been the moment when, at a lunch party, a guest had blithely asked whether anybody had ever been tempted to commit an act of violence, and the hostess unfortunately, in a moment of dissociative aberration, had attacked a former lover and been convicted of assault, to the knowledge of all present except the questioner. Ill-judged remarks led to periods of embarrassment that could be measured in minutes, or sometime even seconds; tonight's awkwardness, by contrast, might be measured in hours, if Cat was going to refuse steadfastly to look at one of the guests. This could be done—Isabel had heard of a woman in Edinburgh who cut another woman seated opposite her by looking through her for an entire dinner. That required some skill, and demonstrated, too, how human effort might be misapplied.

But then Cat suddenly turned to Jamie and said, "My, you're looking fit, Jamie!"

Isabel breathed a sigh of relief; they were not in for the long haul after all. But then Cat added, "Somebody's obviously keeping you rather well."

The significance of this remark took a moment or two to sink in. Isabel, prepared for the worst, immediately saw the concealed meaning: Jamie was accused of being a kept man. The sheer effrontery of this was astonishing, but Jamie, unprepared, appeared not to notice the choice of words, at least not to begin with. As they moved through to the sitting room from the bedroom, he suddenly stiffened and half turned to Isabel. Their eyes met, and she gave a discreet shake of the head, a turning up of the eyes, as if to say, *Don't bother. Rise above it.*

Claudia passed a glass of wine to Isabel and then one

to Jamie. Isabel raised her glass to Cat, who responded halfheartedly.

"We had to bring Charlie," Isabel said. "Grace had one of her migraines. She doesn't get them very often but . . ."

"Charlie sleeps through things," said Jamie. "He's very good."

Both Cat and Claudia turned to look at Jamie as he spoke. Then Claudia turned to Cat and said, "Who had that awful baby? The people who came to dinner, and it screamed and screamed?"

"Oh them," said Cat. "Yes. It was heading for Scottish Opera, that one."

Jamie frowned. "I'm sure it wasn't their fault. You can't stop a baby screaming when it gets going. What can you do?"

He looked at Cat, as if awaiting an answer. She met his gaze, but only for a moment. How does one look upon somebody whom one used to like? Like that, Isabel thought, watching Cat's expression; quick glances, expressing self-reproach, or surprise, perhaps, at the fact that one could have liked the other. And in the case of an ex-lover who had left one, it could be resentment that prevailed—resentment that the other was leading a life in which one played no part, the ultimate slap in the face. Cat, though, had got rid of Jamie, not the other way round, and she could hardly resent his finding somebody else. Perhaps not, but if that somebody was one's *aunt* . . .

Isabel saw that Jamie still appeared to be waiting for Cat to answer his question. A change of subject, she decided, would help.

"Speaking of Scottish Opera," she said, "Did you see their *Rosenkavalier,* Cat?"

Cat's answer was abrupt. "No." And then she added, "No, I didn't."

This, thought Isabel, is going to be difficult; perhaps they should have turned round on the stairway after all.

"*Rosenkavalier* has its moments," said Jamie suddenly.

"Yes . . . ," Isabel began. "I agree. I think . . ."

"I saw *Carmen* in London," interjected Claudia. "English National Opera did it."

For a few moments there was silence. Isabel smiled encouragingly. "*Carmen* is always fun," she said. "Everybody loves it."

Jamie shot her a glance. "Maybe," he muttered.

Isabel persisted. "It's like all the established repertoire," she said. "People like the familiar in opera. *Carmen* fills the house."

For a moment Jamie said nothing. Isabel noticed that his hands were clasped together tightly and that his knuckles showed white. When he spoke, his voice was strained. "Yes, but that's the problem, isn't it? All the old stuff leaves no space for anything new."

"New operas," said Isabel mildly, "can scare people away. It's a fact of life."

"So we shouldn't perform them?" Jamie snapped. "Just the same old stuff? *La Bohème, La Traviata?*"

Isabel glanced at Cat, who was staring up at the ceiling, perhaps to avoid looking at Jamie. She did not want to prolong the discussion that she had started and that had suddenly turned into an argument, but at the same time she found herself resenting Jamie's deliberately provocative stance. She did not disapprove of new opera—he knew that—and it was unfair of him to portray her as a traditionalist. She was not.

"I didn't say that there was no place for new operas," she said firmly. "I didn't. All that I'd say is that opera companies have to live in the real world. They have to sell tickets, and this means doing the things that people come to see. Not all the time, of course. But they do have to do them."

"And that means no new works?" retorted Jamie.

"No," she said. "No."

Isabel felt ill at ease. It was unlike Jamie to be argumentative, but it occurred to her that the tension of the evening was the explanation for his snippiness. She could understand that, but it still hurt her that he should pick a public fight with her, and she was reflecting on this when they heard Charlie begin to cry.

Jamie leapt to his feet. "He's awake," he said.

Cat looked annoyed. "Can't you leave him to settle?" she said. "Won't he drop off again?"

"No," said Jamie, abruptly. "You can't neglect a baby."

Cat's eyes flashed. "I didn't say neglect, for heaven's sake. I said—"

"I'm going to go and get him," said Jamie.

They watched him leave the room. Cat looked at Isabel and smiled conspiratorially. Isabel did not return the smile. In her view, Cat wanted her to be complicit in the judgement that Jamie was overreacting, that he would not really know how to deal with a niggling baby. But she was not prepared to do that.

"He's very good," she said.

Cat turned to Claudia and mouthed something. Isabel caught her breath. It was difficult to tell, and perhaps she had imagined it—surely she had imagined it—but it seemed to her that the words that Cat had mouthed to her flatmate were these: *in bed.*

"THAT WAS A DISASTER."

Jamie nodded. "You can say that again."

They were travelling home in a taxi. Going up the Mound, the lights of the Castle above them and the dark valley of

Princes Street Garden to their right, they watched the late-night life of the streets—the groups of students, boisterous, heading for clubs and pubs, the couples arm in arm, the clusters of people under bus-stop shelters. Charlie had niggled and cried from the moment he had woken up at that early stage, and the atmosphere at the table had been tense and uncomfortable. They had left the moment the meal was over and had gone down the stairs in silence. Jamie was cross with her, Isabel thought, but she did not know what she had to apologise for. For disagreeing with him over new operas? For accepting the invitation in the first place?

"I'm sorry," she said as the taxi crested the brow of the High Street and began to make its way towards George IV Bridge. "I'm sorry for whatever I'm meant to have done."

"You didn't do anything," muttered Jamie. "It's just that I hated the whole thing. I hated the way Cat behaved. I hated her attitude towards Charlie."

Isabel sighed. "It's very complicated," said Isabel.

"Everything's too complicated," said Jamie. "The whole lot's too complicated."

"Why don't we go away then?" said Isabel. She said this without thinking, but after she had said it she realised that it was a good idea. They needed to get away, with Charlie, to be by themselves. A few days would make all the difference.

Jamie did not reject the possibility out of hand.

"Go away where?" he asked.

Again Isabel did not think before she spoke. "Jura," she said.

"All right," said Jamie. He still seemed low, and she reached out and took his hand in hers. She sensed his tension, but he did not draw his hand away, and by the time they reached Bruntsfield Place and were travelling past the darkened windows of Cat's delicatessen, he was stroking her wrist with his

HER SUGGESTION that they should go to Jura for a few days did not look as impulsive in the cold light of morning as she had thought it might. Jamie had been slightly taken aback by the idea—they had not planned to go away together, but now that the idea had been floated, he decided that he rather liked it. "The Hebrides are ideal," he said. "I was on Harris a few years ago—do you know it? I love it there. And we went down to South Uist as well. There's this wonderful feeling that one is right on the edge."

"And one is," said Isabel. "The very edge of Scotland. Of Europe too."

Jamie looked out the window—they were in the kitchen, having breakfast—and the morning sun was streaming in through the large Victorian window, illuminating floating specks of dust that were drifting like minute planets in space. "Isn't it odd," he said, reaching out and creating a whirlwind in the air before him, "how we think of air as being empty, but it's full of things. Bits of dust. Viruses too, I suppose."

Isabel was thinking of the Hebrides. "And Jura?" she asked. "Have you been there?"

Jamie shook his head. "I get the Inner Hebrides mixed up," he said. "Jura is the one which is next to Islay, isn't it? Off the Mull of Kintyre?"

"Yes," said Isabel. "Islay's much bigger. It makes more whisky—it has six or seven whisky distilleries, I think. Then there's Jura. The Island of Deer—that's what it means in Norse."

"Ah," said Jamie. "I've seen it from Islay but I've never been on it." He paused, and looked at Isabel with interest. "But why Jura?" He asked the question, and then he remembered; it was the painting that they had seen in the auction. That had been Jura.

Jamie raised an eyebrow. "It's nothing to do with . . ."

Isabel shrugged. "I've been thinking about it," she said. "I've been thinking about that painting. I suppose that it's made me want to go there again. I have some friends there. I'd like to see them."

"Who?" asked Jamie. He was suspicious. Isabel had a habit of doing things for very specific reasons, even if they appeared to be spontaneous or unplanned.

"Some people called Fletcher," said Isabel. "The Fletchers have had Ardlussa estate up there for some time. I knew Charlie and Rose Fletcher slightly and I got to know their daughter a bit better. Lizzie Fletcher. She's a great cook—she caters for hunting lodges and house parties in the Highlands, that sort of thing. Her brother's taking over the house, but Lizzie still spends time up there when she isn't cooking for people. You'll like her."

"Is that all?" asked Jamie. "Any other people?"

"Well, I went up there only two or three times," said Isabel. "I didn't get to know many people. The manager of the distillery.

The women in the shop in Craighouse." She had been drinking coffee, and now she drained the last few drops from her cup; mostly milk, a few flecks of foam—Isabel liked her coffee milky. "And you do know about Orwell?" she asked.

Jamie did. "He wrote *1984* there, didn't he?"

"Yes, at Barnhill, a house up at the top of the island. He finished it there in 1948."

"And that's how . . ."

Isabel wondered whether Jamie had read *1984*; his reading was patchy, but there were surprises. He had read *Anna Karenina* and *Cry, the Beloved Country,* but did not know who Madame Bovary was—which was half his charm, she suddenly thought; that he should not know about such things. "Who's Madame Bovary?" he had asked once, and Isabel, unprepared for the question, had almost said, *I am,* in jest, and then had stopped herself in time. But it was true, wasn't it? Like Madame Bovary, she had fallen for a younger man, although in her case she had no husband and there was no Flaubert to punish her. Women who fell desperately in love in defiance of convention were punished by their authors—Anna had been punished too; Isabel had smiled at the thought, and wondered whether she would be punished for loving Jamie. She had no author, though. Isabel was real.

Orwell: he punished himself, she thought, by staring at nightmares, and then writing about them. "Yes," she said. "He reversed the figures to get 1984, which must have seemed an awful long way away then." She stood up. "And then when the real 1984 came along, it didn't seem too bad after all. Certainly, it seems quite halcyon when compared with what's going on today. All those cameras constantly trained on the streets and so on. All that suspicion."

Jamie rose to his feet too and glanced at his watch. He was due at the school in an hour or so, and he thought of the boy who awaited him in the music room, a boy who did not enjoy playing the bassoon and who endured his lessons with barely concealed boredom. They disliked one another with cordiality; Jamie disapproved of his attitude to the instrument and was vaguely repelled by the boy's incipient sexuality, a sort of sultry, pent-up energy, just below the surface, manifesting itself in an outcrop of bad skin along the line of his chin and . . . It was hard being a boy of fourteen, and fifteen was just as bad. One knew everything, or thought one did, and it was frustrating that the rest of the world seemed unwilling to acknowledge this. And girls, who were equally uncomfortable, seemed so mocking, so near and yet so far, so out of reach because one was not quite tall enough or one's skin was uncooperative. Jamie shuddered. Had he been like that?

He thought of what Isabel had just said. Had things gone that badly wrong? And if they had, then why?

"Suspicion?" he asked. "Are we more suspicious?"

Isabel had no doubts. "Yes, of course we are. Look at airports—you're a suspect the moment you set foot in one. And for obvious reasons. But we're also more suspicious of everyone because we don't know them anymore. Our societies have become societies of strangers—people with whom we share no common experience, who may not speak the same language as we do. They certainly won't know the same poems and the same books. What can you expect in such circumstances? We're strangers to one another."

Jamie listened intently. Yes, Isabel could be right, but where did her observations take one? One could not turn the clock back to a world where we all grew up in the same village.

"What can we do?" he asked.

"Nothing," said Isabel. She thought for a moment about her answer. It was defeatist, and it could not be right. We could seek to re-create community, we could bring about a shared world of cultural references and points of commonality. We had to do that, or we would drift off into a separateness, which was almost where we were now. But it would not be easy, this re-creation of civil society; it would not be easy taming the feral young, the gangs, the children deprived of language and moral compass by neglect and the absence of fathers. "I don't really mean nothing," she said. "But it's complicated."

Jamie looked at his watch again. "I have to . . ."

"Of course," said Isabel. "It's a major project and you have only ten minutes."

He leaned forward and kissed her lightly on the cheek. She smelled the shaving soap that he liked to use, the smell of sandalwood.

For the rest of that day, Isabel did very little work. She made several telephone calls, though: to the ferry company in the west, to book the car passage on it to Islay and back; to Lizzie Fletcher, to see if she would be on Jura the following weekend, when they planned to arrive; and to the island's only hotel, the hotel at Craighouse, to arrange a room, one that would be large enough for the two of them and Charlie. Then somewhat reluctantly, when it was almost time for lunch, she faced up to the thing that she had been putting out of her mind but which now abruptly claimed her attention. Christopher Dove was coming that afternoon. He was booked on a train from London that would arrive at Waverley Station at three o'clock. He had announced this on the telephone and then had waited, as if expecting Isabel to offer to meet him. That's what people used to do at Oxford; they would meet people at the station and then walk to their college with them. Isabel endured a brief moment of internal struggle. Her natural goodness dictated that she should offer to be there; but her humanity, which, after all, was not restricted to kindness and sympathy—qualities of humanity surely can be bad, because that is what humanity is like—that same humanity now prompted her to be unhelpful. Professor Christopher Dove, after all, was the man who had engineered the coup which had toppled her from her editorial post. He was a ruthless, ambitious man, a plotter, who should have been a politician rather than a philosopher, thought Isabel. And I shall not meet him at the station. He can take a taxi and come to me.

Of course, she relented. Shortly before nine o'clock that morning she telephoned his home to offer to collect him at Waverley. As the telephone rang, she imagined the desk on which it rang, in his house in Islington, where was where she was sure that he lived. There was no reply; he had left for King's Cross and she had no mobile number for him. She rang off. That was a lesson which she should not need to learn at this stage of her life. Do not act meanly, do not be unkind, because the time for setting things right may pass before your heart changes course.

A TAXI HAD DRAWN UP in front of the house. From her study window on the ground floor, Isabel looked out, beyond the rhododendron bushes and the small birch tree to the front gate; a figure in the back of the cab was leaning forward to pay the driver. Well at least he got that right, thought Isabel; in Edinburgh one paid the driver before getting out of the cab—which was the sensible thing to do, the Enlightenment way—whereas in London people got out and paid through the front window, which the driver had to lower. Isabel could not see the point of this, but it was one of those things, like driving on the left side of the road rather than the right, which just *was*. And these things, particularly the side of the road on which a nation drove, was not something that could easily be changed, although Isabel remembered that there had been at least one autocrat somewhere—it was in Burma, she thought, with its odd, unhappy history—who had capriciously insisted that people should abruptly change from driving on the left to driving on the right, with the result that they were confused and had numerous accidents. Rulers should not impose too much on their long-suffering people. Had not the King of Tonga, an extremely large man, insisted that the whole nation should go on a diet when he decided to embark on one? That would surely test the bonds between monarch and people.

She watched as Christopher Dove stepped out of the taxi, holding a small overnight bag and briefcase. He looked towards the front door, to check the number, which was prominently displayed in brass Roman numerals screwed onto the wood. Then his gaze moved to the study window, and Isabel drew back sharply into the shadows. Dove must not, under any circumstances, feel that his visit made her anxious. Isabel had decided that she would remain dignified with Dove and treat him as she would treat any other colleague. That, after all, was the only thing she could do. Anything else—any pettiness or irritation on her part—would compound Dove's victory over her, make it all the more glorious.

She had met him before, of course, and so his appearance was no surprise; the haughty good looks, the high cheekbones and brow; the thick, carefully groomed blond hair like that of one of those men in the perfume advertisements, the men who stood there, shirtless for some reason (the heat, perhaps), looking in such a steely way into the middle distance. That was Dove.

"Isabel!" He had put his bags down on the doorstep and was standing there when she answered the bell, his arms extended as if to embrace her. And he did, leaning forward and putting his arms around Isabel's shoulders, kissing her on each cheek. She struggled with her natural inclination to draw back, but even if she mastered that, he must have felt her tenseness.

"It's so good of you to see me," he enthused. "And at short notice too!"

She thought: It's not at all good of me to see you; I had to see you. It would have been ridiculous not to see you. "It's no trouble," she said. "We have to get the handover right. After all, there are a lot of readers now. A lot. We wouldn't want to lose them."

It was a charged remark. She had not intended to fire off a shot quite so early, but she had. The fact that there were so many readers was attributable almost entirely to her editorship; when she had come to the job, the readership had been perilously small.

"Of course," he said, smiling. "And that's thanks to your efforts, of course. You've built the readership up marvellously. You really have."

Isabel thought, Well, why change editors in those circumstances? Should she say that? She decided not to, and instead invited Christopher Dove in. "Perhaps we should go through to my study," she said. "You can leave your bags in the hall." She looked pointedly at the overnight bag. "You have a hotel?"

She knew that this was a dangerous question. If his answer

was no, then she would be obliged to offer him a bed for the night, and she was unwilling to do that. *I was hungry and you took me in.* Yes, but that was in respect of somebody poor, not somebody *nasty.*

"No," he said, and her heart sank. But then he went on, "I'm going back on the sleeper train. Do you ever use it? I like it."

"Norman MacCaig didn't," said Isabel. "He wrote a poem about it. I think there's a line, 'I do not like this being carried sideways through the night.' "

Dove grinned. "Poets get crotchety," he said. "We philosophers are more sanguine, more stoic."

"Oh, I don't know," said Isabel. "Hume was even-tempered, I suppose, but there have been plenty of unpleasant philosophers." Such as you, she thought.

"I have never fully appreciated Hume," said Dove, not too discreetly inspecting Isabel's shelves. "I understand the appeal, but I take the view that there's so much more to be learned about our emotions from contemporary cognitive science. Hume wouldn't have exactly understood a magnetic resonance scan."

Isabel stared at him incredulously. This was pure nonsense. But she decided that she did not have the energy to engage with Christopher Dove on the point, and she moved over towards the filing cabinet behind her desk. "When I took over the editorship," she said, "I threw out a lot of old files. There were boxes and boxes of papers which my predecessor had done nothing about sorting out. There were all sorts of things which would have been of no interest to anybody. Letters from the printers, and so on. I cleared it all out. There was even an ancient letter from Bertrand Russell about a claim for a train fare to a symposium that the *Review* had organised."

Dove, who had been facing the window while Isabel spoke,

now spun round. "Russell? But what about his biographers? What if they had wanted it?"

Dove's tone was one of subdued outrage, and Isabel bristled defensively. "Would his biographers be interested in a claim for a train fare? Surely not, unless Russell questioned the *reality* of the train journey, or something like that. *I think that I boarded a train at Paddington, but can I be sure?*" She laughed, but Dove did not; he was concerned with posterity, and could not laugh at such things. Isabel wondered what conclusion biographers might draw from such a letter: that Russell was always one to claim expenses? Or that his finances were not in a good state and that he needed to watch even very minor outlays?

"What else?" asked Dove peevishly. "What else did you throw out?"

"I can assure you that I got rid of nothing significant," said Isabel. "It was all what would be called ephemera."

Dove's irritation seemed to mount. Isabel noticed that he was flushed, and that this showed very clearly, given his complexion. And she thought, too, that he was a very good-looking man and that he carried no extra weight. He would be a squash player, perhaps, or a cricketer; he had that look about him.

"Ephemera can be valuable," he said. "Very valuable. The signatures of well-known people on even the most mundane of letters can go for a great deal of money."

Isabel realised that this was true. "I'm sorry," she said. "Perhaps I should have been more careful. It's just that there was so much paper, and I really thought that . . ."

Dove suddenly seemed conciliatory. "Never mind," he said. "I understand your feelings about mounds of paper. It really does accumulate, doesn't it?"

They sat down at the desk, Isabel on her side and Dove on the other.

"I thought that we should go over plans for the next three issues," said Isabel. "Things are fairly far advanced with them, and if the current issue is going to be the last one I do, then you'll be taking over quite a bit of work in progress, so to speak."

Dove nodded gravely. "Yes."

"So shall we start with the next issue?" said Isabel.

Dove said that he thought this was a good idea, and Isabel extracted a thick folder from a pile of papers on her desk. She saw her visitor's eyes go to the pile of papers, and she realised that he disapproved of the clutter.

"I do know where everything is," she said quietly. "It may not look like it, but I do know."

"Of course you do," muttered Dove. "Creative clutter."

She did not like the condescending tone of his comment, but she let it pass. She opened the folder and took out a messy-looking bit of paper on which she had noted the order in which she proposed to put the articles. There was also her editorial, printed out on cream-coloured paper and corrected here and there, in blue ink, by its author. This would be her last editorial, she reflected, and it was about the ethics of taxation. Dove would never write about anything quite so dull, she thought. He would write about . . . what? Cognitive science, perhaps; decision trees and ethics; the question of whether computers had minds, from which Isabel realised the further question might flow: Could one have good computers and bad computers? In the moral sense of course.

They began to work, and worked through until four thirty, when Isabel heard the front gate open. She looked up and saw a visitor coming down the path to the front door. It was

Cat. Dove looked up too. He saw Cat and looked enquiringly at Isabel.

"My niece," said Isabel, getting up from her desk. "I wasn't expecting her."

Dove stretched his arms back and yawned. "I could do with a break anyway."

Isabel left him in the study and made her way to the front door. Cat had her finger poised before the bell when Isabel opened the door.

"I saw you." Isabel smiled warmly. Cat's visit could be a new beginning, and she would not let the memory of that disastrous evening at her flat stand in the way of a reconciliation. But if there was a thaw, it was a slight one, as Cat still seemed distant.

"You left your cardigan at the flat the other night," said Cat. "Here it is."

Isabel took the cardigan, which Cat produced from a small carrier bag. "Come in for a quick cup of tea," she said. "I was just about to make some. Christopher Dove is here."

Cat looked interested. "Christopher Dove? Do I know him?"

"No. He's on the board of the journal. In fact, he's . . ." She trailed off. She was about to say that he was taking over, but at that moment, at the door, she was not so sure. It was complicated.

"All right," said Cat. "But I can't stay long. I've left Eddie in charge and I think he wants to get away early. He's doing a class in the yoga centre near Holy Corner."

"That's a good thing," said Isabel. "Poor Eddie . . ."

Cat did not pursue the subject of Eddie. "Well, Eddie's Eddie."

"That," said Isabel, "is undoubtedly true. And you can probably say the same about most of us, *mutatis mutandis*."

Cat looked at her sideways.

"That is," Isabel continued, "changing that which requires to be changed. In this case, the name."

Cat said nothing. They had entered the hall, and Christopher Dove had appeared from the study. Isabel introduced them, and Christopher stepped forward to shake Cat's hand. Isabel watched and immediately noticed the change in Cat's demeanour.

"We'll have a cup of tea in the kitchen," said Isabel.

Cat looked upstairs. "Where's . . ."

"With Grace this afternoon," said Isabel. She did not want to talk about Charlie in front of Dove. Grace had taken Charlie to the Botanic Gardens to walk him round and get some fresh air. Isabel had been happy for Charlie to be out of the way during her meeting with Dove and had not pointed out her belief that the air in Merchiston, her part of Edinburgh, was every bit as fresh as the air in Inverleith, where the Botanic Gardens were. In fact, the air was fresher in Merchiston and Morningside, which were several hundred feet higher than Inverleith, and there was also that occasional miasmic mist which snaked into Inverleith from the shores of the Firth of Forth and which she would never describe as fresh.

They went into the kitchen.

"Such a large house," said Dove. "In London we have to make do with—"

"You're very crowded," interjected Isabel. "It's most unfortunate."

Cat was watching Dove; a scene enacted in Isabel's garden from time to time when the neighbour's striped cat stalked birds. Isabel smiled at the thought, and turned away to put on the kettle and hide her amusement. But that amusement lasted for only a few seconds, for then she thought: *She can't!*

Isabel went out of the room for a moment on the pretext of

fetching something. But she stopped in the hall and thought: I can't bear it if she falls for him. Dove! She took a deep breath before going back into the kitchen. Cat and Dove were in animated conversation.

"Such a great city . . . Do you know London? . . . A delicatessen? I've got a great one near my place in Islington . . . Hard work, I bet . . ."

And, "I've got a friend there . . . I should get down more often . . . I love it when I do . . . That buzz. Yes. There's a buzz . . . Show you round? Are you staying?"

Isabel busied herself with the making of the tea. It was every bit as bad as she feared. But of course she should have anticipated it. Dove was older than Cat by a few years—eight maybe—but he looked youthful and he was exactly her physical type. She remembered Toby, to whom Cat had been briefly and disastrously engaged. He had looked just like Dove, now that she came to think of it, and so she should not be surprised, and now . . . she could hardly believe it: the invitation to dinner had been extended, and accepted. There would be plenty of time, Dove told Cat, as the sleeper did not leave until after eleven.

Isabel handed Cat her cup of tea with a look into which she tried to pour a wide range of emotions: surprise, pity, and the reproach that went with betrayal. But her efforts were in vain. Cat did not see her. Nor did Dove.

CAT LEFT after half an hour, and Isabel and Dove returned to finish off their work in the study. They did not have much to do, which meant that Dove could leave in good time to meet Cat at the delicatessen and then go out for dinner.

"Cat has very kindly offered to show me a bit of the town this evening," said Dove.

"She's very interested in . . ." Isabel wanted to say *men,* but ended up saying *that sort of thing.* She glanced at her watch. Grace should be back soon, although sometimes she took Charlie to visit her cousin, who lived in Stockbridge, not far from the Botanic Gardens. And Jamie would be due any moment, as he had said that he would be back early in order to see Charlie before his bath time.

They were on the point of finishing when Jamie arrived. The study door was open and he came in, expecting to find only Isabel. "Oh," he said. "Sorry to interrupt."

"This is Christopher Dove," said Isabel.

Jamie knew who Christopher Dove was and a shadow passed across his face, a clouding. "Oh."

Christopher Dove stood up to shake hands with Jamie. He turned to Isabel.

"Your nephew?"

CHAPTER ELEVEN

CHRISTOPHER DOVE left Edinburgh to return to London on the Monday of that week. That left three full days in Edinburgh before she and Jamie—and Charlie, of course—were due to leave for their four days on Jura. It would have been better to leave Edinburgh on the Friday, but they could not, as Jamie was playing in a concert in Perth that evening. So he managed to get the following Monday and Tuesday off, by shifting his pupils to later in the week, something he normally did not like to do but which was just possible, provided that it was not done too often.

The visit of the London philosopher had left Isabel shocked and angry. Her anger, which was more of a simmering resentment, perhaps, was focused on Dove himself and on his scheming ways, his sheer dishonesty. He had coveted her job and had pushed her out; that she could accept, to an extent, if only he had not been so duplicitous about it. Had he taken her job openly, then she might have muttered something about the fairness of all in love and war and left it at that. But he had unctuously congratulated her on her achievements and acted as if the discussions over the transfer were between willing predecessor and willing successor. They were not! thought Isabel. This was what businesspeople called an unfriendly takeover, and no amount of smooth talking and smiling would paper over that unavoidable fact.

The shock that Isabel felt was nothing to do with Dove, or only indirectly so; it had resulted from the sheer, naked concupiscence of Cat's flirting. For a while Isabel had wondered whether Cat knew about the reason for Dove's presence and whether her immediate taking up with him had been intended to rub salt into Isabel's wound, a form of fraternisation with the enemy in full view of General Headquarters. But then she realised that Cat did not know about the change in editorship and that whatever else she might have done in recent months to hurt or offend Isabel, she had not done this. But it was still shocking because Isabel believed that people should be circumspect about picking up other people. One might like somebody and set out to make further acquaintance, but, other than in bars and clubs where everybody went for that precise purpose, one tried not to make one's intentions too obvious. Was this hypocrisy, and an outdated form of hypocrisy at that? She did not think so. The whole point about conventions of this nature is that they affirmed the value of the person; she who advertised the fact of immediate availability—and in Cat's case barely five minutes had passed before the date was made—was suggesting surely, that she was available even to one whom she barely knew. There was such a thing as appropriate reticence, thought Isabel; a reticence that might at least involve a short prelude before the implicit bargain was sealed.

She was shocked by the thought that her niece was—well, there was no other word for it—cheap. She knew that Cat had an eye for a certain sort of man—the wrong sort—and she knew that her boyfriends tended not to last very long, but she had not thought of her before as cheap. Or was there another word? *Fast?* No, a fast woman might not be cheap. They were two different things. Fast women could be stylish and really rather expensive; they might think long and hard before they decided with whom they were going to be fast.

She was distracted for a moment by the conjuring up of an image of a fast woman. She saw, quite vividly, a woman sporting a low neckline, a knee-length silk-jersey dress, close-fitting, expensively draped, an impossibly small bag made of supple green leather; one would smell the quality of the leather. Isabel smiled at the thought, but then her smile faded. Cat was not fast, but she did not want to conclude that she was cheap. What was she then? The answer came to her: confused. That was a third category of women: those who were simply confused. They did not really know what sort of man they wanted, tried many, and found them all wanting.

She tried to put Cat's involvement with Dove out of her mind and thought instead of the absent Charlie. Cat would come round—eventually; even if Isabel could not get through to her, in due course Charlie would. One cannot snub a baby for long, even if he is the product of one's aunt's dalliance with one's ex-boyfriend. As for Dove, he had done nothing to redeem himself and she had decided on a course of action which would deal with him. That required a bit of thought, but Isabel did not want to dwell on it too long. These things, once decided, should be acted upon, as Lady Macbeth pointed out to her indecisive husband. Isabel had not thought that she could do this particular thing; she had not imagined that she had it within her. But now she decided she had, and that she would act.

In the first place it involved a telephone call in which instructions were given. That took rather longer than she had planned, but at the end of the call everything was arranged. Then there was another call, this time to the small private bank, Adam & Company, where Isabel was put through to Gareth

Howlett. That did not take long; liquidity, Gareth explained, was not a problem for Isabel.

"Sometimes people don't quite understand just how substantial their resources are," said Gareth. "You don't really need to worry, you know."

"I don't like to think about these things," said Isabel. She remembered what her friend Max had once said to her: *Money is only a problem if one doesn't have enough of it.* It was one of those observations that seemed self-evident, but which had depths to it that became apparent only when one sat down to think about it. And could one say the same about other things? Was food a problem only if one did not have enough of it? No, that, at least, was not true. Those who had enough food still had problems with it; hence the whole desperate business of dieting—the cures, the pills, the fat farms, the hopelessness of the scales.

That out of the way, Isabel turned to the luxury of spending a couple of days exactly as she pleased. Dove had taken the files on the next issue away with him, which meant that there was nothing pressing for Isabel to do. She could visit the bookshops, go to the galleries, see friends: she felt a heady sense of having choices in what to do with her time, that delicious feeling that there were simply no claims upon her. Apart from Charlie, of course, and Jamie, and the house, Grace, and occasionally, and in a subtle way, Brother Fox.

SHE DID NOT TELL JAMIE where she went the next day, which was to a house in the Stockbridge Colonies. The Colonies were rows of neat, late-nineteenth-century houses, stone-built and terraced, with one house below and one above, the upper front door being reached by an external stone staircase built up against the wall of the house below. They were attractive houses, although somewhat cramped, built for the families of skilled tradesmen at the end of the Victorian era, like the mining cottages one saw in some of the villages of East Lothian, on the plain that stretched out to the cold blue-grey line of the North Sea. At the end of each row of houses, on the gable wall that fronted the street, there were carved representations of the trade of those who occupied the houses beyond: the miller's wheel; the maltman's rake; the calipers, chisel, and hammer of the stonemason. Of course the tradesmen had been replaced by young professionals and advertising people, but these houses were still not too expensive and some of them were occupied by older people who had paid very little for them thirty years ago.

She found Teviotdale Place halfway along the road that crossed over a small bridge. Edinburgh's river, the Water of Leith, not a great river by the standards of many cities, looped its way through Stockbridge at this point. The end houses in the Colonies were all on the edge of the riverbank, a good place to be in summer, when the river was low, but an unsettling place to live when the Water of Leith became overambitious, as it did after heavy rains up in the Pentland Hills. It was a comfortable street, as all these Colonies streets were; proving, perhaps, the proposition that we are happiest when living in courtyards or, as in this case, in streets that face one another and are almost courtyards. Children could play here, in the street, and be watched from both sides; washing could be hung out on the lines that were strung from walls to the black-painted, cast-iron washing posts that emerged from tiny lawns; cats could prowl through lavender bushes and wisteria and along the tops of the pint-sized walls that separated garden from garden.

Isabel had been given the address by Guy Peploe, whom she had seen the previous day, when she had dropped into the Scottish Gallery. There had been a conversation about McInnes—and a further look at the Jura painting which Guy still had—and then he had casually mentioned that he had seen McInnes's widow a few days earlier, that she was still in Edinburgh and he ran into her from time to time.

"Did she marry the man she was having an affair with?" asked Isabel.

Guy looked out of the window. They were sitting in his office in the gallery, and the sun was streaming down into the garden at the back.

"No," he said. "She did not. He went off to London, I think. He was an artist too, but he came into some money, I seem to remember, and he went off with somebody else. Pretty awful for her. She was pregnant when McInnes died, and she had a baby."

"His? Or McInnes's?"

Guy shrugged. "I have no idea. But she had a little boy, anyway. I see her with him from time to time. He must be eight or so, because that's how long McInnes has been dead."

Isabel reflected on the sadness of this, when Guy said, "She lives down in the Colonies. Above that man who plays the fiddle at ceilidhs. You might know him—everybody seems to. He's recorded a lot."

"I do know him," said Isabel. "He sometimes plays with David Todd. He's quite a character."

"Above his house," said Guy. "That's where she ended up," He paused. "And if things had worked out otherwise, and with the prices his paintings command now, they could have been living . . . oh, in the south of France, if they wanted to."

"And that little boy would have had a father," said Isabel.

"Yes," said Guy. "That too."

NOW, standing outside the house in Teviotdale Place, Isabel looked down at her hands. She did that when she was nervous—she looked at her hands—and it somehow gave her courage. She thought, I have no excuse to go and see this person. I don't know her, and she owes me nothing. I am calling upon a complete stranger.

But if that had not stopped her before, it did not stop her now, and she pushed open the small, ironwork gate and began walking up the path to the open staircase to the upper flat. The door was painted blue and there was a small black plaque: MCINNES. She pushed the doorbell, a round, highly polished brass doorbell that was obviously well loved.

Ailsa McInnes answered the door. She was a woman of about Isabel's age, wearing jeans and a brightly coloured striped shirt. She was barefoot.

"Ailsa?"

The woman nodded and smiled. There was a friendliness about her which Isabel picked up immediately and warmed to.

Isabel introduced herself. She hoped that she did not mind her calling round without warning, but Guy Peploe had passed on her name. That was true, thought Isabel; he had provided her name.

"Guy? Oh yes." The woman gestured for Isabel to go into the house. "It's a mess, I'm afraid. My wee boy isn't the tidiest child in the world."

"He's at school?"

"Yes. Stockbridge Primary, down the road. He'll be back

quite soon. We have a group of mothers here who take it in turns to walk the kids to school and back. We put them in a line of five and bring them back like that."

Isabel smiled. "They used to call those lines crocodiles. Walk in a crocodile," she said. And she remembered the nursery school in Edinburgh that used to take the children for a walk all tied together with string; a sensible expedient, but not one, she imagined, of which the modern nanny state would approve— today the state would simply prohibit taking children for a walk on the grounds that it was too dangerous.

"A crocodile. Yes."

They sat down in the living room. There were signs of the small boy everywhere; a construction set, the pieces spilled out across a corner of the floor; a football and a muddy pair of football boots; a couple of children's comics—Korky the Cat, Desperate Dan and his cow pie: the world of a small boy who has not yet been enticed by electronics.

"If you're wondering about why I've come to see you," Isabel began, "it's to do with one of Andrew's paintings."

"I see." Ailsa's voice was quite level, and Isabel thought, Yes, it was eight years ago.

"I don't know if you are aware of this," said Isabel, "but a couple of paintings have recently come onto the market."

Ailsa shrugged. "They do, from time to time. I must say that I don't keep a close eye on what's going on. I have about ten of his paintings myself. I don't keep them here—they're mostly at my mother's house. I might sell one or two later on—depending on whether we need the money." She looked about the room. For all its untidiness, it was comfortable. "At the moment, things are all right. I have a part-time job, which is quite well paid, and I own this house." She looked searchingly at

Isabel. "Are you interested in buying one of my paintings? Is that it?"

Isabel reassured her that she was not. "You must get a lot of approaches," she said.

"A few," said Ailsa. "Especially now that Andy's work is so popular. There was a collector from New York who came round the other day. A very glitzy character. He had three of Andy's paintings and said that he would go for them in preference to a Cadell or an Eardley. He let slip that he hangs one of them next to his Wyeth."

"Good company," said Isabel. "I have one, you know—a small one. I keep it on the stairs. Not next to anything grand, I'm afraid."

"So you don't want to buy one of mine?"

"No. But I have been offered one by somebody who bought it at auction. It's one of the Jura pictures." Isabel reached into her pocket and took out a folded page from the Lyon & Turnbull catalogue. "There's a photograph of it here from the auction catalogue. I wondered if you knew the painting."

Ailsa took the paper and studied the photograph. "No. I don't remember that one at all. But if it was painted on Jura, then it could have been one of . . ." Her voice faltered. "It could be one of his last ones. The ones that he did up there after he left."

The matter-of-fact tone that Ailsa had used before was now replaced by one which was touched with regret; remorse too, Isabel imagined.

"Of course," said Isabel. "But I thought that I might just check up to see whether you knew anything more about the painting."

"No, I don't. But it's his, you know. It's definitely his. Just look at it."

Isabel took the piece of paper back from her and folded it up. At that moment, the front door was pushed open and a boy came in. He was halfway through peeling off a blue sweater, which he tossed down on the floor.

"Not on the floor, Magnus," scolded Ailsa. "We don't throw our clothes on the floor."

But we do, thought Isabel. Charlie will do just that, no doubt.

Magnus was looking at Isabel with that undisguised curiosity that children can show. "This is somebody who likes Dad's paintings," said Ailsa. "She's come to talk to me about them. And you can go into the kitchen and have a chocolate biscuit. *One* chocolate biscuit."

As Magnus dashed into the kitchen, Isabel found herself thinking: *Dad*—that answers that, at least. Whatever the boy's real parentage was, he had been raised to believe that he was the son of Andrew McInnes, whom he never knew, a father who was just a name, an idea, somebody of whom he might even have been brought up to feel proud; but what a poor substitute for the real thing, the flesh-and-blood father who would have helped the little boy with his construction kit and his football, helped him to grow up.

CHAPTER TWELVE

ISABEL DALHOUSIE'S green Swedish car, laden almost to the point of discomfort with the impedimenta that a baby requires, nosed its way gingerly down the ramp onto the deck of the Port Askaig ferry. Charlie was awake, but lying still in his reclining car seat, staring at the ceiling of the car with intense fascination. He had seemed to enjoy the earlier sea journey, which had taken them from the Mull of Kintyre to the island of Islay, and which was now to be followed by the five-minute crossing over to Jura. The rocking movement of the ferry and the noise of the engines made him wave his arms with pleasure. "It reminds him of the womb," said Isabel. "The movement, the noise."

Jamie looked through the window of the car to the hills of Jura on the other side of the sound. They rose steep from the shore, without the normal decency of a cultivable plain, and then became stretches of heather and scree, sweeping up to a feminine curve of skyline at the top. The heather was that characteristically Scottish mixture of soft greens and purples, colours washed and washed again in Atlantic squalls of salt and rain.

Against a growling of engines and a churning of water, the

small ferry docked at the other side to let the three or four cars which it had borne across now drive up the ramp onto Jura. There was a single road, and it led in only one direction.

"That's our road," said Jamie, adding, "I think."

Isabel smiled. "One road," she said. "One hotel. One distillery."

"One hundred and eighty people," said Jamie. "And how many sheep and deer?"

"Numerous," said Isabel. "Thousands of deer. Look."

The road had turned a corner and a stag was gazing down from a bank a few hundred yards away, his legs obscured by bracken, antlers branching upwards sharp and naked, like a tree that has lost its leaves for the winter. They slowed down and he looked at them briefly with that tense mixture of alertness, defiance, and fear. Then slowly he turned away and trotted off into the bracken.

"We'll see him again," said Isabel. "Him or one of his brothers."

"I love this place," said Jamie suddenly, turning to Isabel. "Already. I love it."

She glanced at him and saw the light in his eyes; the car swerved briefly.

"I fell in love with it too," she said. "When I first came here, I fell in love with it as well."

"Why?" asked Jamie. "Why do places like this have this effect on people?"

Isabel mused for a moment. "There must be all sorts of reasons. The hills, the sea, everything really. The dramatic scenery."

"But you find that elsewhere," said Jamie. "The Grand Canyon's dramatic. And yet I don't think that I'd fall in love with it. I'd be impressed. But it would remain platonic."

"I've actually seen the Grand Canyon," said Isabel. "Years ago. And, no, I didn't fall in love with it. I suspect it's rather hard to fall in love with a canyon." Oddly, she thought of lines which said the exact opposite. She did not turn to Jamie, but mouthed, half whispered them anyway: "Love requires an object, But this varies so much, Almost anything will do, When I was a child I loved a pumping engine, thought it every bit as beautiful as you."

Jamie frowned. " 'Pumping engine'?"

"That's Auden's point," said Isabel. "We all need to love something. Anybody can fall in love with anything, or anyone: love requires an object, that's all. Even an island will do."

They were silent for a while. They passed a set of stone gates and a high stone wall, the garden of one of the handful of large houses on the island, houses which stood at the centre of the huge landed estates into which Scotland had been carved. Such places were largely innocuous now, Isabel thought; not much more than outsize farms which were trying to make a living on the sale of sporting rights and various agricultural enterprises. Many had passed into distant hands, so that the lairds, the local gentry, had effectively disappeared, to be replaced by owners who flew in and out for brief periods, or did not even bother to come. There was so much wrong with Scotland; such unfairnesses, pockets of such poverty and desperation, that were so hard to eradicate, no matter what the politicians in Edinburgh might try to do; it was as if they ran with the land, were written into the deeds that gave Scotland to human ownership. And there had been such injury to the soul, too, leaving scars that went down from generation to generation.

They were now close to Craighouse, the only village on the island, and fields of ripening hay, yellow in the afternoon sun, fell away to the east, to the cliffs' edges. Isabel noticed a ruined croft not far away, one of the small stone-built houses that were at the centre of a smallholding. The lichen-covered walls were still standing, but there was no roof, and the window spaces were dark gaps.

She pointed to the croft. "If you love this place so much, you could restore somewhere like that and live here. You could write music, maybe give bassoon lessons to the islanders."

"I just might," said Jamie. "I'm sure that I could be quite self-sufficient. Doing a bit of fishing. Catching rabbits for the pot."

And Isabel thought, Well, if he did that then there would be no place for me, nor for Charlie, but she did not say anything. They were now coming into Craighouse, and she saw the small hotel on the right, opposite the distillery, with its friendly white-washed buildings and its row of bonded warehouses immediately behind.

"That's us," said Isabel, as they came to a halt outside the hotel.

Jamie wound down his window; there was light rain now and the sky had suddenly clouded over, as it could do, so rapidly. The air was warm and smelled of seaweed. The hotel looked out over the bay, which, having a low-lying island at its mouth, was a safe haven for boats; several sailboats bobbed at anchor and a small fishing boat, the sort used for inshore work, sat at its mooring, nets hung up over the boom. There was quiet, that quiet which settles in places where nothing is urgent, nothing is hurried.

They made their way into the hotel. Charlie had begun to niggle, and was taken immediately into the bedroom, where he was changed and fed. From the room, as she was administering Charlie's bottle, Isabel watched Jamie walk down to the pier, where he stood, looking out towards the boats in the bay. As she watched him, she felt a tug of possession that surprised her by its intensity; and she experienced, too, a sense of vulnerability—the feeling that people get when they see that which they love and know that they might lose it. In the back of her mind, there were lines of song, half remembered, their memory triggered by the island scenery, something she had heard sung a long time ago, but which had lodged: *I'm afraid the scorching suns will shine and spoil his beauty.* That was it, but there was more, and it came to her, the melody of it too, not just the words:

> *My love's gone across those fields with his cheeks like roses*
> *My love's gone across those fields gathering sweet posies*
> *I fear the scorching suns will shine and spoil his beauty*
> *And if I was with my love I would do my duty.*

She rose from the bed, where she had been sitting, and stood before the window, holding Charlie across her shoulder to bring up his wind. She looked across to where Jamie was standing in the distance, on the pier, and she waved. He turned round. She waved again, and he raised a hand in salute, and she whispered, *I love you so much. I love you more than you will ever know, Jamie. More.*

THEY HAD ARRIVED in the late afternoon, so there was little time to do much before dinner, which was served at seven. After he came back from the pier, Jamie relieved Isabel of Charlie while she went for a walk along the road that led north past the distillery and the village hall. The sky had cleared again and was now mostly blue, with patches of high white cloud moving in from the Atlantic. At one point, beyond the village school, she saw a flock of Greenland white-fronted geese, coming in off the sound, heading back to Islay; the beating of their wings was like muffled drums. She walked onto the beach, a strand of pebbles interspersed with washed-up bladder wrack and whitened wood.

She knew when she had reached the point she was searching for. If she looked directly behind her she could see the roof of the distillery through the treetops, and behind that the fold of the hills. She took a few steps backwards and looked again, this time from a half-crouching position, as an artist would presumably have had a stool. This meant that he would not have seen the distillery roof, nor the cottage on the lower slopes beside the trees. Yes, it was exactly right.

Back at the hotel, Jamie put a finger to his lips when Isabel came into the room. Charlie was asleep, stretched out in his travel cot. "You've been gone for ages," he whispered. "Where were you?"

Isabel took off her jacket and shook it. She peered down at Charlie and blew him a kiss. "Along the way," she said.

"And?"

She smiled. "Nothing much. I saw some Greenland geese on their way back to Islay."

Jamie looked at his watch. "I'm famished."

Over dinner, when the conversation lagged, she said, "The painting that I almost bought . . ."

Jamie reached for his wineglass. "I knew that you had a reason for coming here. It's something to do with that picture."

Isabel searched his face to see if he was angry, but she saw only the triumph of one whose suspicions have been borne out. "No," she said. "I wanted to come here anyway—sometime. But I thought that . . ."

He grinned. "But you thought that you would interfere in

something or other . . . What is there to interfere with, by the way?"

She thought for a moment. There was nothing, really; and she did not *interfere,* as Jamie put it. He criticised her for *helping,* which was another matter altogether. "I don't interfere," she began.

He cut her short. "You do, Isabel. You can't help yourself."

She looked down at her plate, and he realised that he had offended her. He was about to tell her that the only reason he had said this was that her interfering just did not make sense to him. But he did not get round to this, as she had started her explanation.

"All I'm doing is looking," she said. "It occurred to me that the picture which I was offered by Walter Buie, the picture which was in the auction, was not by McInnes. I wanted to come to Jura anyway, and I thought I would kill two birds with one stone."

Jamie looked at her in astonishment. "A fake? You think it's a fake?"

He had raised his voice, and a woman at the next table looked at him. Her eyes moved to Isabel and then back to Jamie. Isabel noticed the brooch she was wearing, a Celtic whorl design of some sort of sea creature, a kelpie perhaps.

"Yes," she said quietly. "It could be. That's what I thought."

Jamie toyed with the stem of his wineglass. Isabel, he thought, had an overactive imagination. He did not disapprove of this; in fact, it was part of her charm—her imagination and her unexpected, drily witty remarks. He knew no other woman who talked like that, and he was proud of her.

"But why would you think that?" he asked. "Guy Peploe seems happy with it—and he's an expert. And presumably the auction house people must think it genuine—they would never offer anything for sale if they had any doubts about it. So why do you think . . ." He was going to say, "when you really don't know anything much about art," but decided not to. It was implied, though, and he did not need to say it.

"I know it may sound odd to you," said Isabel. "But I just have a feeling that something's not quite right about that painting."

Jamie sighed. "But why? You have to have grounds for thinking something like that. It's not enough to have a *feeling*." He paused, watching Isabel. She had spoken to him before about intuition, and about how it worked; inarticulate knowledge, she had called it. But he had been unable to understand how it was possible to know something but not know how you knew it. That just did not make sense to him. Even with music, he had said, you know why you like something; you can analyse it in terms of musical structure and see why things sound good or not; you know, and you can always work out why you know.

Isabel had decided that there *were* reasons for her suspicions. "Why would Walter Buie want to pass the painting on so quickly?" she asked. "Would you do that? Would you buy a painting and then the next moment try to sell it?" She waited for Jamie to answer, but he was silent, and so she answered for him. "You wouldn't. Unless you had found out something about the painting—something that you didn't know when you bought it."

"Or you had acted on impulse," said Jamie. "Look at how many people take things back to shops after a day or so. Women, mostly. They buy an outfit and then decide that they don't like it. So it goes back."

Isabel looked at him wryly. "And you're saying that men don't do that?"

"They don't," said Jamie. "I worked in Jenners once when I was a student. Everybody knew that men didn't bring things back. In fact, we were taught that in a training course. Somebody from the store had the figures. Men never brought clothes back."

Isabel thought that he was probably right. "So what you're saying is that Walter Buie, as a man, would never take it back to the auction house, but he might try to sell it on?"

"Yes," said Jamie. "But you can't take things back to an auction house anyway. It's not like a clothes store."

"I don't know where this is leading," said Isabel.

"All I'm suggesting is that there could be other reasons he offered it to you. You can't conclude that it's a fake, just because he wants to get rid of it."

She had to admit that this was true. But there was something else. "Guy was surprised that the painting wasn't varnished," she said. "He said that McInnes usually varnished his paintings."

"But he still didn't think it was a fake, did he? So he can't have thought that the fact that it wasn't varnished was all that important."

She had to admit this too. And now, with the two elements of her case reduced by Jamie's scrutiny, she was thrown back on her conviction that something about the painting just did not feel right. She had no idea why coming to Jura should strengthen that conviction, but on her walk today, when she had looked at the very view which appeared in the painting, she had felt it strongly. The painting was faithful to the view from the beach; there was nothing more, nor less, in it than there was in the real scene. But for some reason she was sure that it just did not add up; how she would prove that, she had no idea, and she did not want to talk about it anymore. She picked up her wineglass. "Enough of all that," she said. "I shall keep my suspicions to myself. Let's just enjoy this place."

Jamie raised his glass to hers. "To the next three days," he said. He looked at her, almost reproachfully. "And, Isabel . . . don't. Just don't."

"I'll try not to." She meant it, but somehow she knew at the same time that she did not. Can one want to do something and yet not want to do it? Of course you can, she told herself. Of course.

CHAPTER THIRTEEN

"TELL ME ABOUT LIZZIE," said Jamie.

They were driving up the island, on the narrow road that hugged the coast. Off to their left, now shrouded by cloud, now exposed to shafts of late-morning sunlight, the Paps of Jura towered, crouching lions guarding Scotland against the Atlantic. To their right, across the Sound of Jura, was the Scottish mainland with its mountains in layers, blue beyond blue. The sea was calm, glassy flat, silver in the sun.

"Lizzie?" said Isabel. "Well, I got to know her when I came up here four years ago. I stayed with friends who had rented Ardlussa, where we're going. Her parents were away but she stayed behind to cook. She was in her very early twenties then. She's a genius when it comes to lobsters and crayfish. She caught them herself; she had her own pots. And she knew some men who dived for scallops.

"Then we met again when I was a weekend guest in Glen Lyon. Lizzie had been hired as cook—that's what she does. I've seen her a few times in Edinburgh too. She's great company. Good sense of humour. She'll tackle anything."

"I suppose you have to be like that if you live up here," said Jamie. "You wouldn't last long otherwise." He shifted in his seat;

the wind from Isabel's open window was upon his face. "Could you live somewhere like this, Isabel?"

She thought for a moment. It seemed almost churlish to say that one could not, in the face of such beguiling natural beauty, but she could not. There would be so much that she would miss about the life of the city; the company, the conversation, the places to drink coffee. "I don't think I could," she said. "I'd moulder."

"It might be quite nice to moulder," said Jamie. "And I suspect that people have a very different sense of time here."

"Do you think time slows down?"

He was sure that it did. He looked at his watch; he had no idea what time it was, and had not known all that morning. In Edinburgh his day was sliced into half hours; thirty minutes for a pupil and then on to the next one: sarabandes, suites for bassoon and piano, arpeggios—so many notes, thousands and thousands of notes. "It's different. When you're doing something you really enjoy, it does pass more quickly. And it's the same if people are rushing around you. Everything seems quicker."

"Subjective time," said Isabel. "When we're ten, a week is an awfully long time. Now . . ."

"Yes, it's very odd," said Jamie. "I had plenty of time when I was at music college in Glasgow, and it passed very slowly. Now a week goes by in minutes."

"There's a reason for that," said Isabel. "It's to do with memories and how many you make. When you're doing things for the first time, you lay down lots of memories. Later on, things become a bit routine . . ."

"And you don't have anything to remember?" Jamie asked incredulously.

"Well, you do, but because your life is a bit more routine,

and there are few things which strike you as unusual, you don't feel that you have to remember quite as much. And so it seems that time has passed more quickly."

He said nothing for a while, thinking about a year at school when he had been bullied and he had thought that the time of his oppression would never end, and then, quite suddenly, the bully had not been there one day. Something had happened, and the other boy had simply gone, like a nightmare lifts when one wakes up and realises that it was never real.

She thought, Will I remember this, every moment of this, being here, in this beautiful place, with him—she glanced to her side—and him—she glanced over her shoulder. The green Swedish car swerved slightly, but only slightly, and recovered quickly enough to continue its journey along the side of the island, past startled Blackface sheep and dry-stane dykes, squat walls of stone dividing the fields, built many years ago by hard-working men, poor men, whose names were now long for-gotten.

ARDLUSSA LOOKED DOWN onto the bay of the same name, over lawns, then a field that ran gently down to a pier. Behind it, the River Lussa flowed down from the hills, to spread out, just a mile or so away, and join the sea at Inverlussa. The house had been built in the nineteenth century and added to in Edwardian times, a rambling country house half white, at the front, and half grey, at the back. It was at the centre of an estate that con-sisted of mountain and small forests, the habitat of the deer that provided a living for a handful of people—the family who lived in the big house and a couple of keepers and farm workers. The entrance was typical of that which one would find in any Scottish country house—a comfortable, lived-in hall, with walking sticks, cromachs (the Scottish crooks used by shepherds and hikers), and a bent and dusty green golfing umbrella that would have provided dubious protection against the elements even in its youth. If it rained here, it rained with conviction: shifting veils of water from clouds scudding in straight off the Atlantic; horizontal rain, vertical rain, rain swirling in all directions. Or on occasion the air was just wet: at such times there were no visible raindrops, just suspended moisture like the spray of a perfume atomiser that settled on clothing and skin. And with it came the midges, those tiny fruit fly–like creatures that spurn protective creams and lotions, and nip the skin of any human target in sight. Unfortunate hikers had been known to throw themselves into rivers to escape the clouds of stinging insects.

Lizzie met them at the entrance and took them into the kitchen. She had not met Jamie before and Isabel could see the surprise in her expression; surprise which was quickly and tact-fully masked. When Jamie left the room to find the bathroom, Isabel said to Lizzie, "Yes. We are. And that's our baby."

Lizzie smiled conspiratorially. "I'm happy for you. But where . . ."

"Where did I find him?"

Lizzie blushed. She had not meant to ask that, but it had been what she was wondering. Isabel was an attractive person, and she could understand her being sought after by men, but by men like that . . . Well, somebody would have found him even-tually, and if it was Isabel, then she deserved congratulation. "He's very . . . ," she began, but again trailed off.

"He is," said Isabel. "And he's sweet."

Jamie returned and Lizzie prepared tea for the three of them. A Dundee cake that she had baked was produced out of a tin, and they carried that, and the tea tray, into the drawing room. There were pictures of island scenes on the walls, an old map, and piles of books on the tables. Isabel noticed Bernard Crick's biography of Orwell, and she picked it up and paged through it.

"Do you want to visit Barnhill?" Lizzie asked. She looked at Jamie, unsure whether he would know the story. "It's where Orwell stayed. You can see the room where he wrote *1984*."

Jamie looked interested. "Can we?"

Lizzie nodded. "Yes. And he was in this house, too, you know. He was in this room. My grandfather lived in this house in those days, and Orwell used to talk to him about being a Japanese prisoner of war. Some people think that that's where Orwell got the idea of those awful tortures—the Room 101 part of *1984*. Robin Fletcher, my grandfather, told him about what had happened in the camp. The Japanese were terribly cruel to their prisoners."

"I'd like to see the place," said Jamie. He looked at Isabel, who said that she wanted to go too.

"I can arrange it," said Lizzie. "That part of Ardlussa, and the house up there, the Orwell place, belongs to my uncle now. My cousin Rob's up there at the moment. He could come and fetch us—there are about seven miles of rough track to get to it. You need a four-wheel-drive." She looked at Isabel, with something of the mocking air of a countrywoman addressing a hopeless urbanite. "That car of yours . . ."

"My green Swedish car is very strong," said Isabel. "But no, I agree, it's a bit low-slung for this part of the world."

"I'll get in touch with Rob," said Lizzie. "How about tomorrow? Should we go up there tomorrow?"

They agreed. After they had had tea, Jamie went out for a

walk to the pier, while Isabel and Lizzie stayed in to chat and to feed Charlie, who had woken up and was looking about the room with interest. Lizzie had him on her knee and was entertaining him, rocking him gently backwards and forwards. Isabel watched Jamie through the window; watched as he slapped at his face and ears, under aerial onslaught by unseen attackers. Then he began to run headlong towards the end of the lawn and the pier.

"You can't outrun midges," said Lizzie, laughing.

"But we do outlive them, don't we?" said Isabel.

Lizzie looked at her quizzically.

"Remember drosophila from biology classes?" Isabel said. "The fruit fly? They had two or three weeks, didn't they? Two or three weeks to pack everything in. I assume that the Highland midge has much the same. Not much of a lifespan."

"That doesn't make me feel sorry for them," said Lizzie. "There are limits, you know."

Isabel knew. It was her biggest problem, after all: how to draw limits to the extent of one's sympathy. In the past, she had become involved in all sorts of difficulties by taking upon herself the problems of others; now she had resolved to be more practical about that, and was trying not to get involved in matters that she had no real moral obligation to do anything about. She was trying.

THEY RETURNED to the hotel in the early afternoon. Lizzie had offered them lunch, but Isabel had not wanted to impose, especially as Lizzie had cleared the following day to take them up to Barnhill. They stayed in the hotel while Charlie slept, and then, in the early evening, they went into the hotel bar before dinner.

Jamie ordered a dram of Jura whisky, which he held up to the window and, through the amber liquid, looked at the distillery over the road. The whisky fragmented the lines of the building, making for blocks of white, for impossible angles.

The hotel barman was friendly. "Edinburgh?" he asked.

"Yes," said Isabel. "Sorry."

The barman appreciated this. "There are worse places," he said.

"I'm sure there are. But I don't think that one should name them. Even the worst of places may be liked by the people who actually live there."

It was while the barman was reflecting on this that Isabel said, "It's a long shot, but how long have you been here?"

"I came over from Arran eleven years ago," said the barman. "I married a Jura girl and we moved over here."

Isabel, who had ordered a glass of white wine, raised the glass to her lips. She was aware that Jamie was watching her intently, but she did not look at him. He would not have asked the barman how long he had been there; that was his business, and why, anyway, would one want to know?

"Do you remember an artist who came here? He was a regular visitor until about eight years ago . . ."

The barman, who was drying a glass with a pristine white cloth, held up the glass to examine his handiwork. "McInnes?"

Isabel stole a glance at Jamie, who was frowning at her. Let him frown, she thought.

"Yes. Andrew McInnes."

The barman put down the glass and fished another one out of the sink. "Aye, I remember him all right. I knew him quite well. He drowned—you know about that?"

"I do," said Isabel. "Or I remember reading about it. What exactly happened?"

The barman began work on the second glass. "The Corryvreckan got him. You know about the Corryvreckan?"

Isabel said that she did. She had never seen it, she explained, but she knew.

"You don't want to see it," said the barman. "Or rather, if you do see it, you want to be looking at it from dry land. It's a muckle great whirlpool. The tide comes in, you see, and it sweeps past the top of Jura and Scarba. It creates quite a current, as you can imagine. It's when that current hits the undersea mountain up there—that's called the Hag—that you get those great eddies. And a whirlpool in certain conditions. That's it. That's the Corryvreckan."

Jamie had stopped glaring at Isabel and was listening in fascination. "Would it suck a boat down—even a large one?"

The barman shrugged. "The Royal Navy used to describe the Gulf of Corryvreckan as unnavigable—the only stretch of water in Britain that they wouldn't sail into. Now they say that it can be approached only with great caution and with local knowledge. In other words, people who don't know what they're doing should keep well away. So, yes, boats can go down. People have died. Including McInnes."

They digested this in silence. Then Jamie asked, "I read somewhere—I forget where—about divers going down. Can you actually dive there?"

The barman looked at Jamie. "Just," he said. "You have a window at slack tide. Five or ten minutes at the most. There's a boat that will take you—if you're experienced enough. They drop a ball and line down and you follow the line down to the top of the pinnacle. You watch your bubbles. If they start to go down instead of up, you know it's time to get out pretty smartly. Otherwise you're sucked down six hundred feet." He paused. "You're not a diver, are you?"

Jamie shuddered. "No, thank you."

The barman smiled grimly. "Good. If you were, I was going to suggest that you settle your bill before you tried diving on the Corryvreckan."

"What happened to McInnes?" Isabel asked.

"He used to stay up near Inverlussa," said the barman. "He had an arrangement with somebody up there and they let him a couple of rooms whenever he came to the island. He painted Jura a lot, you know. I hear he was quite famous in places like Edinburgh and London."

Isabel wondered if the barman knew what a McInnes would fetch today. "He's popular," she said. "Very."

"Well, he wasn't doing too well that last time he came up," said the barman. "He'd had wife trouble and he was pretty low about that. But he also told me that his paintings had been slated in the papers. Torn to shreds, he said. He was very cut up."

"The London critics," said Isabel. "They went for him."

The barman shook his head. "Poor Andy. Well, they did him in all right. I think he knew fine well what he was doing when he took that boat of his round the corner to the Corryvreckan. He knew. Everybody round here knows, even the bairns. You go and ask one of those wee bairns outside the shop about the Corryvreckan and how you need to keep well away. It's the first thing anybody tells you about the water round here."

For a while Isabel said nothing. Then, "Suicide?"

"Nobody likes to reach that conclusion," said the barman. "But sometimes what else are you to think?"

Jamie took a sip of his whisky. The conversation had depressed him. McInnes was dead. Why go on about it? "This is a lovely light whisky. But they make a peated one too, don't they?" he suddenly asked the barman.

The barman glanced over the road at the distillery building. "Yes," he said. "In fact, Jimmy over there tells me that they're about to put one in the cask right now. So come back in eight years and you can try it."

Isabel was not paying any attention to this discussion of whisky. She was thinking about what the barman had told her and wondering whether McInnes had had life insurance. If he had, then the money would have gone to his wife. Sometimes people change the beneficiary of their life insurance as soon as they leave their spouse; sometimes they forget to do this. A lot of men live to regret not making the change, she thought; or rather, they die not to regret it.

But why, she went on to ask herself, why choose to commit suicide in a *whirlpool*?

CHAPTER FOURTEEN

LIZZIE HAD PURLOINED one of the estate Land Rovers for the trip to Barnhill. It was normally used for taking deer stalkers up the hill and was equipped with gun and telescope racks. A particularly fine wicker hamper, used for lunches for the sporting clients, was fixed to the floor of the vehicle with leather straps.

With Lizzie at the wheel they made their way along the winding estate road that led to Barnhill. Now there was nothing; no houses, no telephone wires, and the road became little more than a track. Here and there, rain had created deep potholes in the surface, and Isabel put her hand protectively over Charlie's head as the Land Rover bucked and lurched. They made slow progress, but eventually they saw in the distance a white-washed stone farmhouse, with a wooden porch protruding from the front and low slate-roofed sheds on either side. To one side of the house, across a rough field, a thicket of trees stood, and beyond that a hillside of half-exposed granite outcrops. From the angle of the trees and the shape of the gorse bushes, it was evidently a windy place. A battered green Land Rover was parked in front of the house, its tailgate down. A black Labrador was sitting beside the vehicle and it got to its feet and raised its head to bark when it spotted them approaching.

"There's no electricity here," said Lizzie. "No phones. Nothing. They cook on gas and heat the water with one of those coal-fired ranges. And it's really about as isolated as you can get. You could be here for ages and nobody would know. Lovely, isn't it?"

She drew the Land Rover to a halt and they climbed out. Jamie stood still and breathed in deeply; the scent of gorse, like coconut, the sea not far away, salt and iodine.

"Yes," said Isabel, standing beside him. "The air."

She looked at the hills and at the sea a few hundred yards away. Apart from the farmhouse, there was nothing to be seen of the works of man.

A figure appeared from the house and waved. They walked up the gently sloping grass field to meet the young man whom Lizzie introduced as her cousin Rob. There was a modesty about him which Isabel found immediately attractive, and she could see that Jamie warmed to him too. He was about the same age as, or very slightly younger than, Jamie.

They went inside, into a simple, functional kitchen of the sort which was to be found everywhere in rural Scotland—a room for eating in, sitting about in, doing farming business in—the heart of the house. Rob made them a cup of coffee, boiling the water on the hissing gas ring. He and Jamie established immediately and easily, as happens in Scotland, the mutual friends, the points of contact, while Isabel and Lizzie entertained Charlie, who had discovered a button on his romper suit and was fascinated by the discovery. Then, when they had finished, Rob offered to show them round the house.

"I'll show you the room where he wrote *1984*," he said.

"There's not much to see, I'm afraid. And you can see the bath, if you like."

"The bath that Orwell bathed in," Jamie murmured.

"He led a pretty simple life," said Isabel. "A good man, leading a simple life."

"Orwell believed very strongly in social justice, didn't he?" said Rob.

"Everybody does," said Isabel. "These days, at least. Do you know anybody who would say, *I don't think much of social justice?* I don't."

"It depends on how you interpret social justice," said Jamie, peering at a print on the wall. "One person's social justice is another person's social injustice." He tapped the glass that framed the print and Charlie's eyes followed the noise. "He's going to love art."

They moved through the house. "Orwell's bedroom," said Rob, simply, and they looked in on the small room, with its plain bed, like the room of an everyday bed-and-breakfast. "He did most of his writing in there. And in a tent outside. He had TB and the fresh air was thought to be better for him."

They peered into the small room above the kitchen, with its typewriter set neatly on the table and, beyond the clear glass of the window, the day, now sparkling under a sky that again had miraculously cleared. It is so green, thought Isabel; the soft grass, the bracken, the dark viridian of the trees.

She gazed out of the window of the little room while the others moved back into the corridor. She thought about the seeing of what others had seen; this was the view that Orwell had while he wrote that dark novel, with its all-seeing eye, Big Brother, providing the very contrast to the privacy and peace of this place. That was the explanation; the constricting prison of

Winston Smith's world in the novel was so much more of a nightmare when one saw, there, in that place, what had been lost.

She remembered being in Freud's house in Vienna and looking out of the window in his consulting room, seeing the small mirror hanging on the shutter, the only item remaining in that stripped-bare room, and thinking he had looked at that, the great doctor himself; he had looked out onto that particular stretch of sky, that courtyard. And then she remembered seeing James VI's cradle in the bedroom at Traquair, and the thoughts that it triggered; and the bed at Falkland Palace in which James V had died, turning his face to the wall, bemoaning what he saw as the imminent end of a Scottish dynasty—*It began with a lass and it will end with a lass,* the king was reported to have said. Such beds seemed remarkable when we saw them today, although typically what we more often thought was *How small they are,* as if great and important things could happen only in large, imposing beds. Winston Churchill's bed, the bed from which he dictated letters to generals and prime ministers; that had been a small bed. And finally, as she tore herself away from the view, and the room, the thought crossed her mind that a bed was really a very strange thing—a human nest, really, where our human fragility made its nightly demands for comfort and cosseting.

The others had descended the stairs to return to the kitchen. Isabel lingered by a window in the corridor, with another view, similar to that from the small bedroom. She turned away and it was then that she saw it. For a moment she stood quite still, her breath caught. There could be no mistaking it.

She leaned forward and looked at the picture. It was an oil, a rough one, eight inches by ten, perhaps slightly smaller, but even at this reduced scale, there was no mistaking the study for the painting that she had been shown by Guy Peploe. This was Jura, through the eyes of Andrew McInnes.

DOWNSTAIRS, the party had made its way back into the kitchen. When Isabel came in, Rob looked up from the chart that he was showing Jamie, a naval chart, it appeared, with depths, reefs, rocks. They were looking at the Gulf of Corryvreckan.

"I don't like to pry," said Isabel, not looking at Jamie as she said this, "but that picture up there in the corridor, the little oil painting in the grey frame: Do you know who it's by?" She answered her own question. "Andrew McInnes, who often painted on Jura. It's a McInnes oil."

At first Rob looked puzzled, as if trying to work out which painting it was that Isabel was talking about. Then he shook his head. "No," he said. "I don't think so. That's by a man who stayed here. We let this place out, you see. People come up for a week or two. That man was a painter, I think, and when he went he left a rubbish bag full of sketches and stuff that he didn't want. I found that little painting tucked away in it."

Jamie looked at Isabel. "Here," he said, handing Charlie over to Lizzie. Then he turned to Isabel in astonishment. "Isabel?"

She returned his gaze. "You see," she muttered. "A fake."

Rob was puzzled. "That painting?"

Isabel lowered herself onto one of the kitchen chairs. She was thinking. It all made sense now: the forger, whoever he was, had come up to Jura to do some McInnes paintings. He had found the most remote spot available, a place where he would never be disturbed, and he had produced the new, posthumous McInnes paintings. Her intuitions had been right.

"Who was this man?" asked Isabel.

"I didn't meet him," said Rob. He turned to Lizzie. "Did you, Lizzie? Were you around when he was here?"

"When was it?" she asked. "I don't remember a painter anyway."

Rob crossed the room to fetch a small brown file. He flicked through some papers and eventually found one which he took out. It was the list of lettings.

"Last September," he said. "Quite a late let. A Mr. Anderson. Frank Anderson."

"Where was he from?" asked Isabel.

Rob looked through the papers again. "No idea," he said. "We would have known at the time, but we weed out the old letters. We don't keep them."

"A pity," muttered Isabel. She thought of her conversation with Christopher Dove: it was exactly what she had done with the old correspondence of the *Review of Applied Ethics.* She was one to talk.

"Oh well," said Jamie.

"Why are you interested?" asked Rob.

"Because I think that this Frank Anderson, whoever he is, has been responsible for some, well, what shall we call them, some fine *posthumous* works by McInnes."

Rob looked interested. "Done here? Well . . ."

"Did you meet McInnes?" asked Isabel.

"No," said Rob. "I didn't. But I do know who he is. And I do know that he's considered a great painter."

"That often happens after somebody's dead and buried," said Isabel.

"He shouldn't have gone out," said Lizzie suddenly. "People who don't know these waters should be more careful."

Isabel thought: What whirlpools take—they don't give back. Where had she heard that? That was the trouble; there was so much in her mind: philosophy, poetry, odd facts; and they kept surfacing, these odd remembered lines, like corks unexpectedly popping up out of the water.

How would it be to be lost at sea, to sink down into those green depths and deeper, into the dark? Was there a moment of calm when the lungs had filled with water and there was just a heaviness, a moment of clarity, or remembrance, as people said there was, or even that progress towards a light, a gentleness, that was sworn to by those who had near-death experiences? If they were to be believed—those people who had clinically died and then been brought back—the experience was one of great calm, of resolution. And many of them spoke of some form of reunion, a feeling of being in the presence of those they had known, and of being forgiven and made to understand, but gently; not scolded. Nobody was scolded.

THEY DID NOT DISCUSS the matter as they travelled back with Lizzie in the Land Rover, but once they had set off from Ardlussa in the green Swedish car, they talked about little else.

"I hope that you're going to have the good grace to admit that I was right," Isabel said to Jamie as they drove over the Ardlussa bridge and set off on the narrow public road that would take them back to Craighouse.

"Of course. Of course I will." He paused. "But I don't know what we can do next—if anything."

"What do you mean, *if anything*?" asked Isabel. "We can

hardly keep this to ourselves. And why should this man, this Frank Anderson, get away with it?"

Jamie sighed. Isabel was incorrigible; she could not resist setting things right, *solving* things. It was almost as if she felt that life was a chess game in which the end game had to be played out. "We're not the police," he said simply. "We're private citizens. We can report it, of course, to those concerned. So you can tell Guy Peploe that you think that that painting may not be all it looks to be; that's fine. And you do have some evidence, after all. You can tell him about the painting you saw today."

"But what will Guy be able to do?" objected Isabel. "He'll be able to raise it with the person whose painting it is. He'll hand it back, I suppose. And he'll probably ask questions, but he won't be able to do much more than that."

"So you're going to try to find this man?"

For a few moments she was silent. She had been wondering how she would proceed, and had not had any ideas. And yet she knew that she had to do something; her inaction in the face of wrongdoing was hardly an option, provided, of course, that wrongdoing had entered the circle of one's moral recognition, and this, she thought, had done just that.

"Frank Anderson must be a talented painter," she said at last. "You can't do fakes unless you really know what you're doing. Look at that Dutchman, the one who did the Vermeers, what was he called—van Meegeren. He was a real expert. He knew everything there was to know about painting techniques. The pigments, the canvas, the way old paint cracks. Everything. You can't get the exact effect unless you're really good."

"So he knows what he's doing. Where does that get us?"

Isabel was thinking aloud. "Well," she said, "imagine if you had been in the Netherlands at the time and you had wanted to find an artist called van Meegeren. Would it have been all that difficult? Even if he wasn't very well known? You would have asked around and people would have known. Somebody would remember him from art college."

Jamie saw where Isabel's comments were going. "So this man, Frank Anderson, is likely to have been trained?"

"Highly likely. Which means that somebody will remember him from their four years at art college. Somebody will know him—as long as he's in Scotland. If he's in England, then we're on more difficult ground."

Jamie agreed that it might be possible to find Frank Anderson, but he was more worried about what would happen after that. Finding somebody was one thing; unmasking him as a forger was an altogether different matter.

"All right," he said. "Find him. But don't do anything stupid. Frank Anderson will be facing criminal charges if he's found. He's not exactly going to cooperate with you."

Isabel guided her car into a passing place, one of the small bulges in the road that allowed vehicles to pass one another on the narrow strip of tar. A postal van was approaching from the south, and when it passed her, the driver waved in thanks and smiled. That was how it is here, she thought, where there are no strangers.

CHAPTER FIFTEEN

IT SEEMED TO ISABEL that they had been away for weeks. The world of Jura, that self-contained island world, seemed so far from Edinburgh, and yet it was only a drive of half a day or so, and it was the same country. As she stood in her garden on the day after their return, she closed her eyes for a moment and saw the hills, and the burns tumbling down, and the veils of fine rain. And she thought, One can love a country until it hurts.

But one could not stand in one's garden thinking about Scotland. The whole point about being in Scotland was that one was in Scotland, and being in Scotland, for Isabel, meant that she had to get on with those things that required attention, and these were many. Charlie, who might normally have headed the list of those in need of attention, did not do so that morning; Grace had taken him for a walk to Blackford Pond, a pond on the south side of the town popular with dogs, ducks, and children. The resident ducks were overfed by everybody and sailed low in the water as a result, or so Isabel thought. "It's dangerous to feed birds *overenthusiastically*," she had once said to Jamie, when they had taken Charlie on one of his first visits to the pond. "And it's also dangerous to overinvest birds with symbolism. These national eagles that people make such a fuss about must find it difficult to take off under the weight of all that symbolism."

Jamie had looked at her and said, "That's a very strange remark, Isabel. You talk complete nonsense sometimes. Flights of fancy."

She had not minded. "I like to think about things," she said airily. "I like to let my mind wander. Our minds can come up with the most entertaining possibilities, if we let them. But most of the time, we keep them under far too close a check."

Jamie thought about this for a moment. He was trying to recall something rather funny that Isabel had started to say a few days earlier but had been cut off midstream by some protest from Charlie.

"What were you saying about cars the other day? Something about older drivers? Then Charlie started creating a fuss."

Isabel frowned. "Drivers? Oh yes, somebody had mentioned a driver of ninety-three, which I thought was a little bit late to be in control of a car. I'm sure that one must be very wise at the age of ninety-three, but I'm not so sure about one's reactions at that stage. I think I suggested that one's car should become more and more grey as one gets older, which would warn people that one's reactions might be a little slow. They would be like learner plates when one's learning to drive—those are a warning too. So cars would be seen to turn grey, perhaps a little bit slowly, just as people's hair greys."

"And young men would be required to drive red cars?"

Isabel nodded her agreement. "Yes. Red cars would be a warning of the presence of testosterone. We need warning, you see."

"And at intersections the red cars would yield to the grey ones?"

"Of course," said Isabel. "Or that would be the rule in a well-ordered society. Do you know that in Japan, young drivers have to give way to older ones? It can get quite complicated if one can't see the other driver too well and one can't work out whether he's older than you. I believe a certain number of accidents result from this confusion."

Jamie laughed. "Absurd. And completely untrue."

"Perhaps," said Isabel. "Absurd. But fun nonetheless."

"Tell me another absurd story."

"About what?"

They were standing at the edge of the pond, looking at the ducks. Charlie, tucked up in his baby buggy, had dropped off to sleep. Jamie glanced about him. A man farther along the pond side had been helping his young son toss crumbs to the ducks; now he moved away. Jamie had seen that his forearms were covered with tattoos. "Tell me about a tattooed man," he said to Isabel.

"Some other time," said Isabel, looking at her watch.

Now, standing in her garden, her thoughts returned to the day ahead. The discovery that she had made on Jura would need to be dealt with, but there would be time enough for that. Some of Jamie's caution had begun to have an effect on her, and she wondered whether she should hold back before taking any action. All she really needed to do was tell somebody—Guy Peploe perhaps—of her suspicions and then leave it to him, or somebody else, to make further enquiries. For a moment she considered the attractions of disengagement, of a policy of not worrying about the world. Many people lived like that and were perfectly happy. They did not worry about the destruction of our world, about the drift into medieval religious war, about all the cruelties and hypocrisies; they did not think of these things. But what did they think about, these disengaged people? If one looked hard enough, perhaps one would see that the big issues that they ignored had merely been replaced by small concerns that could be every bit as pressing. The successes of a football team—or, more pertinently, its failures—could be the cause of a great deal of anguish; arguments with neighbours, worries over money—all of these could weigh as heavily as the greater matters. So being disengaged was more of an apparent solution than a real one, Isabel decided, although she was still going to put this matter off for a day or two.

There were twelve telephone messages awaiting Isabel on her return the previous evening, and she had delayed dealing with them until the morning. Three were from the same person, a distant acquaintance with whom she had promised to have lunch and who was now wanting to make an arrangement. Isabel slightly regretted the original promise; she had not really intended it but it had been taken seriously by the other person. This was a cultural misunderstanding. The acquaintance was a New Zealander living in Scotland, and New Zealanders meant what they said, much to their credit, and thought that everybody else did too. As a general rule, Isabel certainly meant what she said, but she was as guilty as everybody else of using language which was really intended to be no more than an expression of general goodwill. Suggesting a meeting for lunch might be a real invitation or it might not, depending on the tone of voice used, and the context. She remembered the late Professor Glanville Williams, whom she had met at Cambridge, once saying to an Italian visitor that they should meet for lunch. Whereupon the Italian had fished in his pocket for his diary, opened it, and said, "When?" Glanville Williams had been quite shocked, in the same way in which those who automatically wished one to have a nice day would be shocked if they were asked in what way they thought this might be achieved.

Isabel returned the telephone call, arranged the lunch, and then went through the remaining messages, skipping over several until she found the one she was waiting for, the voice of her lawyer, Simon Mackintosh. "You asked me to act quickly, Isabel, and I have. And a good result too, I'm happy to say. Could you please get in touch when you get back?"

She played the message and then replayed it. The news made her feel elated but concerned at the same time. She had acted impulsively before she had left for Jura, and she had not really expected a result so quickly. But now, when she reflected on the instructions she had given Simon, she experienced that curious feeling, that mixture of elation and dread, that comes from having done something very significant.

She replaced the telephone handset and said to herself, *I own it; it's mine.* And that thought occurred to her again when she found herself in the waiting room at Turcan Connell, in their offices at Tollcross, waiting for Simon to appear and lead her into the small conference room which the firm used for clients and lawyers to talk. Tea was served, and shortbread biscuits, and Isabel had already poured herself a cup by the time that Simon arrived.

They exchanged small items of news. Simon's wife, Catriona, an artist, had just finished a successful show, and there was news of that, and Isabel reported on Charlie's sleeping habits. Then Simon opened a blue cardboard folder and took out a page of notes he had made on a sheet of paper.

"Now then, Isabel, those instructions of yours." She wondered whether he was reproaching her, but it was not reproach—just surprise. "What you asked me to do was, how

shall I put it? Fairly unusual. At least it's unusual to do something like this so quickly. In fact, the whole thing . . . well, I suppose it's just a case of doing something in record time."

She shrugged. "Sometimes . . ."

He smiled. "Yes, sometimes there are things that one feels
one has to do. And lawyers should always assume that their
clients know what they want, even if sometimes, on rare occasions, it may not seem that way. But I've never thought that
of you."

Isabel laughed. "I did think about this, you know. It didn't
come totally out of the blue. I thought about it for at least"—she
blushed—"an hour or so."

Simon wagged a finger playfully. "Well, I did what you asked
me. And thank heavens we were dealing with a small private
company. They proved very easy to negotiate with. And very
quick. Of course we still have to do various things before the
contract is finally signed—warranties, indemnities, that sort of
thing—but we've got agreement in principle."

"They're nice people."

Simon agreed. His conversation with the chairman had
been brisk and to the point, and there had certainly been an air
of civility about it. "When I asked them what sum they had in
mind, I must say that I was pleasantly surprised. It was considerably less than the limit you had suggested. Sixty thousand
pounds for the title and the goodwill." He paused and consulted
a printed sheet in the file. "And I suppose we have to accept
that, even if last year the *Review* made a profit of a grand total of
four hundred pounds . . . and eight pence."

"They wanted rid of it," said Isabel. "I thought they might
hold out for more."

"Not when they knew I was offering on your behalf,"
said Simon. "They think very highly of you. And so there we

are, you're the new owner of the *Review of Applied Ethics.* Congratulations!"

Isabel looked at her teacup. She had shamelessly used her superior financial position to deal with Christopher Dove and his machinations. Did she deserve congratulations for that? She thought she did not, but if she were to try to explain her feelings to Simon, she was not sure whether she would be able to convey to him the guilt that she felt. She had done nothing wrong. Things were for sale or they were not, and the *Review,* as she had suspected, was for sale if one were to pay enough. Money, she realised, was an instrument of crude power; a conclusion that she had always sought to avoid, but which was demonstrably and uncomfortably true.

Simon was studying her with a slightly bemused expression. "I know you can well afford this, Isabel," he began. "But do you mind my asking, why do you want to own it? Wasn't it enough just to be the editor?"

For a moment, Isabel did not reply. Now she looked up and met Simon's gaze. "To set right an injustice," she said simply.

Simon slipped the piece of paper back into the file. "Ah," he said. He thought for a moment, fingering the edge of the blue file. "That's a very good reason for doing anything. Well done."

She reached forward and poured him a fresh cup of tea. Nothing more needed to be said about the transaction and so they spent a few minutes discussing the weather, which was perfect, and the world, which was not quite.

Just before she rose to leave, though, it occurred to her that it might be easier for Simon to write a letter that needed to be written. "There's one thing more," she said. "There's a letter that needs to be written to the chairman of the editorial board. Could you do that for me? As my lawyer?"

"Of course."

She explained that the letter needed to go to Professor Lettuce. "A ridiculous name, I know, but that is his burden in life. I'll write down the address here. Please tell him that you are acting for the new owner of the *Review of Applied Ethics* and that she—and please remember the *she*—is very grateful to him for all his services to the *Review.* However, it will be necessary to appoint a new editorial board, and this will be done shortly."

Simon made a few notes and then looked at Isabel. "Should I mention your name at this stage?"

Isabel hesitated. One part of her wanted the satisfaction of letting them work it out; she could imagine their anxious discussions. But another saw the pettiness of this, the wrongness. Plato's white horse and dark horse. She closed her eyes. Revenge was sweet, but it was wrong, and she should not repay them in the coin they had used on her. No, she should not.

"Tell them who I am right at the beginning," she said. "That would be better."

Simon, who sensed that he had just witnessed a great moral struggle, nodded his assent. "I'm sure that you've made the right decision," he said.

Perhaps, thought Isabel. But then she went on to think, Oh, Lettuce and Dove—you did ask for this, you really did.

ISABEL LEFT the offices of Turcan Connell shortly before midday. Their building, a new one, was made of green and blue glass, like sheets of thinly sliced ice; looking up from the small square to its front, one could see through the upper storeys to the sky beyond. Around it, though, was the Edinburgh with which Isabel was more familiar—the stone tenement buildings, the predominant note of grey. She walked up Home Street, past

the vegetable shops, the watchmaker, the sellers of cheap orna-
ments, the bars. She passed the King's Theatre and Bennet's
Bar beside it, with its elaborate stained-glass windows, where
singers and musicians would meet after rehearsals in the theatre, sitting on the long red benches, reflected in the large brew-
ers' mirrors.

Farther up the road, she suddenly felt hungry as she
approached Cat's delicatessen. She was in no hurry to get home;
Charlie was off somewhere with Grace and they would not be
returning until after lunch. There were things to be done in the
house—correspondence and a long list of small chores—but
she did not feel like doing anything yet. She felt awkward about
going into the delicatessen now, with Cat in her current mood,
but she knew that she had to persist: the ice would melt, as it
always did.

Eddie was behind the counter and there was no sign of Cat.
He was slicing Parma ham for a customer and he nodded to
Isabel. She picked up a copy of a newspaper from the table—
somebody had left that day's *Guardian,* and she would read that
at one of the coffee tables until Eddie could serve her. Eddie
made good focaccia and olive plates and she would have one of
those when he was ready.

She was absorbed in a *Guardian* article when she became
aware of Cat's presence. She lowered the paper and saw that
her niece was smiling. The thaw, she thought.

Cat looked over her shoulder towards Eddie. A couple of
customers were peering into the display case below the counter,
pointing at cheeses. "It looks as if he's going to be busy for a
while," said Cat. "I'll look after you."

"I was hoping for focaccia and olives," said Isabel. "But
there's no hurry. There's always *The Guardian.*"

Cat did not think it would be any trouble. "And how's Charlie?" she asked.

It was the first time that she had shown any real interest in her cousin, although Isabel suspected that the interest, or curiosity at least, had always been there but had been repressed. "Thriving," she replied. "Sleeping. Eating. Doing all the things appropriate to being a baby."

Cat smiled. "He's very sweet," she said. "He looks a bit like . . ." Isabel held her breath. "Like Jamie."

That, Isabel thought, was extraordinary progress. Isabel herself not did not think that Charlie looked remotely like Jamie, but that did not matter now: the air, she thought, was filled with the sound of shifting logjams.

"Yes, well, perhaps he does. In some lights."

Cat went off to prepare Isabel's lunch, leaving her with *The Guardian*. She was reading an article on the Middle East and the prospects for peace, which were slim. What acres of newsprint, she thought, what lakes of ink, had been expended on that topic; and always it came back to the same thing, the sense of difference between people, the erection of barriers of religion, clothing, culture. And yet there were differences, and it was naïve to imagine that people were all the same—they weren't. And everybody needed space, physical space, to live their lives amongst those with whom they shared an outlook and values; which led to the depressing conclusion that the recipe for social peace was keeping people separate from one another, each in his own territory, each in the safety of fellows. She was not sure if she could accept that—and *The Guardian* certainly did not. The problem was that we could no longer have our own cultural spaces: everybody was now too mixed up for that and we had to share.

She was wrestling with these issues when Eddie came

across to her, bearing the plate of focaccia and olives which Cat had prepared.

"She seems to be in a good mood today," said Isabel, nodding in the direction of Cat, who was now dealing with a customer at the counter.

Eddie's lip curled in mock disdain. "Guess why," he said. "Have three guesses. Or shall I just tell you? She's found a new man."

Isabel had a feeling that she and Eddie had had this conversation before; and they had, she decided, some time ago, when the man was . . . she could not remember.

"Yes," said Eddie. "He came in here not long ago. And he's coming up to see her again this weekend. That's why she's all smiles."

It had not occurred to Isabel, for reasons of denial, perhaps. Or because she had thought of him as a flash in the pan— somebody temporary. Now the thought of it appalled her. She looked up at Eddie, who was grinning knowingly. "A tall man," she said. "A tall man with blond hair slicked back like this." She made the gesture.

"Yes," said Eddie. "But they all look like that, don't they? All of her men are the same. Except for . . ." He looked embarrassed.

Isabel stared down at her plate. Christopher Dove. She had imagined that the dalliance between him and Cat had been limited to the evening in Edinburgh; she had not contemplated that anything further would come of it.

"Anyway," said Eddie, "long may it last."

Isabel shook her head. "I doubt if he's right for her."

Eddie sniggered. "They get along." He took a step backwards. "I've got to go."

Isabel ate her meal in silence. Dove would know by tomorrow that the *Review* had changed hands, and he would realise immediately, even if it weren't for the wording of the letter to Professor Lettuce, that he would never become editor. He would be angry, of course, and his anger would be directed at her. And if Cat heard about it—as she would—then she would assume that Isabel had fired Dove to spite her. Cat was quite capable of believing that, thought Isabel, and of course there might be people who would do such a thing, even if she was not one of them.

She knew, of course, that she should not allow herself to be governed by thoughts of what her niece would think—particularly a niece who was growing into such an unpredictable person as Cat was. And yet she was not sure that she could face more of Cat's moods or hostility. It would be like living with Schopenhauer, not an easy task for anybody, and certainly not for Schopenhauer's mother, to whom the philosopher refused to talk for the last twenty-three years of her life.

She stood up and crossed the room to pay for her lunch. At the till, Cat waved her aside. "No need," she said.

"But I must," said Isabel.

Cat shook a finger. "No, it's a thank-you."

Isabel's heart sank. "For what?"

"For introducing me to such a gorgeous man the other day!"

CHAPTER SIXTEEN

THE QUEEN'S HALL that evening was packed, and although Jamie had tried to get Isabel a good seat, she ended up in the gallery, on one of the benches in which one could never quite relax. And there had been a purpose behind that discomfort; the Queen's Hall had been a church, and the Church of Scotland had never been one for excessive comfort, lest it lead to somnolence during sermons. Jamie was playing in the orchestra, as he sometimes did, and he was keen that Isabel should hear this particular programme.

"It's a very adventurous mix," he explained. "Fauré's *Requiem* in the first half, and then new or newish pieces in the second. Various offerings from Peter Maxwell Davies, Stephen Deazley, and Max Richter. It'll be interesting, to say the least."

Jamie had given Isabel a recording of Max Richter's *Blue Notebooks,* and she had played it time and time again, absorbed by the haunting, enigmatic music. And then in Mellis's cheese shop one day, she and her friend Rosalind Marshall had seen the composer himself, who lived in Edinburgh; he had come in to buy a piece of Dunsyre Blue, and, recognising him from the sleeve of *The Blue Notebooks,* Isabel had said, "You don't know me, but *The Blue Notebooks* . . ." She was not sure that he had heard her, in fact she thought that he had not, as the cheese-monger had started to speak, extolling the virtues of a particular cheese, and then somebody else had come in and it was too late.

"I'll talk to him some other time," Isabel said to Rosalind.

"Yes, perhaps," said Rosalind. "I almost had a conversation with the prime minister once. He was paying a visit to the Portrait Gallery and I said something to him about one of the pictures, but he was distracted by somebody else and so I'm not sure he heard me."

Isabel smiled. "There are probably many of us in Edinburgh who have almost conversed with prominent people, but not quite." She paused, remembering something that had been said to her some time ago. "I was in Ireland, once, staying at a place called Gurthalougha House, near Shannon. And the woman who ran the hotel had an aunt, or so she told me, who had been walking in the Black Forest in the nineteen thirties when she met a small walking party coming along the path towards her. And she recognised the man in front—it was Adolf Hitler. So apparently she said, 'Good morning, Mr. Hitler,' and he just nodded and continued on his way."

Rosalind shook her head. "What a strange story. I'm not sure what we can take from that, but it certainly is rather strange."

"Had her aunt been armed," mused Isabel, "she could have changed the course of history, for the better."

"By murdering Hitler?"

Isabel hesitated, but only briefly. "Yes. Although I'm not sure that I would use the word *murder* there. Murder is intrinsically wrong, isn't it? The word carries a lot of moral baggage."

"So what should we call it? Execution? Assassination?"

"We could just call it *killing*," said Isabel. "That's neutral. A person defending himself from an attacker kills the aggressor, and that's morally justifiable. We don't say that he murders the person attacking him. Murder is one of those words with strong moral associations."

Rosalind frowned. "So nobody could ever be said to have *murdered* a tyrant—is that what you're saying? Even if somebody had ever succeeded in removing him?"

"Not unless somebody killed him for the wrong reasons," said Isabel. "Take Stalin, for instance, or Chairman Mao. Let's say that a rival, an even bigger monster, had disposed of Mao or Stalin in order to become leader himself, then that could be described as murder, I suppose. But if a relative of one of his victims took a shot at him, then I'm not so sure that I would call it murder. Assassination, perhaps, and even a justifiable one, if it saved lives."

Their attention reverted to their purchases. Rosalind was inspecting a very small square of cheese. "I wonder," she said, "whether this comes from that cheese maker I met in Orkney who has only one cow. She can't produce very much, you know."

Now, remembering their conversation about Stalin and the rest, Isabel thought: Yes, people should condemn the crimes of tyrants equally. The problem was that people were selective in their moral outrage or simply did not know.

She sighed. Moral evenhandedness was rare, but that was another issue, and she had often been troubled by it. Moral evenhandedness suggested that one should treat one's friends and strangers equally, and that was very counterintuitive. You are outside a burning building. At two adjacent windows appear two people, both calling for help. One of these is your friend, the other a stranger. You have enough time to use your ladder to rescue only one of them. Some would say that both have an equal claim on you, and that you should toss a coin to decide who should be saved. But who amongst us would do that? Isabel asked herself.

But back to homicide, which she and her friend had started to discuss. An image was forming in Isabel's mind of the contents page of a special issue of the *Review of Applied Ethics,* which she would title "Good Killing." She would ask Professor John Harris to contribute because his writing was so lively, and he had once titled a chapter of one of his books "Killing: A Caring Thing to Do?" That had not been as provocative as it sounded; John was a kind man—and a very subtle philosopher—and he was talking there of mercy killing, which might be carried out precisely because one cared about the suffering of another; to acknowledge this was not so much to condone it as to recognise why people did it. She liked John, whom she knew quite well, and had enjoyed several intense debates with him in the past. If he was at a window in a burning building, she would be very much inclined to rescue him. But would a moral impartialist—a hypothetical moral impartialist, not John—do the same and rescue her? He would surely have to make a random choice, toss a coin perhaps, which might mean that he could rescue the stranger, if the stranger won the toss. But he would be apologetic about it, of course, and would shout up from below, "Isabel, I would have loved to have rescued you rather than this stranger, but your needs, you see, are equal, and I must not prefer you simply because I know you. I'm so sorry."

During the first half of the concert, while the chorus sang the Fauré *Requiem,* Isabel's mind wandered. Jamie was not due to play until the second half of the concert, and she imagined him in the large green room behind the stage. Before the performance he often said that he read to divert himself—something unconnected with music. She saw him sitting there with a book that he had picked up in the small bookshop at the corner of Buccleuch Place, a book of tiger-hunting memoirs. She had looked at him sideways when he had produced it, but he had explained, "All of them were man-eaters. Those are the only tigers he shot. He went round villages in the north of India back in the twenties and thirties and shot the man-eaters who were terrorising the villagers." But it had still puzzled her that Jamie would read about that; no woman would read a book like that, and then she thought, He's not a woman.

With the "Pie Jesu," which was sung by Nicola Wood, whom Isabel knew slightly, her mind came back to the music. *Dona eis requiem;* grant them rest. It was not complex music, with its cautiously developed melody and its utter resolution; it was a lullaby really, and that, she thought, was what a requiem really was. If one were to be taken up to heaven, then it would be Fauré who might accompany one. Again her mind wandered to the death of McInnes, his watery death; if it had been suicide, then would he have welcomed that death, abandoned the body's natural struggle for life, and embraced what lay ahead? *Grant them rest, rest everlasting;* they were such kind words, even in their finality, and the music that accompanied them, as in this requiem, should be gentle.

They reached "In Paradisum." Behind the words, the organ's question and answer provided a tapestry of sound that was almost mesmeric, weaving delicately about the words. But it was the words themselves which engaged Isabel: *May the angels lead you into paradise / May the martyrs receive you / In your coming / And may they guide you / Into the holy city, Jerusalem.* There was really no consolation for death, she thought, just the various anodynes. But even if one could not believe in Paradise, or in angels, this was music which might, for a few sublime moments, nudge one towards belief in just that.

The last notes died away, and there was applause. Isabel sat quietly for a moment while members of the audience filed out for the intermission. A woman sitting beside her caught her eye for a moment and said, "Sublime."

Isabel nodded. "Yes, it was. Yes."

When the rush for the bar had subsided, she got up from her seat and made her way downstairs. In the lobby below, the wide double doors had been thrown open to the street, to allow the cool night air into the hall. Her feet always felt sore at concerts for a reason that she had never quite worked out; perhaps it was the heat, or the fact of sitting motionless for a long period. Whatever it was, she always yearned to be barefoot, or to have, as now, fresh air about her ankles.

She stood immediately outside the hall, watching the traffic go by. A small group of students, engaged in earnest conversation, walked past on the pavement, and one of them, a boy with glasses and a small goatee, was holding forth in an animated way. He must have said something to amuse his companions, as they laughed raucously.

Then a poor man walked past. Isabel knew that he was a poor man because he had a regular beat, selling a magazine that homeless people sold in the streets. From time to time she bought a copy from him, not because there was anything in it that she wanted to read, but in order to support him.

"Lazarus," she muttered.

She had intended to think the word rather than utter it, but it had slipped out. She froze. Had he heard? If he had, he would wonder, surely, why she should call him Lazarus.

He had. He stopped and stared at Isabel, separated only by the low stone wall between the forecourt of the theatre and the pavement on which he had been walking.

"Lazarus?" he said in a thick, nasal voice. "I'm not Lazarus."

Isabel felt flustered. "I'm sorry," she said. "I was thinking aloud."

The man frowned. "Well, I'm not him," he reiterated. "I'm not Lazarus."

"Of course not."

He swore, not quite silently, under his breath. Isabel began to edge away, imperceptibly, but it was unnecessary, as he had turned and started to walk away. Isabel thought: What does he think of me? And all I was doing was thinking of Lazarus at the end of the Fauré: *et cum Lazaro quondam paupere / Aeternam habeas requiem. (And with Lazarus, once poor, may you have eternal rest.)* Lazarus once poor, led off to Paradise by angels, as in the parable.

Somebody tapped her on the shoulder. Peter and Susie Stevenson had come out to join her. Susie was holding a small glass of iced water in which a twist of lemon was submerged. She passed this to Isabel. "I saw you from down below," she said. "I thought you might like this."

Isabel thanked them. "Why are concerts so hot?"

"All those people," said Peter. "And a general lack of air-conditioning. Which is maybe no bad thing. The more we air-condition, the hotter the world gets—or so we're told."

They discussed the Fauré and the pieces that were to come; Isabel only half followed the conversation because she was thinking of the embarrassing encounter with the homeless man. Don't think aloud, she muttered to herself.

"What was that?" asked Peter.

She said, quickly, "I was going to come to see you. There's been something on my mind." She took a sip of the water. "It's about that painting."

"Ah," said Peter. "You're still tempted? You know, I think that you're going to buy it. And why not? It won't break the bank, I imagine."

"I'm not going to buy it," said Isabel, "because it's a fake."

"Hold on!" said Peter. "Have you any evidence?"

He had not expected her to reply so firmly, but she did.

"I have," she said. "And what's more, I know who did it. A man called Frank Anderson."

She had spoken with some conviction, and, as she uttered the forger's name, with some anger. The strangeness of that struck her; why should she feel that way about something which, as Jamie would be quick to point out, had very little to do with her? But it is to do with me, she told herself; I was *almost* a victim, in that I would have bought it had it not been for Walter Buie. He is the victim and . . . and he sought, in turn, to make me his victim.

Susie broke her train of thought. "Frank Anderson?"

Isabel looked at her keenly. "Do you know him? An artist?"

In the distance, the sound of a wailing ambulance siren seemed to be drawing closer. Peter looked at his watch anxiously; the intermission had five minutes to run.

Isabel had to raise her voice now against the sound of the ambulance. "Do you?" she pressed. "Do you know that name?"

Susie looked at the passersby. The light from the door was behind her, and her shadow fell upon the low wall. Somewhere in her mind there was a memory of Frank Anderson. But she could not say who he was or why she should remember the name. The ambulance went past, dodging a car which had stopped awkwardly in the middle of the junction, its driver paralysed by the emergency of the moment.

"It's not an uncommon name," said Peter. "There must be lots of Frank Andersons in Scotland." He looked again at his watch. "But the point is this, Isabel: How do you know?"

She wondered how convincing her explanation would

sound; probably not very, she decided. "We've been on Jura," she said. "You know that these two paintings are of Jura? Well, a man called Frank Anderson stayed in a house there and left behind a painting that he'd done. It was pure McInnes. I saw it, Peter. I'm absolutely certain. It's the same scene as that painting which Walter Buie has." She shrugged. She had made her case.

Peter was watching her, but she could not tell whether he believed her.

"Right," he said. "That's evidence of a sort, or at least it's a reason to be suspicious, I suppose."

A bell rang within, warning of the end of the interval. They turned round and went back into the vestibule.

"I don't like this," said Susie. "This is a criminal offence you've stumbled upon, Isabel. I'm not sure if you should get involved, you know. These things . . ."

"What Susie's saying is that it's dangerous," said Peter. "And I think she's right. So I think you should go and talk to Guy Peploe. Hand the matter over to him. He'll know what to do."

She did not take much persuading. "All right."

"And you'll definitely do this?" asked Peter. "I know about your tendency to . . ."

"Interfere?" asked Isabel, playfully.

"You said it rather than I," said Peter.

LATER THAT NIGHT, well after the concert, when Isabel lay sleepless, Jamie turned to her. He took her hand, stroking it gently. The room was in darkness apart from a sliver of moonlight that penetrated the chink in the curtains, like a searchlight in the night sky.

"You played so beautifully," said Isabel. "Particularly in the Maxwell Davies."

Jamie pressed her hand to his chest. His skin, she thought, was so smooth—like satin.

"Every note was perfect," she went on. "It was."

He moved her hand across his chest. She felt the beating of his heart, somewhere below her fingers, and that felt the most intimate of all. She might possess him, but she might not touch his heart.

"You shouldn't say that," he whispered. "Flatterer."

"No, I mean it. I don't give compliments I don't mean." She paused. They were whispering, though for no reason; but in the dark it seemed right to whisper, so as not to disturb the silence.

"When I was a boy I used to think that talking in the dark was what it would be like talking to God," said Jamie. "Odd. I thought that he could hear us in the dark."

Isabel was not sure about this. "The difference is that we can hear ourselves," said Isabel. "That's the difference." It was that, she thought; that, and something to do with the accentuation of the hearing in the absence of other stimuli for the senses.

He turned and kissed her on the forehead. The back of his hand was upon her cheek.

"Tell me a story of a tattooed man," he whispered. "You promised that you would."

"Did I?"

"Yes, you did."

She shifted slightly, so that his hand fell from the side of her cheek. She thought of a tattooed man, the sort of man one saw in Edwardian photographs, those photographs of side show exhibits of the past, every square inch of the body covered with inked designs, the sacred, the demoniacal, the confessional. What could she say about this tattooed man? That he loved his wife, the tattooed lady, and was proud of his son, the tattooed baby? It sounded like a couple of lines from a poem, but it was not; it was from nowhere. And such a story would be trite, she thought; trite and tragic at the same time.

"Your tattooed man, Jamie," she began. "Let me see, now. All right, the tattooed man."

He sounded drowsy. "I'm listening."

His drowsiness communicated itself to her, as a yawn will pass like an infection, from one to another. She felt a wave of tiredness coming over her. She wanted only to lie there with him, close to him in the darkness, and drift off to sleep. It was hard to speak, she was so tired, and anyway she thought that he was now asleep, with his breathing getting deeper, more regular. She let her eyelids close, so that even the sliver of moonlight was blocked out. Before sleep claimed her she thought: We forget so many stories in our lifetime, some told, some that remained untold; some that we did not really know in the first place. *The tattooed man / Who loved his wife, the tattooed lady / And was proud of his son, the tattooed baby.*

CHAPTER SEVENTEEN

HE'S WEARING his Macpherson tartan rompers, I see," said Grace, bending down to tickle Charlie under the chin. "Have you bought him his first kilt yet?"

Isabel had not, but would do so, she thought, when he was about three.

"To wear a kilt one must first be able to walk," she said. "And his little legs would get rather cold, I think."

"What a figure he'll cut," said Grace, admiringly. "Charlie Dalhousie, apple of every eye at the school dances . . ." She broke off. Would Charlie be Charlie Dalhousie, taking Isabel's name, or would he . . . She smiled nervously, in the awkwardness of the moment. There were few things that embarrassed Grace, but illegitimacy was one of them, even if the word had been more or less retired. Nobody spoke of illegitimacy anymore, and there were, fortunately, no legal consequences of any significance. But corners of shame remained in some parts of Scotland, even if so many children now were born out of wedlock. And Grace belonged to a section of society where these things were still felt.

Isabel immediately understood and put Grace at her ease.

"Yes, Charlie Dalhousie will be quite the young man about town, won't you, Charlie?"

"Good," said Grace, and went on to the business of the day. Isabel was taking Charlie out, into town, she said, and she would stay in the house and tackle the upstairs bathroom, which she thought had been allowed to become a mess. There was a line of mould tracking its sinister way along the line of grout at the bottom of the shower—Jamie's fault, Grace suspected—as he showered far too much in her opinion and left the cubicle too damp. Grace did not believe in showers, except for when a bath was for some reason unavailable: then one might have a shower, a quick one, remembering to wipe down the tiles after use to prevent the formation of mould.

"I've bought something for that shower," said Grace. "It's—"

"I know," said Isabel quickly. "Mould."

For a few moments there was silence; Isabel called such interludes *Grace's moment of censure,* and this was one. But the point had been made, and she wheeled Charlie out under a smiling farewell from her housekeeper. As Isabel walked up the road, she thought about mould. Grace had made her feel responsible for it because Jamie used the shower and Grace considered Isabel to be responsible for Jamie. Grace wanted her employer to feel *guilty* about the presence of mould, but she felt that she could not add mould to her burden of guilt. She already felt guilty about the use of her money to buy the *Review,* and she felt guilty about the sheer pleasure she had taken in the thought of Lettuce's face when he read the letter from Simon. She could just see him, opening the letter dismissively—having seen the Edinburgh postmark and assuming that it was some inconsequential communication from herself, but no! There it was, in Lettuce's now trembling hands, a letter from none other than Simon Mackintosh, WS, partner in the large law firm of Turcan Connell. Lettuce would not know what WS stood for, but she would be delighted to tell him, if asked: it was Writer to the Signet, which meant that Simon was a member of that august legal society with its splendid library overlooking St. Giles Cathedral in the very heart of Edinburgh. Let Lettuce contemplate that for a moment in his London fastness. So might the Hanoverian have quaked at the news that Bonnie Prince Charlie had put his generals to flight.

But sweet as such thoughts were, they were not thoughts which a conscientious moral philosopher could entertain. Schadenfreude in any shape or form was, quite simply, wrong. The discomfort of others should never be delighted over, she reminded herself; it was wrong to gloat. But then she saw Lettuce's face again, caught in a moment of shocked disbelief, and she allowed herself to smile at that. Charlie looked up at her from his supine position and smiled too.

Isabel's destination that morning, determined upon after the concert the previous evening at the Queen's Hall, was Dundas Street and Guy Peploe. She had decided that with Charlie present it would be better to meet at Glass and Thompson, the café a few doors up from the gallery. Charlie could be fed there and would like the colours and bustle of a restaurant.

She was there first, sitting on one of the bench seats at the back, watching the two young men making coffee and preparing bread and quiches for the lunchtime rush that would come in a couple of hours. Suddenly Guy was in front of her, looking down at Charlie with amusement.

"Macpherson," said Isabel. "My maternal grandmother was a Macpherson and we liked that tartan."

"That purple is very fine," said Guy. "He's quite the lad."

He sat down and fixed Isabel with an expectant look.

"Yes," she said. "McInnes."

Guy looked apologetic. "It's been sold, I'm afraid," he said. "A couple of days ago. The buyer I mentioned to you has taken it. It's going abroad. I'm sorry—had I known that you were still interested . . ."

He hesitated, seeing her dismayed expression. "I'm really very sorry, you know," he said. "I thought that you had decided against it."

Isabel was lost in thought. The information that she had to give to Guy would be even less welcome now.

Guy was solicitous. "Isabel? Are you really upset?"

"No," she began. "Not upset. And I wasn't going to buy it. I came to have a word with you about . . . well, something that I think I've found out about that painting."

"I'd be most interested," said Guy. "As I said to you, I think that it's a very fine McInnes."

Isabel shook her head. "But it isn't, Guy. It's not a McInnes at all."

The proprietor of the restaurant had caught sight of Isabel and had come to greet her. She asked him for two coffees and then turned back to Guy. "I believe that that painting was painted by a forger by the name of Frank Anderson. I don't know exactly who he is, or where he is. But that painting was painted by him and not by McInnes. I know that, Guy. How I came to know it is a bit complicated, but I do."

The coffees arrived. Guy flattened the milky top of his with a teaspoon, staring into his cup as if to find the solution there. Isabel watched him. "You're asking me," he said at last. "You're asking me to distrust my own judgement on a painting's authenticity. On what grounds? What are these complicated grounds?"

She told him, describing the moment when she stood before the fake McInnes in Barnhill, and of how certain she was that it was by the same hand that did the larger painting he had just sold. "You say that you can tell just by looking," she ended. "Well so can I. In this case, at least."

Neither said anything for a full minute. Then Guy sighed. "What do I do now?" He was thinking aloud, rather than asking Isabel. "I suppose I contact the purchaser and tell him that we have some doubts about the painting. And then?" He looked at Isabel, waiting for a suggestion.

"It's not just me," she said. "If I thought I was the only one with reservations about these paintings, then I would feel a little less convinced. But I think that the person who bought the McInnes at auction thinks the same."

Guy looked sceptical. "So you're suggesting that that's a fake too?"

"Walter Buie offered to sell it to me more or less immediately after he got hold of it," said Isabel flatly. "I think he did that because he'd tumbled to the truth and wanted to get rid of it."

Guy shook his head. "Walter Buie? Nonsense, Isabel. Walter is . . . well, he's just not that type. He simply wouldn't . . ."

"Why would he try to sell it, then?"

Guy laughed. "I could tell you of numerous occasions when people have changed their minds—more or less immediately. They take the painting home and discover that it's not right for the room. Somebody makes a remark about it and they decide that it's not to their taste after all. There are a hundred and one reasons why people change their minds."

She listened to this. Of course people could change their minds, but in this case there were just too many factors suggesting otherwise. And Walter Buie might be a paragon of respectability in the eyes of the public, but such people often had a dark, private side which was very different. There were so many cases of that, and this was, after all, Edinburgh, which had spawned the creator of Dr. Jekyll and Mr. Hyde.

"Anyway," said Guy, "I'll do what's necessary. I suspect you're wrong about all this, but I'll do my best to find out more—if there's any more to find out. I'll tell the purchaser. And I'll make enquiries about this Frank Anderson."

"The name means nothing to you?" asked Isabel.

Guy looked thoughtful. "It rang a distant bell," he said. "But I can't bring anything to mind. I'll ask about, though, and I'll let you know." He paused. "Do you want me to speak to Walter Buie?"

It was tempting. If Guy did that, then there would be no need for her to do anything further; she would have handed the whole matter over. But Isabel was not one to abandon responsibilities quickly, and so her answer was no; she would do that herself. She had become involved in this business, and she would see it through. It was a question of principle. And it was also, she decided, slightly exciting. Not very exciting; just slightly exciting, which, as she started to walk back up Dundas Street, past the elegant gardens that lay along the north side of Queen Street, was just right for Edinburgh. One did not want too much excitement in a place like Edinburgh. One could go to Glasgow for that, or even London, if one had the urge.

WHEN SHE RETURNED to the house, Grace whisked Charlie away. She wanted to take him out into the garden, she said, as the weather, which had been fine, could change at any moment.

"That fox," said Grace, "has dug up half the small rose bed. You know the one near the garden shed?"

"The summerhouse?"

"Whatever you call it. Yes, there. He's dug a great big hole and put the soil all over the lawn."

Isabel peered out the window. The grass near the summerhouse certainly looked darker. "He must be thinking of a new burrow," she said. "Even foxes must have their plans for the future. Presumably they face the same sort of dilemmas that we do: renovate, or dig a new burrow."

Grace stared at Isabel with a look that was half disbelief, half scorn. "They don't think that way," she said after a while.

Isabel returned the stare, but did not say anything. The trouble with Grace, she thought, is that she is so literal. But that was the trouble with most people, when it came down to it; there were very few who enjoyed flights of fantasy, and to have that sort of mind—one which enjoyed dry wit and understood the absurd—left one in a shrinking minority. Isabel remembered being at a conference at Christ Church in Oxford and sitting next to a Japanese woman over breakfast in the Great Hall. The Japanese woman, who was accompanying her husband, a philosopher, to the conference—*Kant for Our Times*—had suddenly turned to her and said, "I am so old-fashioned. I am a dodo."

The heartfelt comment had been triggered by the hall and its table lights, by its paintings of past masters and benefactors of the college, by the presence of what seemed like a quieter past, and Isabel had felt a surge of sympathy for the other woman.

"I am sure that there must be a club for dodos," she said. "The dodos club. And it would meet in places like this."

The woman's eyes had widened, and then she had burst out laughing. "The dodos club! That's so clever."

It was not very clever, thought Isabel, but for a moment there had been a sense of contact across cultures, of kindred spirits reaching out to one another. And that happened from time to time, when she met somebody who could look at the world in the same way and see the joke. But not now, in this conversation with Grace about Brother Fox and the mess that he had made of the small rose bed.

"We'll have to watch that fox when Charlie's around," said Grace.

Isabel frowned. Was Grace suggesting that Brother Fox would *harm* Charlie in some way? Did foxes do such things?

It was as if Grace had heard the unspoken question. "They carry off lambs," she said darkly.

The thought that anything should *eat* Charlie appalled Isabel; even the thought that a dangerous world should lie ahead of him, filled with creatures that might wish to harm him, was in itself bad enough, but eat . . .

"Brother Fox would not harm him," she said. "Foxes don't bite unless you corner them. And nor for that matter do wolves." Although at the back of her mind there was a vague memory of reading of a fox that *did* bite a child, in London. But that must have been a very stressed urban fox; Brother Fox was not like that.

If Grace had been prepared to accept this defence of foxes, she was not prepared to do so with wolves. "Wolves do," she said simply. "Wolves are very dangerous. I have a sister in Canada."

Isabel raised an eyebrow. The fact that one had a relative in Canada did not, she felt, automatically entitle one to pronounce on the subject of wolves, even if it gave one authority in some other areas.

"Wolves," said Isabel, "have never been recorded as attacking man. They keep well away." She felt tempted to add that she had been in Canada herself and had never seen a wolf, which was true and would therefore add empirical strength to the claim that wolves avoided people, but the full truth might require her to add that she had only been in Toronto, which somewhat diminished the force of the observation.

"Well, all I'm saying," said Grace, picking up Charlie, "is that we would be better off without that fox. Particularly with Charlie. That's all I'm saying."

The matter had been dropped, and Isabel had gone off to her study to deal with the mail. The fact that she had thought that she was soon to stop being the editor of the *Review* meant that she had let things slip, and the unopened correspondence had mounted up. Now she would have to think again in terms of future issues, have to deal with the unsolicited submissions, and would have to think, too, of the appointment of a new editorial board. She already had her list and was adding to it: Jim Childress in Charlottesville would be a great catch, and Julian Baggini, too, who already edited *The Philosophers' Magazine* but who might be persuaded to join. They would all be her friends, which would make the task of consulting the board so much more pleasant—no Lettuce or Dove. *Of Lettuce and Dove I am freed,* she said to herself, savouring the words, which sounded so like a line—and title—of a sixteenth-century English madrigal in the Italian style. It could be sung, perhaps, by the Tallis Scholars:

> *Of Lettuce and Dove I am freed*
> *And of their schemings no more shall be heard*
> *For they are gone with the morning dew*
> *Yea, Lettuce and Dove are both departed . . .*

There was a letter from Dove.

Dear Miss Dalhousie,

I have heard from Professor Lettuce that you have persuaded the owners of the *Review* to sell it to you. I have heard, too, that you will be appointing a new editorial board and that it is unlikely to include current members. I am, of course, sorry that you are seeing fit to dispose of the services of those who have given so much time to the *Review* over the years and who have always had its best interests at heart. I suppose that this is the prerogative of those who have the economic power to acquire assets which should, in a better-ordered world, be owned and operated for the common weal. However, I must say that I am surprised that a moral philosopher, which you claim to be (although I note that you have no academic position in that field), should act in a way which is more befitting of the petulant proprietor of a chain of newspapers. But that, I regretfully conclude, is how business is conducted today. I wish you, nonetheless, a successful further tenure of the editorial chair to which you have, it seems, become stuck.

Yours sincerely, Christopher Dove

She read the letter, and then reread it. It was, she had to admit, a small masterpiece of venom. To anybody who was unaware of the background, and who therefore did not know that the letter was from the pen of an arch-schemer, it might even have seemed poignant. But to Isabel, who knew what lay behind it, it was pure cant. *Cant for Our Times,* she thought.

She laid the letter to one side and picked up the envelope. Dove, she remembered, was famously keen on recycling and reused envelopes, sticking new address labels on them and sealing the flap with adhesive tape. Sure enough, this envelope had been used before and had a small label with her name and address stuck on the front. Idly she held the envelope up to the light and saw the writing underneath. The envelope in its first incarnation had been addressed to Dove at his home address. "Professor and Mrs. C. Dove" read the original.

CHAPTER EIGHTEEN

THERE WERE two difficult tasks now. One was to speak to Cat—not an easy thing to do in her niece's current mood, but rendered doubly difficult by the Dove problem—and the other was to visit Walter Buie. She had spent the previous evening in a state of anxious anticipation, trying to concentrate on reading, then work, then a television adaptation of a novel she liked, but had failed in all three, as her mind kept returning to the difficult encounters that would take place the next morning. She had telephoned Jamie, who had been working late in rehearsal and had been unable to be present for Charlie's bath time. She had decided that she would tell him about Dove and Cat and seek his advice, but then had changed her mind. And then she decided that she could not broach the subject of her impending meeting with Walter Buie, but again had changed her mind. Jamie would tell her to avoid further involvement with that matter now that she had passed on her misgivings to Guy Peploe. She had found no comfort there, and had been reduced to saying to Charlie, as she picked him up to change him, "What am I to do, Charlie? What do *you* think?" But Charlie had simply gurgled in a noncommittal fashion, which provided at least some reassurance. It would be many years yet, she thought, before Charlie started to disagree with her.

Cat was first on the list, because it was potentially the most painful encounter, and it would be best, she thought, to get it over and done with. In spite of Cat's recent jauntiness, Isabel felt that their underlying relationship seemed so bad now that any further deterioration was unlikely. They still spoke to one another, but Isabel could never gauge in advance what Cat's mood would be. Sometimes it was as if nothing had happened, but for the most part there was a simmering unforgiveness. If she had thought that this would last forever, Isabel would have felt despondent; but she knew that Cat would come out of this, as she had done before. There would eventually be a reconciliation following a gesture of some sort from her niece. Last time, it had been a basket of provisions from the delicatessen, left on the doorstep as a peace offering, and largely consumed by Brother Fox, who had found it before Isabel had. She thought that for him it must have been akin to the cargo awaited by the members of a Pacific island cargo cult, unasked for, delivered by an unseen hand.

Charlie remained behind with Grace—one did not take babies into a war zone—and Isabel walked, sunk in thought, along Merchiston Crescent to the delicatessen in Bruntsfield Place. Cat was behind the counter when she entered; there was no sign of Eddie or of any customers.

She received a reasonably warm welcome—the Dove effect, Isabel thought—and Cat offered to make her a cup of coffee. "Eddie's gone to the dentist," she said. "I asked him when he had last been and he said two years ago. I made the appointment myself."

"You shouldn't have to," said Isabel. "One's own teeth are enough to look after. One should not have to worry about the teeth of others."

Cat smiled. "But we do, don't we? I can imagine that you worry about others' teeth. It's exactly the sort of thing you worry about."

" 'The loss of one tooth diminishes me,' " mused Isabel. " 'For I am involved in mankind.' "

"John Donne," said Cat, looking triumphant. "You think that I don't know anything. But I do know about John Donne."

"Well done. But I have never thought of you as one who knows nothing about Donne."

"Good."

They looked at one another for a moment and Isabel saw in Cat's eyes a yearning that they should return to their previous, easy ways with each other; when jokes like this, absurd, silly, could be made without thinking. For there was love there—of course there was—and it was a canker of resentment that had obscured it, a canker that could so easily be put out of the way, altogether excised. But now she had to risk provoking it again, by deliberately rubbing in salt, and she had no alternative, she thought. She had to warn Cat about Dove. She had warned her before about a man; now she had to do it again.

She looked down at the counter. There was a fragment of cheese that had been caught at the edge, a tiny bit of blue cheese, a miniature colony of organisms detached from its polis. She reached forward and wiped it away. "Christopher Dove," she said.

Cat smiled at her. "Christopher. Yes."

Isabel was not sure what to make of that. But now she had to say it. She could not put it off. "You know he's married?"

Cat stood quite still, her eyes fixed on Isabel, who looked away; she could not bear this. Oh Cat, she thought. Oh Cat.

"Married?" Cat's voice was small, and Isabel's heart went out to her.

"Yes. There's a Mrs. Dove, I'm afraid."

Cat closed her eyes. "Why are you telling me this?"

Isabel reached out across the counter. She wanted to take Cat's hand; if her voice could not show how she felt, her touch would. But Cat withdrew her arm.

"I'm telling you this because you ought to know it. You'd tell a friend, wouldn't you? You'd tell her if you knew that some man—some married man—was going to deceive her."

Cat opened her eyes again. "You think he's deceiving me?"

It had not occurred to Isabel that Cat might know that Dove was married. She had assumed that Cat would not get involved with a married man, but that assumption she now realised—and it was a sudden, shocking realisation—was perhaps unjustified. Cat belonged to a generation that did not feel particularly strongly about marriage, in that many of them did not bother about getting married, and so perhaps they did not regard married people as being off-limits. I have been so naïve, she thought; so naïve.

She struggled to find the words. "Well . . . I thought that . . . I thought that you might have believed that he was single. It's difficult sometimes if . . ."

Cat interrupted her. "It's just fine for you," she said. "You come here and tell me this . . . You're not content with taking Jamie from me; now you come along and . . . and spoil this. Why can't you just . . ."

Isabel couldn't believe what she was hearing. *Took Jamie from her?* She drew in her breath; there was so much to be said, as there always is in the face of an outrageous accusation. "I did not take Jamie from you. You can't say that. You got rid of Jamie. *You* got rid of him. He wanted you to take him back for ages,

ages, and you wouldn't hear of it. Then you stand there and tell me that *I* took him from *you*."

"No," said Cat. "It wasn't like that."

Isabel reached out again, but Cat turned away. "Cat!"

"Just leave me. Please, just leave me."

The door of the delicatessen opened. Isabel looked round and saw that it was Eddie. He came over to the counter and smiled at her. Then he started to address Cat, whose back was turned. "My teeth are fine," he said. "The dentist didn't have to do anything, except polish them. Look."

He opened his mouth in a wide grin. Isabel made a gesture towards Cat. "I'm going," she said. "Look after Cat, please."

She left the delicatessen and began to walk down the street in the direction of Chamberlain Road. The brow of Church-hill rose gently in front of her, and at the end, beyond the rise, were the Pentlands, blue at this distance, with a mantle of low cloud. She had once read a poem somewhere, by an Irish poet she seemed to recall, which suggested that we could all be saved by keeping our eye on the hill at the end of the road. What he meant by being saved was not clear. We could not be saved, she thought, from anything just by looking at a hill; certainly not from the raw pain that came from divisions between people, between brother and brother, sister and sister, aunt and niece. Then it occurred to her: one might be saved from taking one's petty concerns—and one's petty feuds—too seriously if one looked up at the hills. That must have been it.

WALTER BUIE'S DOG, a Staffordshire terrier, mesomorphic, muscle-bound in the way of a small pugilist, growled at Isabel, baring stumpy, discoloured teeth. Such was his halitosis that even from where she stood, a good three feet from the unfriendly animal, she could smell him.

"Now then, Basil," said Walter, reaching down to pull at the dog's collar. "We must not be unfriendly."

He pulled the dog away and it slunk off, with the air of a small-time thug whose plans for a fight have been defeated, but only temporarily.

"Such a nice dog," said Isabel. "Staffordshires have such character."

The compliment pleased Walter Buie, who beamed back at her. "How kind of you to say that. Some people find Basil a bit . . . a bit difficult to get to know. But he's got a good heart, you know."

Isabel raised an eyebrow involuntarily. "Every dog has something to offer," she said. She was going to say something more, but could not.

"Exactly," said Walter. "But look, do come in. I didn't mean to keep you on the doorstep."

They made their way into the drawing room.

"My mother," said Walter. "I don't believe you've met her."

Isabel had not expected to find anybody else in the room and was momentarily taken aback. She recovered quickly, though, and moved over to the window where the elderly woman was standing. Walter's mother had half turned round and extended a hand to Isabel. Taking it, Isabel felt the dry skin, the roughness. She looked at Mrs. Buie and saw the recessed eyes, the folds dotted with liver spots.

"I was going to make tea," said the older woman. "Walter, let me do that. You stay and talk to . . ."

"Isabel."

"Of course." The eyes were fixed on Isabel, but they were still. There was little light in them. "I knew your mother, you know. We played bridge now and then."

Isabel caught her breath. Her mother; her *sainted American mother*.

"She was such an attractive woman," said Mrs. Buie. "And amusing."

Isabel thought: Yes, she was. So many people said that—that she made people laugh.

"And your poor father," Mrs. Buie added.

Isabel said nothing. She wondered what would follow. Did Mrs. Buie know about her mother's affair—the affair that Isabel herself had found out about only when her cousin had revealed it to her, on being pressed to do so by Isabel herself? Perhaps she did, but it seemed strange that she would mention it on a first meeting, unless, of course, she had become disinhibited. Age brought that sometimes, with the result that all sorts of tactless things might be said.

But Mrs. Buie had nothing more to add and made her way out of the room to make the tea.

Walter Buie gestured to a sofa near the window.

"The painting?" he said as they sat down. "You said you had some information for me."

Isabel looked past him to a picture on the wall above his head. It was, she thought, a McTaggart. He caught her eye.

"McTaggart," he said. "My mother's." He gestured around the room. "These are all hers. She's the one with the collection."

"But you bought the McInnes?"

He nodded. "I did."

She decided that she should wait no longer. "I don't think it's a McInnes," she said.

She watched him very closely. At first it seemed that he had not heard her, or had mistaken what she had said. He had been smiling when their conversation had started, and he was still smiling. But then it was as if a shadow had passed over his face. The face has a hundred muscles, she thought; even more. It has such a subtle surface—like that of water, sensitive to changes of light, to the movement of wind—and as indicative, every bit as indicative, of the weather.

"I don't understand," he said.

"You don't know that it's a forgery?" She felt her heart beating within her; she was accusing him now, and she was suddenly aware that it was the wrong thing to do. But the accusation had slipped out.

"Are you suggesting—" He broke off. He was looking down at the carpet, unable to meet her eyes. But it was not guilt, she decided; it was pain.

"Please," she said, impulsively reaching out to lay a hand upon his sleeve. "Please. That came out all wrong. I'm not suggesting that you tried to sell me a forgery."

He seemed to be puzzling something out. Now he looked up at her. "I suppose you thought that because I wanted to sell it quickly."

"I was surprised," she said. "But I thought that there must be a perfectly reasonable explanation." That was a lie, she knew. I am lying as a result of having made an unfair assumption. And I lied, too, when I paid a compliment to that unpleasant dog of his. But I have to lie. And what would life be like if we paid one another no compliments?

Isabel thought now that he was debating with himself whether to say something. When he spoke, it was with hesitation, and his voice was lowered. "I have to sell it," he said. "Or, rather, had to. If what you say is true, then . . ."

"You need the money?" It seemed unlikely to her. This was

an expensive house and the furniture, the paintings, the rugs on the floor—none of these suggested financial need.

He stared at her. He had the look of one who has said enough and is reluctant to say more. But there was more.

"I need to raise slightly more than one hundred thousand pounds," he said. "I didn't need to when I bought the painting. Then I did."

Isabel waited, and he continued. "It's my own fault," he said quietly. "I gave a personal guarantee for a friend who was involved in a management buyout of the company he worked for. It all seemed very solid when I agreed to back him, but an accountant somewhere along the line had deliberately misrepresented the liabilities. My friend goes under if I don't come up with the money. He loses his house—everything. And I'm godfather to his son."

She was silent. It was utterly convincing, and it was while she was thinking of how unjust she had been in her assumptions that she heard Mrs. Buie behind her. She was standing in the doorway, holding a tray. She took a step forward and put the tray down on a side table. She looked at Isabel.

"That painting is not a forgery," she said.

"Mother . . ."

Mrs. Buie raised a hand. Her eyes flashed angrily at her son, who was silenced in the face of her disapproval. "Do you imagine that we would attempt to sell a forgery? Is that what you think, Miss Dalhousie?"

Isabel felt the power of the older woman's disapproval. Her reply was conciliatory. "No. I'm sorry—I didn't suggest that. But it's quite possible, isn't it, that one might in good faith sell something which is not genuine? I could imagine that happening to me. I might sell something which I thought . . ."

Mrs. Buie shook her head vigorously. "With all due respect,

Miss Dalhousie, that would happen only when one didn't know much about the artist. I've known Andrew McInnes for a long time. I'm very familiar with his work. There's probably nobody else who's as familiar with it."

"Knew him," said Walter Buie. "Knew him, Mother."

This intervention was ignored. "And I assure you that the painting that Walter bought is absolutely genuine. It is the work of Andrew McInnes. There's just no question about it." She paused. "And there's another thing. That particular painting of Walter's is really very good. It's far better than anything that he painted ten years ago. Far better."

"It's unsigned," said Isabel. "And it's unvarnished."

"That's because he didn't have the time," said Mrs. Buie. "There's nothing more to it than that."

There was a silence. Isabel frowned. She was intrigued by something that Mrs. Buie had said. What did she mean when she expressed the view that the painting was better than anything painted ten years previously? She decided to press the point. "So you know when it was painted?" she asked.

The question took Mrs. Buie by surprise, and for a moment she seemed flustered. "I'm not sure . . ."

"But you said that he didn't have time to varnish it," pressed Isabel. "Forgive my asking, but how do you know?"

Then it dawned on her. It was so obvious. Andrew McInnes was not dead. *I've known Andrew McInnes for a long time.* People like Mrs. Buie, with her precise speech, did not mix up their tenses.

"He's alive, isn't he?" Isabel spoke so softly that she barely heard her own voice, but Mrs. Buie heard it, as did Walter; he gave a start and spun round to stare at his mother.

"No," said Mrs. Buie. "Andrew died. He was drowned off Jura."

Isabel watched her as she spoke, and saw the lie. It was evident, exposed; a person of Mrs. Buie's nature, she thought, finds it hard to lie, impossible even.

"I'm sorry, Mrs. Buie," she said quietly. "I know that it's rude of me, but you did seem to imply that you knew when the picture was painted. And then you said that you *know* Andrew McInnes, not *knew*. Forgive me for thinking that he is alive, and that you are finding it really rather difficult to continue to claim that he isn't."

Mrs. Buie looked away. When she spoke, her voice was distant. "Yes. You're right."

Walter glanced at Isabel. "Mother is perhaps not well," he muttered.

Mrs. Buie turned to look first at Walter and then at Isabel. There was irritation in her voice. "I'm perfectly well," she said. "And yes, Andrew is alive. You believe that you know a great deal, Miss Dalhousie, but I'm sorry to say that from my perspective you don't really know very much at all. If you had bothered to go to the library and read the papers, you would have seen the reports. And you would have read that the body of Andrew McInnes was never recovered. It was assumed that he had been devoured by that whirlpool, but he was not. He made it to the shore after his boat capsized and it was then that it occurred to him that he had the ideal opportunity to make a fresh start—as somebody else. And who can blame him?"

There was silence. "Well?" prompted Mrs. Buie. "Can you blame him?"

"No," said Isabel. "I can understand."

Mrs. Buie appeared pleased. "Well, that's something," she said. She turned back to face her son. "That painting, Walter, which you so foolishly bought, was sent down to Lyon & Turnbull by me. Yes, by me."

"You should have told me. You should have told me about that . . . and about Andrew."

Her answer was snappy. "I couldn't. I couldn't tell you something that I had given my word not to reveal. Nobody was to know that Andrew survived."

Walter was shaking his head in disbelief. "And you let me offer the painting to somebody else—to Miss Dalhousie here—although you knew full well that it was not what I thought it was. You let me carry on."

"It is exactly what you said it was," said Mrs. Buie. "You were deceiving nobody. And if you had told me that you were going to buy it, instead of going off by yourself, then you wouldn't have found yourself in this mess in the first place. Why did you suddenly get it into your head to buy a McInnes? Why didn't you discuss it with me? I would have told you then. I would have put you off."

Isabel thought she knew the answer to this. Walter Buie was trying to lead his own life, which was difficult, she imagined, with Mrs. Buie still being in the house. She felt a momentary surge of sympathy for him; he did not seem a weak man, but he was still a boy as far as his mother was concerned. The pictures on the wall were his mother's, bought by her; perhaps he wanted something of his own.

That was Walter; his mother, though, was a different matter. Mrs. Buie was such an unlikely conspirator, and Isabel wondered how she had been drawn into this elaborate deception. "Why did Andrew McInnes get in touch with you?" she asked. "If he wanted to disappear totally—which he must have—then why . . ."

Mrs. Buie cut her short. "As you may or may not know, I was his . . . well, I suppose you might call me his patron. I bought his paintings before he disappeared, and I have been supporting

Andrew for the last eight years or so, not in a big way, but supporting him nonetheless. He needs some money for an orthopaedic operation which he is having to wait a rather long time for on the national health service. He is in pain and can get it done privately more or less when he wants it. So I arranged for a couple of paintings to be sold."

She glared at Isabel. "I had not imagined that somebody might make things difficult for us by concluding that the paintings were forgeries. They are not that."

Walter Buie was staring at his mother, his lower lip quivering. "You could have told me," he said reproachfully. "You could have told me that he was alive. You said nothing. Yet you saw the painting."

Her voice was sharp when she replied. "As I've said, I have always respected Andrew's desire for privacy. And your trouble, Walter, is that you are rash. If you hadn't backed Freddy like that, you wouldn't be in this mess. John told you not to do it. Remember? He spelled out the danger."

"Freddy was my friend. *Is* my friend."

"Friendship and business are not always compatible," she snapped back at him. Then, reaching up to finger a string of pearls around her neck, she turned to Isabel. "Is it too much to ask you to respect Andrew's wishes? If you spread this and he is outed, as they say these days, then I can tell you one thing: I am quite sure that he will do something foolish."

"Disappearing in the first place was rather foolish, I would have thought," said Isabel.

"Don't joke about it, Miss Dalhousie," said Mrs. Buie. "Suicide is not a joke."

WHEN ISABEL RETURNED from the Buie house, she saw the light on the hall telephone blinking at her, signalling that a message had been left. There were two.

"May I come round for supper tonight?" asked Jamie. "I've got some fish that I could bring. Two pieces of halibut. They're quite small, but they'll taste really nice. I'll cook them."

And then, in the next message, before which a recorded voice said it would take twenty-two seconds to deliver, Cat said: "Look, I'm sorry. I really am. I make a mess of everything and you're always so nice about it. But that's what you're like. You're kind and understanding and all the rest, and I'm just stupid. Will you forgive me? Again? One more time?"

Isabel smiled at this. She had expected it, of course, but had not known exactly when, and how, it would come. She put down the handset and walked into the morning room, her head light with relief. It was late morning now and the sun was shining in through the skylight overhead, making a square of strong, buttery light on the faded red of the Turkish carpet, or Turkey carpet, as her father had called it. It was warm.

She went over in her mind what she had heard that morning; there would be a great deal to tell Jamie that evening, over their two pieces, small pieces, of halibut. So Andrew McInnes was alive; well, his body had never been found—she had been told that—and so she should have thought of the possibility that he was still alive. But she had not, however obvious it appeared with the judgement of hindsight. But then she thought: I have only Mrs. Buie's word for that, and I barely know her. It could be that . . . She stopped and looked up through the skylight, into the empty blue. It was perfectly possible that Mrs. Buie and

Walter had made up the whole story in order to conceal their being party to forgery or to the attempted sale of a painting they had decided was forged. It would be a neat solution for them. Walter might have suspected that Isabel had stumbled across the real reason for his try at a hasty sale. He might then have discussed it with his mother, who might have helped him concoct the story of the failed management buyout and his friend's desperate need for money. It was all too pat, all too neat. And she had swallowed it—even accepting Mrs. Buie's melodramatic warning of a suicide attempt by McInnes. That was a crude threat: the notion that somebody might take his life if we proceed with some course of action is a guaranteed way of stopping things in their tracks. And I fell for it, thought Isabel. I fell for it so very easily.

CHAPTER NINETEEN

GRACE WOULD SNATCH any chance of time with Charlie, so she did not hesitate to agree to continue to look after him that afternoon while Isabel attended to what she described as "urgent business." She needed to go out of town, she explained, up to Perthshire, and might not be back until very late. Would Grace mind staying overnight?

The prospect of having unfettered possession of Charlie over so long a period clearly appealed. "Don't you worry," she said. "You go ahead. Take as long as you like. Charlie and I will go and see my friend Maggie. She's been ill—nothing infectious, don't worry—a gallstone, actually, and a visit will cheer her up. She hasn't met Charlie yet, and she'll love him. We might even have our dinner down there."

Isabel tried to place her. Grace had many friends, whose exploits and affairs she occasionally narrated in detail to Isabel. Now, who was Maggie?

"You remember Maggie, of course," Grace went on. "I told you about her. She was a medium once, but she had a terrible fright and gave it up. She saw something unpleasant."

"Like Ada Doom," said Isabel. "Who saw something nasty in

the woodshed and never quite recovered. *Cold Comfort Farm.*" It was very funny, but she did not think that Grace would find it so.

"No," said Grace. "Not that. It's nothing to do with woodsheds. But a very disturbing thing nonetheless. She doesn't talk about it, but I know she thinks about it from time to time."

"That's the problem with mediums," Isabel ventured. "The future may be unpleasant, for all we know, and I wonder if that knowledge is really . . ."

She did not finish; the message conveyed by Grace's look was unambiguous. She did not like to discuss her spiritualist beliefs: this was a matter of faith.

"Oh well," said Isabel, cheerily. "I hope that Maggie feels better. A gallstone can be very uncomfortable."

She had a late lunch and fed Charlie. Then, when he dozed off—he was to have a sleep before the visit to Maggie—she went out to the garage at the side of the house. It was dark inside the small, windowless building, and she had to feel for the switch. But once she had turned it on, the light revealed the mysterious shapes for what they were: the curves of her green Swedish car, the upside-down bunches of last year's lavender that she had hung to dry from the exposed roof beams and had then forgotten, the neatly rolled coils of hose pipe, the bicycle that she never used now.

She slipped into the car and savoured, for a moment, the smell of the leather seats. It was a reassuring smell—the smell of something individual, and therefore rare in an age of moulded plastic. Somebody, some Swedish hand, had stitched that leather to make these seats; and it had been done with the same care that had been lavished on the engine, which never let her down, and started now, obediently, making the chassis of the car tremble slightly, as if in anticipation of the trip.

The traffic was light as she drove up Colinton Road and out onto the Stirling road. To her right, stretching down towards the Firth of Forth, the fields were full of ripening oilseed, patches of extravagant yellow. And beyond them, over the Forth and to the west too, were the hills of Fife and Stirlingshire, blue-green, indistinct in the warm afternoon light. She opened the window on her side of the car and savoured the rush of the wind, heavy with the scent of the country—mown hay, water, the soil itself. The sky, she noticed, had some cloud in it, but this cloud was thin and wispy, travelling fast in some high, invisible airstream; beyond that there was nothing—just an inverted bowl of blue over Scotland.

She did not rush. It would take her an hour and a half to reach Comrie by the back road past Braco, and she decided that she would enjoy the journey. There was enough to think about, of course, but she knew that if she dwelled too much on what she was doing she would think only of complications and reasons she should not do it at all. She was going in search of Frank Anderson, not because she was in any doubt that he was McInnes, but because she had come this far. She had taken it upon herself to look behind the paintings, and she had found out a closely guarded secret about the artist's survival. It was not clear to her what it was that had been achieved—other than satisfying the curiosity that had been raised in her when she had first begun to question the paintings' authenticity. One result was that the paintings had been shown to be completely authentic. When Guy Peploe had looked at them and pronounced them to be by McInnes, he had been absolutely right. His eye had not failed him; he had seen McInnes in the paintings, and indeed McInnes had been there.

In one sense, Andrew McInnes and his friend Mrs. Buie had not deceived anybody. McInnes had painted a McInnes—

he could do nothing other than that, whatever he did—and Mrs. Buie had offered a McInnes for sale, both to the gallery and to the auction house. The only deception—on the part of Mrs. Buie—lay in the fact that the paintings were offered as the work of an artist thought to be dead. She was uncertain what to make of that, but at least she was sure that it would not be repeated; Walter Buie himself had made that clear enough as he saw Isabel out of the house.

"My mother has never apologised about anything," he had said, looking back over his shoulder. "I'm ashamed of her. Really ashamed. I know that she's getting on, but . . ."

Isabel looked at him. Peter Stevenson had been right; Walter Buie was an upright man. People might be rude about old-fashioned Edinburgh, but it was upright. Reserved, proud, perhaps; but upright.

"I feel that I should apologise for her," Walter went on. "And I promise you this: there'll be no more McInnes paintings coming from her. I promise you that."

"You shouldn't reproach yourself," said Isabel. "She did it only to help him. He's the one who chose to deceive everybody with that disappearance of his. Your mother was only trying to help."

Walter thought about this for a moment. "There are times when one shouldn't help," he said. Yes, thought Isabel. And perhaps one of those was when your friends ask for major financial guarantees. But then she thought, Of course I would do exactly as he did. I am not one to lecture him on that; I would not turn a friend away either.

Now, as she turned onto the road that led from the village of Braco across the hills to Comrie, her anticipation over her meeting with McInnes increased—if there was to be a meeting, she reminded herself. She did not know exactly where he lived or whether he would be in when she arrived. It was ridiculous, travelling all that way up into Perthshire without any certainty that the person she was hoping to see would be there; ridiculous, she thought, but that's what I choose to do because . . . because I am a free agent and doing something like this is exhilarating and underlines my freedom.

The road crossed a moor; on either side, rising up gently, dotted with grazing sheep, were the slopes of heather-covered hills. There were no houses, no sheep byres, nothing to show the hand of man but a few fences marching off into the distance. It was a lonely place, but a gentle one, not desolate, as some northern places can be. And then the road began to dip down towards Glenartney and the River Earn, and Comrie was before her, grey-slate roofs among trees, small white-gabled houses, a village typical of that part of Scotland—well ordered, quiet, a place where nothing much may happen, but where that suited the inhabitants well enough.

She drove into the High Street, the road which ran directly through the village from one end to another, and parked the green Swedish car near the Royal Hotel. On the other side of the road was a newsagent's shop, its front window filled with local notices stuck to the inside of the glass with pieces of tape. Isabel could never resist these for their social detail. In Bruntsfield the equivalents gave news of vacancies in shared flats, suitable for those with a good sense of humour, nonsmokers, the easygoing; news of virtually new computers being sacrificed; of kittens requiring dog-free homes. Here there were offers of grazing for ponies, of jam-making pans now surplus to requirements, of fishing tackle. The Royal Hotel needed waiters and waitresses and invited applications from "hard-working applicants only"; a plaintive advertisement asked for news of Smoky, "a grey cat with half a tail" who had absented himself from home ten days ago and whose disappearance had led to "heartbreak, regret, tears." Isabel gazed at that final notice; that a cat should leave such things behind him.

She went inside. A woman in late middle age, hair tied back, emerged from behind a curtained door. In the background somewhere, music played softly. Mahler, guessed Isabel.

"Yes? What can I do for you?" The woman's voice was soft, the accent of somewhere farther west, Oban perhaps.

Isabel explained that she was looking for Frank Anderson. He lived somewhere nearby, she said, but she was not sure where. Did she know him, by any chance?

"Not exactly know," said the woman. "He hardly ever comes into town. But of course I know where he lives. It's a house along the road, out beyond Cultybraggen. You know the old training camp with all those funny wartime Nissan huts? Out beyond that about two miles. There's a track up to the left—you don't see the house from the road. But it's up there."

Isabel thanked her and left. She had asked the woman whether she thought that he would be in and she had replied that it was highly likely. Frank Anderson, she said, appeared never to go anywhere, although she had seen him in Perth once or twice. "He hirples a bit," she said, using the Scots word for limping. Isabel nodded; the hirple would be why he needed the orthopaedic operation that Mrs. Buie had mentioned—the operation that the state was failing to provide. We care for one another, thought Isabel, but we still don't care quite enough.

She drove out of Comrie, back along the road by which she had entered the village and away in the direction of Glenartney. The road was empty, a snake of black tarmac heading up the glen, and without any difficulty she found the turnoff to which the woman in the newsagent's had referred. The surface of this road—which was really little more than a track—had been neglected, and in one or two places the grass growing in the middle, between the two tyre tracks, brushed against the bottom of the car, making it sound as if Isabel was driving through water.

The house was unexpected, or at least unexpected in that place. It suddenly appeared from behind a rise, a small white-painted house that would have been a farmhouse or, more likely, a shepherd's house. In front of the house a wooden high-backed bench had been placed, and beside this a peony was in full flower, a flourish of pale red against the white wall of the building. Isabel noticed that at the side of the house, half obscured by a small trailer, was an old, dusty-looking car.

She parked and went up to the front door. It was open. There were voices within—a discussion on the radio.

"Mr. Anderson?"

Inside the house, the radio was switched off abruptly. A bird called behind her, the clicking sound of an alarmed grouse. She half turned round. The sun was in her eyes.

"Yes?"

He was standing before her in the door, and she knew immediately it was McInnes. The face had changed, in a way that she would have found difficult to describe, but behind the beard were the eyes that she recognised from the pictures.

Isabel stared at him. "Mr. McInnes?"

McInnes said nothing, but she saw the effect of her words. He seemed to take a step back, but then corrected himself. He closed his eyes.

"Are you from . . . a newspaper?" His voice was strange, mellifluous even—the rich voice of a classical actor.

She shook her head. "No, I'm not from a newspaper. Certainly not."

Some of the tension seemed to go from him, but his voice when he spoke was still strained. "Do you want to come in?"

"Only if you don't mind," said Isabel. "I haven't come to . . . to be difficult. Believe me, I haven't."

McInnes gestured for her to follow him into the sitting room at the front of the house. It was not a large room, but it had been made to be comfortable. Against one wall was a sofa bed, strewn with cushions; on the walls, Isabel immediately saw, there were paintings by McInnes and others; a paint-bespattered easel was propped up against a wall. It was an artist's room.

"I can make you some tea, if you like," he said. "But please sit down. Anywhere where's there's a space."

"Thank you."

He stood and watched her as she moved a couple of the cushions on the sofa bed. "Why have you come?" he asked.

She detected a note of fear in his voice. And that was understandable, she thought; I have broken in upon his privacy—the privacy that must have cost him so much to create. And why? Can I even begin to answer that question in a way which will not make me sound intrusive?

"I saw one of your paintings," she said. "A recent one. My curiosity was aroused."

For a moment he said nothing. "So it's just curiosity?"

Isabel nodded. But in what light did that show her?

McInnes sighed. "I should not have agreed to their being sold," he said. "I have sold nothing by . . . by McInnes since he died."

"He died?"

He turned away. "Yes. He did. The man who was McInnes died."

Isabel was about to say something, but McInnes continued: "It may sound odd to you, but that's what it felt like to me. Everything seemed hopeless, tainted. I decided to make a fresh start." He paused and looked at Isabel as if to challenge her to refute what he had to say. "And I've been perfectly happy, you know? Living here as Frank Anderson. Doing a bit of painting. And I've even managed to earn a living looking after sheep and driving a tractor for two of the farmers up here."

Isabel waited for him to say something more, but he became silent. "I can understand," she said. "I can understand why people might want to reinvent themselves."

"Understand, but not approve?"

"That depends," said Isabel.

"You disapprove of what I did? Misleading everybody into thinking that I had drowned?"

Isabel shook her head. "Not really."

"There was no insurance, or anything like that," said McInnes. "I did no wrong."

"You were presumably mourned," said Isabel. "Somebody must have suffered."

"No," said McInnes flatly. "I had no close family. My parents were dead. I was an only child."

Isabel spoke gently. "But you had a wife."

"Had," said McInnes. "She . . . she went off with somebody else. And anyway, she hurt me more than I hurt her."

There was silence for a moment. Isabel wondered whether McInnes knew that his wife had herself been left by her lover. And if he did know, would it make any difference?

She looked at him. He was standing in front of the window, his crop of unruly hair outlined in the afternoon light. There was something about him that was indisputably the artist; however hard he sought to change his identity, she thought, that part would remain—that hair, and those eyes. It was the eyes of the artist that could be so very powerful, as they were with Picasso. She had read about one of Picasso's friends telling the painter not to read a book lest his eyes burn a hole in the paper.

For a moment she said nothing. Then, very quietly, "And a son too."

"A son." It was not a question; just a statement.

"Yes," said Isabel. "Magnus."

"That's the child she had by him," McInnes said. "Not my son."

Isabel was surprised by his response. "You knew about him?"

When he answered, McInnes's voice was full of disdain. "She came to see me," he said. "When her boy was quite small. I told her that I did not wish to change my mind."

It took a few moments for Isabel to digest this. So Ailsa knew all along that her husband was still alive; that surprised her. That made at least two people who knew his secret: his wife and Mrs. Buie. And now her.

McInnes seemed eager to change the subject. "It was Flora Buie who persuaded me to sell those two paintings. I didn't want to. She went on at me. I have some medical expenses, you see . . ."

"I know about that," said Isabel. "But I suspect that everything will be taken care of."

He looked at her quizzically.

"You see," explained Isabel, "Walter Buie bought one of the paintings and another collector bought another. Walter Buie knows that the painting is by you . . . in your posthumous period." She could not resist the joke, and she was pleased to notice that McInnes smiled. "And he knows that you are still alive. I propose to buy that painting from him, and I know very well that you are still with us. So the money from that transaction is quite untainted. Nobody has been deceived. And the same applies for the collector who bought the other painting. The gallery is going to get in touch with him and tell him there is some doubt about its authenticity. But at least you'll get money for the one that was sold at auction."

"Some of it yours?" asked McInnes.

"In a sense," said Isabel. "The fact that I am going to buy the picture from Walter means that indirectly my money comes to you. But I get a McInnes, which I know was painted by you. So I'm happy too."

McInnes nodded. "All right."

"But there is one other little thing," said Isabel. "In fact, it's quite a major thing. That little boy. Magnus. He's your son, you know."

"He's not."

"He calls you Dad," said Isabel. "That's what he calls you. And I think he's proud of you."

McInnes stood quite still. Then, quite suddenly, he raised a hand to his face and covered his eyes. Isabel heard his sobs and stood up. She placed an arm around his shoulders. He was wearing an Arran sweater, and the wool was rough to the touch.

"You have to see him," she said. "He is your son, you know. He looks just like you."

He took his hand away from his eyes and shook his head. "No. He's not."

"I think he is," said Isabel. "Because he looks like you. He really does."

She watched the effect of her words on him. It was not easy, but now she knew why it was that she had come, and why it was that she needed to finish what she had to say.

"You have two things to do, Andrew," she whispered to him. "Two things. The first of these is that you have to go and forgive your wife. After eight years, you have to do that. You have to tell her that you have forgiven what she did to you. You have that duty because we all of us have it. It comes in different forms, but it is always the same duty. We have to forgive.

"And then the second thing you have to do is to go and see your son. That is a duty of love, Andrew. It's as simple as that. A duty of love. Do you understand what I'm saying to you?"

She had a few minutes to wait before he answered her. During that time she stood where she was, her arm about his shoulder. Outside, through the window, she could make out the shape of a cloud moving in the sky beyond the summit of the hills. Low stratus.

She looked at him, and then, almost imperceptibly, she saw him move his head in a nod of agreement.

THAT WAS TUESDAY. On Wednesday nothing of importance happened, although Grace found a ten-pound note in the street and this led to a long and unresolved discussion of the level at which one is morally obliged to hand lost money over to the police. Isabel suggested thirty pounds, while Grace thought that eleven was about right. On Thursday she received a letter which made her think—and act too—and a telephone call from Guy Peploe. Then on Friday, which had always been her favourite evening of the week, Jamie obtained a further two pieces of halibut, slightly larger this time, which they ate together at the kitchen table, under guttering candles.

Thursday's letter, innocent in its beginnings, contained a bombshell halfway through. It came from a person whom Isabel had sounded out about joining the new editorial board. He was an old friend from Cambridge days, and he now occupied a chair of philosophy at a university in Toronto. She had told him the story of Dove's foiled machinations—she knew that he had a low opinion of Dove, whom he had once described as a charlatan. "I saw the Dove himself about five months ago," he wrote in reply. "We were together at a conference in Stockholm. The Swedes were wonderful hosts, as usual, and the city was so beautiful in its late-winter clothing; white, the harbour still frozen over, everything sparkling. I had the misfortune of sitting next to the Dove at one of the dinners and he went on about himself the whole evening. He has a big book coming out, he said. A huge book, he implied. And then he went on about the fact that he was about to be divorced. There was some sort of hearing coming up and he gave me all the details of his wife's iniquities. But who can blame her, Isabel? Being married to the Dove would be a pretty stiff sentence for anybody."

Isabel had put the letter aside and stood for several minutes in front of her study window, uncertain what to do. Of course there was only one proper course of action, and she took it, although she had been tempted to do nothing.

"Cat," she said. "I was misinformed. I owe you an apology."

"Misinformed about what?" said Cat.

"Christopher Dove," said Isabel quickly. "He's not married. He's divorced. I jumped to conclusions."

There was a silence at the other end of the line. But only a short one. Then "Makes no difference," Cat said. "I'm seeing somebody else, actually."

Now it was Isabel's turn to be silent.

"He's called Eamonn," said Cat. "He's Irish, originally. And he's lovely. He's gentle. You'll like him."

"I'm sure I shall," said Isabel. But she was not sure. "What does Eamonn do?" she asked.

There was a further silence, this time quite a long one. "Well," said Cat at last, "he's a bouncer for a bar at the moment, but he's going to stop being a bouncer and do a stonemason's apprenticeship. There's a builder called Clifford Reid who's taking him on. Clifford has been doing up a building near the delicatessen. He's the most highly sought-after builder in town. You might have seen the scaffolding. That's how I met Eamonn. He came in for coffee with Clifford."

Isabel did not know what to say, but Cat had to cut some cheese and so that brought the conversation to an end. Isabel felt relief over the Dove affair; she had done her duty and confessed, but it had made no difference. And if anxiety should be felt over Eamonn, there would be time enough for that in the future. A former bouncer–stonemason could be an improvement, though, on some of the men in Cat's past; both required solid qualities in their practitioners, contrasting good qualities perhaps, but solid qualities nonetheless. Ireland gave so much to the world; perhaps Cat was learning at last.

The telephone call from Guy Peploe started briskly, but led to at least one silence. "The purchaser of that painting was very understanding," he said. "I told him that I had reason to think that it was not what I had been led to believe it was. He said that he still liked it, and would keep it. I adjusted the price, of course: a nice painting in the style of another artist is still a nice painting, but shouldn't cost as much. He was perfectly happy with that. Very happy, in fact."

"And the consignor?" said Isabel. "Was she happy with getting a smaller sum?"

"She was very relieved," said Guy. "She said—" He stopped. "How did you know it was a woman?"

"You told me. And I've met Mrs. Buie," said Isabel.

That was when the silence occurred, and Isabel decided that she would have to take Guy into her confidence. He was discreet and she knew that he could keep a secret. But she had involved him, and she would have to give him a full explanation.

"May I see you next week?" she said. "There's a long and rather complicated story that I have to tell you. But I'm going to tell you only if you give me your word that you won't tell a soul. Not a soul."

"You have my word," said Guy. "But can't you give me a hint of what it's about?"

Isabel laughed. "It's about a whirlpool," she said. "And human oddness."

Now, sitting with Jamie in the kitchen, enjoying a glass of the chilled West Australian wine that he had brought with him, along with the slightly larger pieces of halibut, Isabel recounted the week's events. Jamie listened attentively, and with increasing astonishment.

"So Mrs. Buie gets away with it?" he asked at the end. "And McInnes continues to pretend not to exist? Hardly a very satisfactory conclusion, is it?"

"But Mrs. Buie did no wrong," said Isabel. "She sold two McInnes paintings painted by McInnes. Nothing wrong with that. Although I think that she won't try it again."

Jamie frowned. "But there is," he said. "She put up for sale two paintings which were meant to be by an artist who was dead. He wasn't dead. What would the lawyers call that? A material misrepresentation, or something like that?"

"That sounds like a rather fine point," said Isabel.

"Oh really?" Jamie expostulated. "You're one to accuse *me* of making fine points." But his tone was one of amusement, and he was smiling.

"What worried me more," said Isabel, "was the fact that McInnes had ignored his son. That was the real tragedy."

"You persuaded him otherwise?"

"I think so," said Isabel. "In fact I'm sure of it."

She looked at Jamie, silently daring him to accuse her of unjustified interference. But he did not; instead he glanced at her, smiled, and said, "Well, that's fine then."

He was thinking of his own son; how could anybody deny love to a child?

"So would you say, on balance, that on this occasion at least it was worth interfering?" Isabel asked.

Jamie hesitated. She should not meddle in the affairs of others; he was sure of that. But when he looked at what had happened here, well, would it be anything other than churlish to deny the good effects? So he merely said, "Yes. You did the right thing in this case."

"Thank you," said Isabel. "But here's something to think about: I realised it was the right thing to do only after I had done it."

They finished their dinner. And later, upstairs, lying still wakeful with the moonlight falling through the chink of the curtains that did not quite meet, they suddenly heard outside the yelping of Brother Fox. "He's out there," whispered Isabel. "That was him."

Jamie remembered a line of song: *Prayed to the moon to give him light.* That was about Mr. Fox, wasn't it? Yes, said Isabel, it was. Does he pray to the moon, do you think?

Jamie got up and went to the window to look out over the lawn. She saw him standing there, in his nakedness, and she thought of the beauty that somehow he had given her. A gift of beauty.

He came back to the bed. "He sticks to the shadows," he said. "But that was him, all right. Praying to the moon."

He held her hand lightly. "You promised something, you know. You promised that you would tell me a story about a tattooed man. Remember?"

"Did I?" She was beginning to feel drowsy.

"Yes, you did," he whispered.

"All right. A story about a tattooed man."

She put a hand on his shoulder. She felt the movement of his breathing; so gentle.

She whispered the lines, close to his ear. *"The tattooed man / Who loved his wife, the tattooed lady / And was proud of his son, the tattooed baby."*

She stopped, and she heard him breathing.

"Is that all?" he asked.

"There are some stories that are very short," she said quietly, "because they say everything that there is to be said."

In the silence of the room he thought about this. She was right.

"Thanks for that story," he said. "I liked it very much."

Isabel closed her eyes. There is a sea of love, she thought. And we are in it.

VISIT THE WONDERFUL WORLD OF

Alexander McCall Smith

© Chris Watt

- **AlexanderMcCallSmith.com**
  Join the official Alexander McCall Smith Fan Club to receive email updates on author events and book releases. Click on "Newsletter" on the home page to sign up!

- **facebook.com/AlexanderMcCallSmith**

- **twitter.com/mccallsmith**

THE ISABEL DALHOUSIE NOVELS

"The literary equivalent of herbal tea and a cozy fire....
McCall Smith's Scotland [is] well worth future visits."
—*The New York Times*

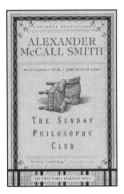

The Sunday Philosophy Club

Isabel Dalhousie is fond of problems,
and sometimes she becomes interested in
problems that are, quite frankly, none of her
business—including some that are best left
to the police. Filled with endearingly thorny
characters and a Scottish atmosphere as thick
as a highland mist, *The Sunday Philosophy
Club* is an irresistible pleasure.

Volume 1

Friends, Lovers, Chocolate

While taking care of her niece Cat's deli, Isabel
meets a heart transplant patient who has had
some strange experiences in the wake of his
surgery. Against the advice of her housekeeper,
Isabel is intent on investigating. Matters are
further complicated when Cat returns from
vacation with a new boyfriend, and Isabel's
fondness for him lands her in another muddle.

Volume 2

The Right Attitude to Rain

When Isabel's cousin from Dallas arrives in Edinburgh, she introduces Isabel to a bigwig Texan whose young fiancée may just be after his money. Then there's her niece, Cat, who's busy falling for a man whom Isabel suspects of being an incorrigible mama's boy. Isabel is advised to stay out of it all, but the philosophical issues of these matters of the heart prove too tempting for her to resist.

Volume 3

The Careful Use of Compliments

There's a new little Dalhousie on the scene, and while the arrival of Isabel's son presents her with the myriad wonders of life, it doesn't diminish her curiosity about other things. While attending an art auction, she discovers a mystery revealed in one of the paintings, launching her into yet another intriguing investigation.

Volume 4

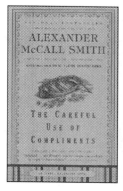

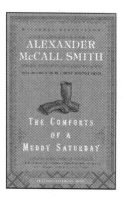

The Comforts of a Muddy Saturday

A doctor's career has been ruined by allegations of medical fraud and Isabel cannot ignore what may be a miscarriage of justice. Meanwhile, there is her baby, Charlie, who needs looking after; her niece, Cat, who needs someone to mind her deli; and a mysterious composer who has latched on to Jamie, making Isabel decidedly uncomfortable.

Volume 5

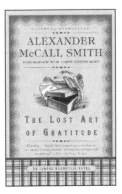

The Lost Art of Gratitude

When Minty Auchterlonie takes Isabel into
her confidence about the complicated troubles
at the investment bank she heads, Isabel
finds herself going another round: Is Minty
to be trusted? Or is she the perpetrator of an
enormous financial fraud? As always, Isabel
makes her way toward the heart of
the problem.

Volume 6

The Charming Quirks of Others

Old friends of Isabel's ask for her help in a
rather tricky situation: A successor is being
sought for the headmaster position at their
alma mater and an anonymous letter
has alleged that one of the candidates has
a very serious skeleton in their closet.
Could Isabel discreetly look into it?

Volume 7

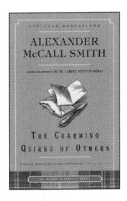

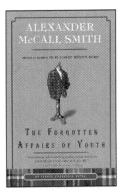

The Forgotten Affairs of Youth

A visiting Australian philosopher asks Isabel's
help to find her biological father. As usual,
Isabel cannot help but oblige, even though
she has concerns of her own. Her young son
Charlie is now walking and talking, and her
housekeeper Grace regularly attends a
spiritualist who has taken to providing
interesting advice. And could it finally be
time for Jamie and Isabel to get married?

Volume 8

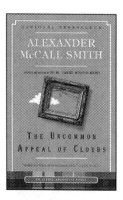

The Uncommon Appeal of Clouds

Isabel answers an unexpected appeal from a wealthy Scottish collector, Duncan Munrowe, who has been robbed of a valuable painting. Never one to refuse an appeal, she agrees, and discovers that the thieves may be closer to the owner than he ever would have expected. Isabel also copes with life's issues, large and small, and finds herself tested as a parent, a philosopher, and a friend.

Volume 9

The Novel Habits of Happiness

Isabel Dalhousie takes on a unique case with paranormal implications. The mother of a six-year-old boy, who has been experiencing vivid recollections of a past life, asks Isabel to investigate. But Isabel's desire to find rational explanations comes up against the uncanny mystery unfolding before her when she locates the house where the boy claims to have lived, on an island off the Scottish coast?

Volume 10

THE NO. 1 LADIES' DETECTIVE AGENCY SERIES

Read them all....
"There is no end to the pleasure."
—*The New York Times Book Review*

**The No. 1 Ladies'
Detective Agency
—Volume 1**

**Tears of the
Giraffe—Volume 2**

**Morality for Beautiful
Girls—Volume 3**

**The Kalahari Typing
School for Men
—Volume 4**

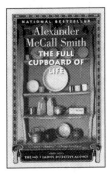

**The Full Cupboard
of Life—Volume 5**

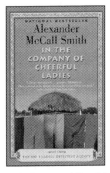

**In the Company of Cheerful
Ladies—Volume 6**

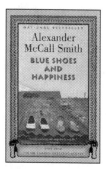

Blue Shoes and Happiness—Volume 7

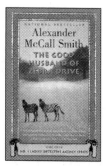

The Good Husband of Zebra Drive—Volume 8

The Miracle at Speedy Motors—Volume 9

Tea Time for the Traditionally Built—Volume 10

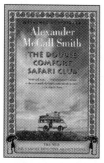

The Double Comfort Safari Club—Volume 11

The Saturday Big Tent Wedding Party—Volume 12

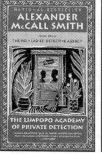

The Limpopo Academy of Private Detection—Volume 13

The Minor Adjustment Beauty Salon—Volume 14

The Handsome Man's De Luxe Café—Volume 15

The Woman Who Walked in Sunshine—Volume 16

THE GREAT CAKE MYSTERY

In her first case as a young girl, Precious sets out to find the real thief of a piece of cake. Along the way she learns that your first guess isn't always right. She also learns how to be a detective.

Volume 1

THE MYSTERY OF MEERKAT HILL

Precious has a new mystery to solve! When her friend's family's most valuable cow vanishes, Precious must devise a plan to find the missing animal! But she needs the help of another to solve the case. Will she succeed and what obstacles will she face on her path?

Volume 2

THE MYSTERY OF THE MISSING LION

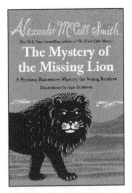

Precious gets a very special treat: a trip to visit her aunty Bee at a safari camp. On her first day there, a new lion arrives. But this is no average lion: Teddy is an actor-lion who came with a film crew. When Teddy escapes, Precious and her resourceful new friend Khumo decide to use their detective skills to help track down the lion and find out where he has gone.

Volume 3

Illustration © Iain McIntosh

THE 44 SCOTLAND STREET SERIES

**"Will make you feel as though you live in Edinburgh....
Long live the folks on Scotland Street."**

—*The Times-Picayune* (New Orleans)

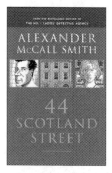

44 Scotland Street
—Volume 1

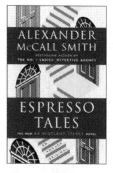

Espresso Tales
—Volume 2

Love Over Scotland
—Volume 3

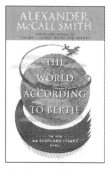

**The World According to
Bertie**—Volume 4

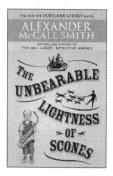

**The Unbearable Lightness of
Scones**—Volume 5

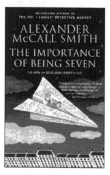

**The Importance of Being
Seven**—Volume 6

Bertie Plays the Blues
—Volume 7

**Sunshine on Scotland
Street**—Volume 8

**Bertie's Guide to Life and
Mothers**—Volume 9

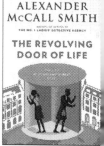

**The Revolving Door
of Life**—Volume 10

THE CORDUROY MANSIONS SERIES

"McCall Smith returns with a new cast of characters to love."
—*Entertainment Weekly*

Corduroy Mansions
—Volume 1

The Dog Who Came In From the Cold—Volume 2

A Conspiracy of Friends
—Volume 3

THE PORTUGUESE IRREGULAR VERBS SERIES

"A deftly rendered trilogy . . . [with] endearingly eccentric characters."
—*Chicago Sun-Times*

Portuguese Irregular Verbs—Volume 1

The Finer Points of Sausage Dogs—Volume 2

At the Villa of Reduced Circumstances—Volume 3

Unusual Uses For Olive Oil—Volume 4

MORE NOVELS AVAILABLE IN PAPERBACK AND EBOOK:

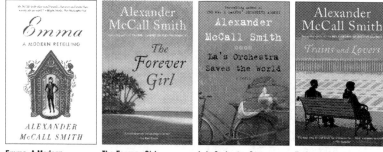

Emma: A Modern
Retelling

The Forever Girl

La's Orchestra Saves
the World

Trains and Lovers

SHORT STORIES AVAILABLE IN EBOOK:

The Perils of
Morning Coffee

Fatty O'Leary's
Dinner Party

At the Reunion Buffet

STORY COLLECTIONS AVAILABLE IN HARDCOVER AND EBOOK:

The Girl Who Married a Lion
and Other Tales from Africa

Chance Developments

Printed in the United States
by Baker & Taylor Publisher Services